# BLOOD ASCENDANT

SONS OF NAVARUS
BOOK 7

K.M. SCOTT

WRITING AS
GABRIELLE BISSET

## BLOOD ASCENDANT

I am everything. I am vampire.

Theron has grown into adulthood knowing he is the war machine the Sons will need to defeat their enemy. The most powerful vampire ever, he's finally ready for what the Prophecy of Idolas foretold all those centuries ago. But is he destined to ascend to power forever alone?

For ages, the Sons and the Archons have known all-out war was inevitable, a fight for the domination of their world. The Archons have nothing less than a god on their side, but the Sons and their allies have something more to fight for, more than just control of the vampire world.

The Sons fight for family, for friends, and for love, but their duty to the vampire world is clear. Stop the Archons. No matter who must die and what they must sacrifice, the Archons must be defeated.

ISBN: 978-1-955335–47-8

# 1

---

*I am everything.*
*I am the Alpha and the Omega.*
*The beginning and the end.*
*I am vampire.*

Noele had only been in the Underworld for a short time, but she'd already grown accustomed to how busy Hades' realm was. She couldn't remember ever thinking about what being there would be like, although she was sure it had entered her mind more than once in all her time she was alive, but she had a feeling her imagination had never conjured up a place so industrious.

Then again, as she watched soul after soul hurry in and out of Hades' chamber, she wondered if all this commotion could be due to the war between the Archons and the Sons beginning. She listened carefully each time one of Hades' daemons approached his throne to inform him of some bit of news, hopeful to glean even the tiniest detail that might let her help the Sons. So far, little of what they bothered him about had much to do with anything other than the daily running of the Underworld.

Who had arrived. Who was being sent where. Who the king of the realm should bother with. It all seemed like the type of clerical work that could easily happen without bothering Hades.

Not that she disliked anyone interrupting him from his near obsession with her. Hour after hour of his attention exhausted her, so any respite was appreciated more than any of his minions could know.

His sexual appetite had no end, boundless in its style and methods. Every moment with him sickened her and forced Noele to repeat the mantra she'd chosen for her task in the Underworld from the first moment he laid his hands on her.

*I'm doing this for Ramiel and the rest of the Sons. This won't be in vain. I'll learn something from Hades or one of his daemons that will help them defeat this bastard.*

Over and over, she silently said those words as Hades did with her what he chose. Sometimes the mantra was all that got her through her time with him, and when he released her to go with another or to sate his hunger for something other than fucking, she could do little more than pray to forget as she tried to convince herself that what she was doing would eventually pay off.

But all the while, no matter what she believed, she thought of Ramiel and the sadness in his eyes as she watched him fade into nothingness when she died. She wanted to remember all the wonderful moments with him, but all she could ever think of was that look in his eyes.

It was probably this place. Hades likely did something to make sure she couldn't remember how happy she and Ramiel were. That sounded like something the son of a bitch would do.

She hated that it worked so well and all she could imagine of Ramiel now was his sadness at her death. They were so much more than that singular moment. She knew that, even if she couldn't picture anything else in her mind. She felt it inside in a place Hades could never reach.

They were happy and meant for one another. And now, he had a war to win, and she had her own work to do to help him and his fellow Sons.

As she thought of that, she wondered if Nico had finally gotten his way and taken her son to be that war machine he was so sure he'd be. Even though she couldn't say for sure, she had to believe that Ramiel wouldn't put Theron in harm's way unless he could handle himself.

What did he look like now, she wondered. Unlike with her memories of Ramiel, she could see her beautiful son as clearly as if he stood in front of her at that very moment. His dark eyes looking into hers seeking the answers to all those questions he had because of how fast he was growing up. She could only imagine how difficult his life was now that she wasn't there to help.

Ramiel would, though, so she could rest easy knowing that. For all his Visigoth nature, he knew how to love and was no doubt taking care of Theron right now.

"What is my pet thinking of so intently?" Hades asked as he dragged his fingertip along Noele's jaw.

Quickly, she recovered from her daydream and

smiled just as she knew she should. "Nothing, my lord. Just waiting for you to have a moment for me after all this work you have to do."

She hated that she had to be so obsequious, but she'd learned very early with the god of the Underworld that servility was what he required from her to remain happy. She didn't dare take the chance that he grew unhappy. Noele had made that mistake once and would never do that again.

Hades looked into her eyes and grinned in that way that never failed to terrify her. She'd seen that wicked smile come before his summoning his daemons and torturing a new arrival to his kingdom. She'd seen that same smile when he was unhappy with one of them and tore him to pieces in front of a room full of them.

That smile could mean anything, but all too often, it meant something bad was about to happen.

Patting his lap, he looked at her standing behind him and then down at his hands. "Come. I want to feel you on me."

Noele did as he ordered and sat herself across his thighs. Lean and strong, they provided her stability as she quivered in fear at what would come next.

Naked, except for the black pants he routinely wore, he ran his hand along the inside of her thigh, making her wish he'd let her wear something more than the tiny black dress that allowed him to touch any part of her body easily. Still shaking in fear, she forced a smile for him to hide her terror.

"What's my pet frightened of?" he asked, as if he didn't know the answer.

"Nothing, my lord. I simply tremble at your touch."

She'd become so good at lying in her time in the Underworld. Untruths slid from her mouth with utter ease that she had a hard time believing she could say such things.

His grin grew, showing his straight white teeth. "So perfect. I love that about you, Noele."

Rarely did Hades refer to her by name, so instantly, every nerve in her body went on alert. She looked at him smiling at her and worried something terrible was about to occur.

Then it dawned on her. Had Ramiel died in the battle against the Archons and in just moments she'd see him standing in front of Hades on his first night in the Underworld? Her body yearned to leap off his lap so her husband wouldn't see what she'd been forced to be in this place, but she knew she couldn't show Hades her true feelings.

For what seemed like forever, she waited for him to say something that would indicate why he was in such a good mood while she silently prayed that she wouldn't see Ramiel. Finally, Hades lifted her off his lap and set her on her feet on the cold stone floor.

"I have a surprise for you. Would you like to see what it is?" he asked as he stood and ran his hand down over his chiseled abs.

Happy it likely wasn't anything to do with Ramiel arriving in the Underworld, she nodded eagerly. Her anticipation may be met with something horrible, but at least it wasn't her worst nightmare come true.

Not yet, at least.

Taking her by the hand, he led her to a passageway that grew darker and darker by the step. Within minutes,

Noele couldn't see anything and squeezed his hand tighter. Where were they going?

In the darkness, his whisper surrounded her. "You have no reason to fear, pet. I rule even these darkest of hallways. When you're with me, you're safe."

Normally, she wouldn't ask questions of him, but the moment got the best of her and she asked, "Where are we going?"

He lifted her hand to his lips to softly kiss her knuckles, brushing his mouth against her skin as he answered, "To the depths of the Underworld."

Terror raced through her. Tartarus? She'd heard horror stories of that part of the Underworld. Only creatures Hades wanted to punish were sent to Tartarus. Why would he take her there?

Immediately, she slowed her pace until he practically had to drag her forward. In the pitch black, she shook her head and struggled to hold back tears.

"What have I done, my lord? Please don't send me away."

The fear that clung to each word wasn't an act. To be consigned to Tartarus would be tantamount to solitary confinement. She'd never be able to help the Sons from there!

She felt him stop, and then he pulled her close to his side. "I would never send you to Tartarus, my pet. I adore you over all others in this place, so don't cry, Noele."

Unable to keep the tears from coming as relief swept over her, she sobbed against his chest, ashamed at how weak she felt in this place. He kissed the top of her head like a lover would to show affection, but since Hades had no capacity for love that she'd seen, she took his gesture as one meant to calm her so he wouldn't have to deal with her growing hysterical.

Whatever the reason behind it, she welcomed it since it meant she wasn't being sentenced to that horrible place. But if that wasn't why he was taking her there, then what was?

"Now come with me and no more crying," Hades whispered into the darkness around her.

She let him lead her down stairs carved of stone that seemed to go on forever. Noele wondered how far Tartarus existed below the Underworld as they continued to walk step by step into the depths of the earth.

Finally, they reached the bottom and began walking down a hallway lit by torches on both sides. Deep scratches and pits marred the walls, like the beings that had been sentenced to this place fought with every ounce of their strength to not enter Tartarus. Streaks of red told of violence worse than what she'd seen up above as Hades would never allow evidence of that to remain where he could see it. The Underworld was his kingdom, his realm he ruled over, and while it was a prison for many, he saw it as a place of beauty and opulence.

In the distance, Noele heard noises that sounded like they came from giant beings. Instinctively, she tightened her hold on his hand, and he chuckled.

"Don't be frightened. That's just the Titans complaining, like they always do. You'd think after all the time they've been here that they'd be used to it by now."

Noele thought back to what she knew of the Titans and remembered they were the gods who came before the Olympian gods. They had given birth to Hades and his brothers and sisters, and after Zeus overthrew Cronus and the Olympians won the War of the Titans, those first gods were imprisoned in Tartarus, joined by the worst the world had to offer as the eons passed.

Clearly, he hadn't brought her all the way down here to see them since he had such disdain for them, so was she there to see the criminals that had been sent to Tartarus?

Hades was nothing if not unpredictable, but he'd seemed to genuinely care about her happiness back in that dark hallway. Then again, his being capricious meant he very well may have dragged her down there to show his displeasure for something she'd done and never even realized she'd offended him. Gods were like that, and mere mortals like her, even if she was a vampire, simply had to endure the lightning quick changes to their moods.

They passed the cages holding the Titans, but she squeezed her eyes shut, too afraid to look in at them. He stopped a few cells away and tapped his knuckles against the bars. "Don't be afraid. You can look into this one."

Noele tentatively lifted her eyelids to see a man alone in the cell. Light-haired and muscular, he looked like every image she'd ever seen of Apollo. Leaning forward, she studied him for a moment. He was nothing less than beautiful.

"I think you'll know who this is when I tell you his name. Noele, I'd like you to meet Idolas, famous for his prophecy. Idolas, this is Noele, the born vampire who gave birth to the child you claimed would overrun the Archons in their little war with the Sons."

The man stood from his stone bench and walked toward them. As much as Noele didn't know what to expect, she didn't fear him. He was the one who foresaw her and her son's part in the world centuries ago.

"You forget I also saw that he would defeat you, Hades. You conveniently left that out."

The god of the Underworld threw his head back and laughed at the comment. "Ridiculous nonsense. This is my realm, and only a god could dethrone me. Your little born vampire isn't a god, Idolas."

"You underestimate him at your peril, Hades."

In the next cell, another male pressed his face against the bars and beckoned Noele to him. Consumed by the back and forth with Idolas as their insults grew louder, Hades didn't notice her move around his side so she could be closer to the prisoner.

She looked into the cell and saw a dark-haired man who looked nothing like Idolas. Leaning forward, she whispered to the being with dark eyes much like hers, "Who are you?"

"I am Nikitor, one of the original Sons of Navarus. We don't have long, so listen carefully. I heard what Hades said about you. You're the born vampire of my bloodline who joined with one of my brother's to conceive the child he prophesized would save us all. You clearly have a protected position in the Underworld, so take advantage of it to help the Sons defeat the Archons when the time comes."

Noele hung her head and answered quietly as Hades bellowed about the Prophecy of Idolas and how he'd never be overthrown. "I haven't been able to do much of anything yet, but I'm trying. I'm sorry to tell you I think the time has come, and the war has begun."

"Then it's more important than ever that you do all

you can to help them. You're strong. You're of my blood-line, so you can save them just like I saved my brother. Find a way."

Nikitor stepped back as Hades barked at Idolas, so Noele quickly hurried back to his side before he noticed she had stepped away. Finished with taunting his grandson, Hades looked at Noele and smiled.

"I thought you might like to see where the original Sons of Navarus live. These new ones will join them once they're all here."

Noele didn't say a word, not knowing how to respond since she couldn't defend Ramiel and the rest of the vampires she believed in. Better to simply force a smile for the god of the Underworld to placate him.

He took her hand in his again and turned to leave. "Time to get back, pet. I don't like to spend much time down here. Gods belong in better places."

They walked out the way they came, but now she heard a female's voice calling to them. Hades stopped for a moment and then turned to face a cell near the entrance to Tartarus.

"Let me out!"

Pointing at the dark-haired woman who gripped the bars of her cell so tightly her knuckles were stark white, he rolled his eyes. "Love, this is Macaria, my daughter and the cause of all my troubles with vampires."

Noele stepped forward to fill her eyes with the vision of the female. Beautiful, even after God only knew how long she'd been imprisoned in this horrible place, she smiled and loosened her grip on the bars in front of her.

"Hello, Macaria."

Before she could say anything more, Hades huffed in

disgust. "I had to put them down here after they gave birth to those sons of theirs. The fruit of my loins and she gives birth to vampires."

"Are you alone in there?" Noele asked as she searched the back of the cell for Navarus.

As if she read her mind, Macaria nodded and sadly said, "He separated us. I haven't seen him in ages. He's a vicious tyrant. Don't trust him. He will hurt you like he hurt me, his flesh and blood."

Hades groaned like this encounter bored him and took Noele by the hand again. "Time to go, pet."

She had so many questions she wanted to ask Macaria, but how could she when Hades stood right there? Reluctantly, she let him pull her away from the cell.

They made it a few feet away before Macaria yelled, "The child will defeat you, father. Your time ruling this world is nearly to an end!"

Her threat didn't seem to faze Hades, and as they left through the gate to Tartarus and began walking back up to his throne room, Noele wondered if Macaria knew that for sure. She so wished she could ask her, but she knew she had to keep pretending to not care about her claim or risk the pain that would surely come from Hades' anger.

Even more than that, Noele worried her son wasn't ready for the destiny that would come from defeating the god of the Underworld. He was only a little boy, no matter how fast he'd aged. How would he ever deal with the power that came from defeating Hades?

## 2

The Order's headquarters buzzed with excitement, making Theron want to just begin this fucking war and stop all this meeting and planning bullshit. The rest of the Sons had been anticipating this war with the Archons for decades and centuries. How much more talking had to happen before they just accepted it had begun and they did what they had been chosen to do?

Elders hurried past him as he headed toward the main conference room, and he watched with amusement as their long black robes made it hard for them to move as fast as they wanted to. Not exactly active wear. He couldn't even imagine how they sat around in those things all the time. His mind drifted to things other than the impending battle, like did they wear clothes under their robes, or did they let everything hang free under them?

With a chuckle, he thought maybe if he could free ball, he might consider being an Elder someday. Well, only if those robes weren't scratchy. No one wanted prickly fabric rubbing up against their balls.

That thought was quickly replaced with the reality he knew all too well.

If he got out of this Archon war alive, he would never have the luxury of just lolling around the Order's headquarters naked under those long black robes and discussing issues of the vampire world. His fate held a far different future. If he survived the war, he was to be the ruler of the Underworld.

Not that the idea held a whole lot of pleasure for him. He'd never been down there, but just the name said it all. Underworld. No sun. Beneath the world where all the life existed. For a young clyten vampire, the thought of being bound to that place did little to make him look forward to much of anything.

So while the rest of the Sons of Navarus made plans for their lives after the war, lives full of hope and anticipation they willingly wanted to fight to protect, all Theron had to fight for was the fact that he was born for this very purpose and had only the present to live for.

He walked into the main conference room and saw everyone had arrived already. Well, not everyone. Nico was missing.

"I think we can put away any hope that your friend Nico has remained loyal to the Sons of Navarus," he said as he made his way across the white marble floor toward the table where all the Sons and their mates sat.

Not a single one of them responded to his statement, but they didn't need to. They knew as well as he what Nico was. Traitor. The Son who had been there the longest mentoring generations of warriors had given up and gone to the other side.

Theron stopped at the spot at the head of the table they'd left empty for him. Leaning down, he firmly placed his hands on the table and looked at each of the vampires gathered there in front of him waiting for what he had to say. Just two years ago, they'd come to see him as his mother held him lovingly in her arms, proudly showing off her baby boy. Now they'd come to listen to him as their leader.

If only his parents could see him now.

"I hope you all had an enjoyable final night and got everything you needed to in order. The time has come."

Terek leaned forward and looked down the long table at him. "We've heard nothing to indicate the war has begun, Theron. Have you heard something?"

Christ, this one in particular seemed to want to drag his feet. What was with this guy? He knew how to fight. He was revered in the vampire world as a great warrior who'd vanquished thousands in battle. Why the hell did he seem to be so intent on avoiding this war?

Theron only had to look to Terek's left to know the answer. The beautiful blond who sat next to him, a petite thing who looked at her mate like the world revolved around his every thought. He didn't mind Ilona, especially since she took such good care of his sister, but Theron didn't have time for lovesick vampires too afraid to fight because they had so much to lose.

Just as he opened his mouth to tell Terek the time had come to fucking step up, an Elder hurriedly shuffled across the floor toward them, breathing heavily like he'd run all the way there. When he stopped next to Theron, the old vampire with the wrinkled face sighed and his whole body seemed to collapse under the weight of his task at that moment.

"I come with news, terrible news. Reports have come in that Ramiel has attacked Archons across the continent, killing dozens. Archon headquarters has gone into lockdown mode."

Then he took a deep breath and hung his head. "The war has begun."

For a moment, it felt like time stopped as no one around the table, including Theron, moved or even breathed. The Elder's words hung in the air all around them.

The war has begun.

As the old vampire slowly walked away, all Theron could think of was how happy he was that the time had finally come. Good. Those fuckers had killed his mother. It was high time they paid for that.

His father had done the right thing. Attack the Archons before they attacked the Sons and their allies. Leave it to Ramiel to step up like a Son should.

Looking down the table at Terek, who now sat with his head hung and frowning, Theron answered his question from a few moments earlier. "There's your indication, courtesy of my father."

Seated next to Terek, Vasilije smiled. "Leave it to that Visigoth to take things into his own hands. I have to admit I'd expected this to come before now. He must have been planning his attacks all this time."

"Well, whatever he was doing, the war's begun, thanks to my father, so now we move. We don't have time to drag our feet or discuss what should happen anymore. We're at war, so now we attack."

He half expected some kind of resistance from one or more of the other Sons, but not a single one said a word, so he continued. "Vasilije and Terek, you'll fight with the dragons in the east. Aim for any and all Archons you can find. The dragons will be up against the European witches who likely know the geography as well as the dragons and you two do, so don't underestimate them. And you should expect Hades and his creatures to come to the witches' rescue if things start looking good for you."

Terek slowly nodded but didn't say anything. Vasilije smiled and shrugged before nudging his friend. "Looks like we get to fight with our friends this time. You ready?"

"As ready as I'll ever be," Terek said in a somber voice.

Before that vampire's worry could infect everyone around the table, Theron turned to Saint and Solenne who sat closer to his end of the table holding hands. Neither one had ever appeared unwilling to fight, which he liked, so he expected less feet-dragging from the two of them.

"Saint, you and Solenne will be fighting with the weres in Italy, Spain, and Portugal. Expect things to get nasty fast since the witches will be bringing out the big guns when it comes to spells to keep the weres down. I suspect that most of the Archons in those areas have already made their way to Archon headquarters, but knowing the weres prefer to keep to their home turf in that region, I think you should expect the witches to come at them hard. I wouldn't put it past Hades and his daemons to show up too."

Nearly as serious as Terek but nowhere as reluctant, Saint nodded. "That's all fine and good, but I need everyone here to understand that Verrater is mine and Solenne's. That goes for you too, Theron. I don't care who thinks they have more right to that bastard. You don't. He's hurt my family the most, so we get to kill him. I'm not willing to negotiate on this."

A quick glance around the table told Theron no one disagreed with Saint's claim to Verrater's death. "I don't care what you do to him. He's no one to me other than another goddamned Archon who needs to be eliminated. Whoever finds him will hold him for you two. Then it's just a matter of what you want to do to him."

Unlike most of the Sons, Saint ran on pure vengeance when it came to that Archon, but Theron could appreciate that. He knew what it felt like to eat, sleep, and breathe pure hatred for another being and think of nothing but how you planned to wipe them from the world, except his rage wasn't focused on any one Archon. He wanted all the motherfuckers dead.

Next, he turned to Sion and Kali. His mechanical army would help them against the witches. Their fucking spells wouldn't be as effective on machines like they would be against the weres and dragons.

"Sion, we're going to need your drone army up and running as soon as possible. Kali, keep working on the Prophecy of Idolas for anything that might be able to help us."

Smiling, she sighed. "I just hope I can find something, anything to help."

Her mate turned to look at her and shook his head.

"You cracked that thing practically all on your own. You've already helped more than you can know."

For the first time, Dante spoke up. "Yeah, nobody thinks Sion, Ramiel, and Thane did the heavy lifting on that."

As always happened when anyone mentioned Thane's name, the feeling amongst them all changed. Theron had never met that Son and had heard enough about him to know he'd betrayed them nearly as badly as Nico, so he struggled to understand why any of them ever looked sad when his name came up. Well, all but Vasilije, the one he'd betrayed the most. Whenever he was around and Thane's name was mentioned, all he did was narrow his eyes to angry slits.

Recognizing what he'd said and seeing the reaction of his fellow Sons and friends, Dante quickly asked with a smile, "So do I just get to hang out here with the robed dudes or what?"

"No, you will head up the clytens and join with Scarlett and the American witches. After what happened with her coven already, I expect them to be in danger now that the war has begun. I also expect that your friend Nero, the Archon from New York, might not be so friendly now that the fighting has started. If he's still on our side, all well and good, but if not, take him out along with any other American Archon. They don't get spared just because they're over there. They made their choice. Now they'll have to die for it."

Dante had no joke to follow that, so Theron continued. "I'm going to follow my father's lead and take out as many Archons as I can in Europe. Keep in mind that Nico is the enemy now, so if I see him, he'll get the same treatment the Archons will. The sooner we eliminate all of the other side, no matter who they are, the sooner this war ends. That means if any of us find him, he needs to be killed."

All of them reacted with shock at how plainly he stated the truth, but Theron quickly read each of their minds to find out what they planned to do about Nico. Each one understood the necessity of treating their old friend as the true enemy he now was. Even Terek, whose mind was filled with sadness at the thought of what he must do because of the choices Nico had made.

While he visited each of their thoughts, he found Kali's not focused on Nico but on what he must do with Hades. Of course, she'd be thinking about that. She'd spoken to him several times about that very topic since she deciphered his future in the prophecy and saw it entangled with the god of the Underworld's.

But he needed to keep his eye on the immediate fight in front of him. The Archons needed to be eliminated first before any defeat of Hades could happen.

"As Kali will be back here at all times, if any of us need help, let her know. For now, we understand what we have to do."

With that, he turned to leave as the rest of the Sons and their mates said their goodbyes. He didn't know if any of them would ever see one another again, so he didn't begrudge them these final few moments together. For him, though, he had another place in the world to be.

Just as he stepped out into the dark hallway, Kali and Dante caught up with him. Quickly, he scanned their minds and saw what they were thinking. Neither one seemed to have war in their thoughts, oddly enough.

Dante pushed him on the shoulder and smiled. "Hey, tell that crazy father of yours I miss him and his miserable ways, okay? And tell him I want to see him again, so don't do anything stupid. That goes for you, too. Got it?"

"Still trying to boss me around like you used to when you were my babysitter," Theron said, remembering those happy days he and his clyten friend used to spend together in the sun as his parents slept.

"Old habits die hard, you know? So just don't get yourself killed, all right? And if you find yourself looking for excitement, the clyten regiment can always use another one, and since you fit the bill on that..."

He let his sentence trail off before wrapping his arms around Theron in a hug that surprised him. "Seriously, though, find your father and get those fuckers who took her away, okay?" he whispered in his ear before backing away. "Take care, Theron. See you soon."

As he watched Dante walk back into the conference room, he thought about how good his friendship with him had been, even when he didn't deserve any kindness back when they were in the States. Theron hoped after the war ended and life for vampires changed for the better that they'd see one another again.

Alone with Kali, he didn't have to consider what she wanted to say to him. He read it perfectly in her mind, so he said it first. Looking down at the small female who had done so much for the Sons and the Order, he smiled. "I know what you're thinking, and you don't have to worry so much. That whole Hades thing will happen when it happens. Until then, I have to focus on helping my father kill as many Archons as possible."

She took his hand and gave it a sympathetic squeeze.

"I don't have much more to do with the prophecy when it comes to this war. The sides have been drawn, and the battles will be fought. I worry about the effect of Hades' daemons when it comes to our side, but I believe in the Sons and our allies. What's left for me to figure out all revolves around your defeat of Hades, Theron, so that's what I'll be working on."

He saw tears well in her eyes and wondered why. She'd already told him the Prophecy of Idolas said he'd defeat Hades, so what was the problem?

"Have you kept something back from me about my beating Hades?" he asked, sure she couldn't have since he'd read her mind over and over and found nothing she'd hidden from him.

She smiled and shook her head. "I know you can read my mind, but I have a feeling that gift of yours might allow you to see what you want. I've been worried about you fighting Hades since I first deciphered that part. Hades is a god, Theron. For all your gifts and abilities, you're only a vampire. I'm afraid of what you'll have to endure to end his reign in the Underworld."

For a moment, he thought about that very idea of what Hades was and what he wasn't and smiled. "I don't have a choice, do I? I never have before, so if I do on this, give me a head's up."

Kali rolled her eyes. "I'm not kidding. This is a huge thing. He's a god, Theron."

"And I'm not, yet still the prophecy says I'll defeat him. Since the prophecy predicted I'd be born from the only born vampire who could give birth to me, and then it predicted all the abilities I'd have, which I do have, I'm putting my money on Idolas and his prophecy. He says I'll defeat Hades. So I'll defeat him."

She grabbed his forearm, and with a grave look in her eyes, stared up at him. "That's not how prophecies work. If that were the case, this war wouldn't be a big deal at all. But it is. Vampires will be killed. And I'd like to remind you that the Prophecy of Idolas said nothing of the Bliss epidemic the Archons have set loose on the vampire world. Prophecies give us the rough outlines. Real life and now fills in the details. Please don't forget that, Theron."

"Okay, Kali. I won't forget. If you find out anything about what will happen with Hades, let me know."

She sighed and then opened the door to the conference room. Light spilled out into the hallway, and Theron took one last look at the rest of the Sons of Navarus. His father belonged there with them, and now he had to find him so the two of them could exact their revenge on those fucking Archons for what they took from them.

As for Hades, he'd get to him when the time came. Whatever was to happen, Theron knew one thing for sure. He'd been born to fight the evil in the vampire world, and that's what he'd do.

He didn't have a choice.

# 3

Marc Verrater stood silently in Magistrate Consera's office wondering if he had organized the attacks on the Archons himself considering how beneficial they'd been for him. Any stragglers who weren't sure now was the time to go to war with the Sons instantly came over to the magistrate's side when they heard about what that fucking animal Visigoth had done to so many of them.

So much for any opposition on their side. Now that all the Archons had been persuaded of the necessity for unity and the witches were fully on board, along with Hades' daemons, all that was left was for the fighting to begin.

Not that Marc had any goddamned intention of being a part of it. He was an Archon stationed at their headquarters. Fuck, he'd struggled long and hard to get to where he was, and one of the benefits of that was he didn't fight. Hell, he barely worked, especially ever since the success of Bliss had shot him to the top of the pile in Corsica.

No, he wouldn't be bothered with the actual battles or whatever Consera had planned for this war to defeat the Sons so they could finally subjugate all the vampire race. While the rest of the world set itself on fire, he planned on enjoying his success in his office, with his feet up on his desk and a stiff drink in his hand, away from all the madness his kind seemed hell bent on inflicting on themselves.

Looking around Consera's office, he thought about how much nicer it would be instead to relax there while the fighting raged on. It was bigger than Marc's, and since he wasn't an Archon, it didn't have to be stark white. He took a deep breath in and let his gaze roam over the pale blue walls that instantly relaxed him, unlike the walls in his office with their boring white that made him feel like he was sitting in some hospital room.

Life would be even better in his boss's position. Maybe someday.

Archons weren't allowed to be magistrates, but things could change. Anything was possible, and once the Sons were eliminated, who knew what could open up for him?

The door opened as Marc daydreamed about a leisurely life as a magistrate, and Consera strolled in grinning, followed by his vampire Nico and that witch who had become a far too frequent fixture in Marc's life recently. Clearly, something had gone well already by the smile on his boss's face.

"Marc, I'm glad to see you. Do you know what today is?" Consera asked as he sat down behind his desk and poured himself a glass of red wine.

Shaking his head, Marc quickly tried to remember if

that day was anything special. Nothing came to him, so he shrugged. "No. What?"

Consera took a deep breath in and exhaled slowly, blowing the air out of his mouth. "It's independence day, my obtuse friend. Today is the day we declare our freedom from those troublesome Sons of Navarus."

Obtuse friend? What the hell did that mean? Marc knew he'd been insulted, but why? Why the fuck was Consera mad at him now?

Irritated, he knew he had to play the game with his boss, so he smiled and nodded like he agreed. "Ah, independence day. Good. Soon we'll be rid of the Sons and the vampire world will finally begin to run like it should."

"Exactly!" Consera said excitedly, pointing at Marc to punctuate his agreement with what he'd said.

Jesus. One minute he was obtuse and then the next minute he was exactly right. How the fuck was anyone supposed to know how to act with this guy?

"Marc, why do you seem like you're off in la-la land today? You haven't been getting into the Bliss again, have you? I swear if you have I'm going to stake you myself."

And just like that he'd moved from being stupid to being right to being threatened.

"No, I'm just a little overwhelmed with what's happened today. I guess I didn't expect the Sons to attack first. I also mourn the loss of my fellow Archons at the hands of that fucking monster."

Only the part about being surprised that the Sons attacked first was true. Little overwhelmed Marc since he cared for next to nothing, and he didn't give a fuck about those Archons the Visigoth had killed. They should have worked harder to get ahead so they weren't stuck out there on the Continent, wide open to attack by virtually anyone instead of being safe and sound at Archon headquarters.

For barely a second, Consera showed the tiniest hint of unhappiness at the mention of the Archons' deaths, but then the feeling passed, and his smile returned. "We'll make sure every one of the Sons and anyone they care about pay for the attacks on the rule of law, Marc. Don't worry about that. For now, just know that they didn't die in vain."

Marc didn't respond because he didn't know what to say. He didn't care about the ones who'd been killed. All it did was give him a reason to call for an even more painful death for the Visigoth Son. Other than that, it mattered nothing to him. He didn't even know the names of those Archons. They meant nothing in his life.

Consera leaned forward and looked over toward the witch. "Let's get down to business. I want your witches to get rid of the weres, first and foremost. I don't want them just immobilized. I want them eliminated."

Lucinda's round eyes opened wide, making her even uglier than usual. "Eliminated? How many of them?"

Without missing a beat, Consera answered her question as coolly as if he was ordering a drink. "All of them. Wipe them off the board so we don't have to deal with them."

A chill ran down Marc's spine at the magistrate's answer. Extermination.

No one said a word in response to Consera's statement for the longest time, but as Marc looked around the room, he saw the witch and Nico understood as well as he did what their boss's order meant.

Then he added, "The same goes for those American bitches. They made the wrong choice. Now they will have to pay for it."

Lucinda staggered back a few steps, clearly shocked by that order. "All of my fellow witches you want dead too?"

Jumping up from his chair, the magistrate came around his desk and got in the witch's face. "Did I stutter? All of those bitches. I don't want a single one of them alive when this is over. Got it?"

She looked around the room like she couldn't believe what he'd just ordered her to do. Kill all the American witches? Marc didn't understand why any of this confused her, though. This was a war for control of the supernatural world. They made their choice. Too bad it was the wrong one.

"Now go and be ready when I call for you," Consera barked, making the witch jump at the sound of his voice bellowing off the walls.

She hurried out of his office, clearly flustered. Marc rolled his eyes at how ridiculous witches could be.

"God, this war forces us to associate with such shit."

"The witches?" Consera asked with a chuckle as he turned to walk back to his chair.

"And those fucking daemons too. I can't wait until we win this war and then we're rid of them."

Just then, Hades appeared in front of them and glared at Marc. "Careful, vampire. You saw what happens when I let my daemons do what they do best. Another insult like that and I'll set them on you."

Fear tore through him as the memory of what those damn daemons had done to the magistrate raced through

Marc's brain. Fuck! The last thing he needed was the goddamned god of the Underworld pissed at him.

He stammered out a pathetic sounding apology as Consera dropped to his knees in deference in front of Hades. Lowering his head, the magistrate said, "My sire. I'm sure he simply misspoke."

Hades broke his stare from Marc to look down at the one kneeling at his feet. His face twisted into an expression of disgust. "You know, I hate when you call me that. I didn't make you vampire. I'm a god, not some two-bit royal either, so don't use that word around me again."

Eager to change the subject, Consera looked up at him and pointed over toward where Nico stood silently staring down at the floor. "I want to introduce you to one of my vampires. Nico has been invaluable in bringing about this war with the Sons of Navarus since he was one for years. He's been my eyes and ears the whole time."

All traces of his earlier anger disappeared, and a look of surprise settled into Hades' expression. "A Son of Navarus. Traitor to your brothers. I can appreciate that. I've done the very same thing to my own brothers. Do they know you've sold them out?"

Nico simply nodded and continued to look down at his feet. "I'm sure they do by now," he said quietly.

Turning to look at Consera who had gotten himself up from the floor, Hades smiled. "Your vampire's heart doesn't seem to be in this."

"No need to worry. Nico has always been my most obedient vampire. We have him to thank for getting the born vampire Noele."

Suddenly, Hades seemed to be very interested in Nico. "Really? You did that?"

Still, Nico didn't look up and simply nodded.

"Then I have to thank you, Nico. She's settled in nicely in the Underworld. I really can't say I've ever had a better whore. Very good work."

Marc noticed Nico winced at Hades' description of his newest plaything and wondered why. He gave her up easily from what his sire said, so why would he be bothered what the god of the Underworld thought of her, or for that matter, what he did with her? She was the mate of a Son of Navarus and the mother of the child the Prophecy of Idolas claimed would defeat not only the Archons in this war but Hades himself. Nico shouldn't have been surprised if he tore her limb from limb and flayed her alive just for kicks. The fact that he was simply using her as his fucktoy meant she was getting off easily.

"I was just explaining how the war will go. The witches are to eliminate the weres and the American witches. Your daemons will be invaluable in helping us fight the Sons and the dragons. One battle and this will be over, and we'll have the vampire world to ourselves."

The magistrate seemed downright pleased with himself, practically gloating before he'd even sent a single witch or daemon out to avenge those slaughtered Archons all over the Continent. Marc wondered if Hades liked that level of smugness, but he didn't have to wait long to get his answer.

Raising his eyebrows up into his forehead, the god of the Underworld grinned. "Very good. And since you've been plying your own kind with that Bliss shit, you'll be rulers of zombies. You've left nothing to chance, Consera."

Clearly, smugness didn't offend Hades like Marc thought it would.

"Thank you. It just took some planning, but I expect this to be over practically before it begins."

Hades' smile faded just a touch. "Be careful, though. I've got more than a few humans in my realm who were just as sure about their own military success before the battle began. Sometimes the best laid plans are blown to smithereens by one underestimated variable."

Consera waved his warning away before sitting down behind his desk. "Those were foolish humans, who are always fucking things up. Invading Russia and not anticipating the effects of the Russian winter? Leave it to a human to be that colossally stupid. We aren't them, though. Between your daemons and the witches, we can defeat all the Sons and their allies. They are, after all, only six vampires, no matter how impressive they may be."

For the first time, Nico lifted his head. "Seven, sire. Theron is a Son now."

"The born vampire's child?" Consera asked with utter disdain.

"I promise you he's not a child anymore. The last time I saw him, he had surpassed everything I'd believed he'd become, and he wasn't finished. He has abilities no vampire has possessed together, and most of all, he was born for a single purpose. To defeat you and the Archons. Do not underestimate him."

Hades threw his head back and let out a deep laugh. "And there, my myopic friend, is your Russian winter. Listen to your vampire, Consera. I've seen the child, and I can assure you he's no toddler, despite being only two years old."

Clearly offended by the insult, Consera quickly said, "True, but we're not the only ones the prophecy said had to worry about the child. His ultimate goal is you and your kingdom."

Marc held his breath in anticipation of Hades calling his daemons to torture the magistrate once again for his impudence, but instead, he simply rolled his eyes at Consera.

"You continually make the mistake of believing we're equals. We are not. You are a vampire. I am a god. That child of the prophecy can wipe out your entire plans now that he's joined with the Sons of Navarus. Defeating me won't be as easy. Gods don't die, so whatever our young opponent has planned might be a passing irritation I have to deal with but little else."

As the thought of Hades' immortality settled into Marc's brain, he wondered why that idiot Idolas had thought some born vampire would ever be able to dethrone Hades and take over his kingdom. Since gods couldn't die, how would he ever defeat him?

"Well, this has been fun, but I've got better things to do with my time," Hades said dismissively. "Call me when you need my daemons, but don't expect them to do all the heavy lifting, Consera. Let those witches handle that, along with any other ragtag creatures you've convinced to help you. I'll be sitting on the sidelines watching it all happen."

The magistrate hurried around his desk to guide Hades into the anteroom of his office where he preferred to conduct private business, leaving Marc and Nico standing there. He had no idea what the traitor Son was thinking, but all Marc could think about was how the Archons' main ally had just announced his daemons wouldn't be coming into the war to support them any time soon. That left only those nasty witches to help defend them against the Sons and their allies.

Is that what Consera had planned? If it wasn't, then this war had just gotten a hundred times worse, and the damn thing had just begun. Fucking witches wouldn't be enough. Even Marc knew that.

When the magistrate returned without Hades, Marc considered asking about what the god of the Underworld had just said but decided against it. The less he knew about what was involved in this whole war with the Sons of Navarus the better. All he wanted to do was get back to his office and crack open that vial of Bliss he had stashed in the bathroom behind the toilet.

"Well, I'm going to get going. Lots of work to get done," he said as he made his way toward the door.

"Not so fast, Marc. I want you to go to Lucinda and find out how she's doing with her witches and their preparations. They need to strike the weres quickly, as in as soon as possible, but I didn't get the feeling she was one hundred percent on board with our plans. Check up on her and report back to me tomorrow night."

He couldn't believe it. Go to where the witches were and check up on them? He had to be kidding. He was a fucking Archon, not some minion who should be sent out on errands for him.

Picking his mouth up off the floor, Marc scrambled to think of a suggestion better than the one his boss had just offered. Who could go instead of him?

Then he spied Nico standing in the same spot he'd been in for the entire meeting and pointed at him. "Don't you think he might be a better choice? What if the witches decide they don't have to listen to me? They're loyal to you, not the Archons. Nico was a Son for hundreds of years. He can handle them better than I can. Plus, he's one of your vampires, which means it will be like they're dealing with you through him. I really think Nico would be better to go."

For a moment, Consera looked like he'd explode in a fit of rage at Marc's disobedience, but then he nodded and looked over toward his vampire. "You might be right about the loyalty issue, Marc. Very well. Nico, I want you to go to Lucinda and the European witches. Make sure they're ready to go by tomorrow night. I want to strike at the weres and the Americans hard and fast. The sooner we get rid of them, the sooner we can show Hades how much we need his daemons to close the deal and end this war."

Nico simply nodded and quietly walked out, leaving Marc standing there relieved he'd been able to talk himself out of that awful assignment. Imagine him, an Archon, having to go deal with witches. Just the thought of it turned his stomach.

Then his boss's words about Hades and his daemons settled into his mind. When he and the magistrate left to go into the anteroom, the god of the Underworld made it clear their side had to prove themselves before he'd send his daemons into war for them.

Marc couldn't help but wonder if the alliance the Archons and magistrate Consera had constructed would withstand this war with the Sons. As it was, it seemed to be getting more and more fragile by the minute. First, reluctant witches, and now, Hades holding back his troops until Consera showed him they weren't going to depend entirely on the daemons to win this war.

Their side could only hope the alliance between the Sons of Navarus and their allies was even less stable. If not, this war might end with one single battle, but not in the way Consera predicted.

In that case, Marc knew he better have a backup plan to ensure whatever happened to the rest of his fellow Archons and their side, he would end up safe and sound. Now was the time to formulate that plan before it was too late.

# 4
---

Closing his eyes, Theron tried to sense where his father was at that moment, but his mind filled with memories of his mother. He'd read Dante's thoughts to find out how she died, and he wished he hadn't the second he saw how she'd suffered at the hands of those fucking Archons. She lay on the filthy ground like some castoff creature, her dark brown eyes filled with pain after they tortured her to find out where he was. He didn't know how long she endured that agony, but Theron wished she'd just told them what they wanted to know instead of giving her life to protect him.

His chest hurt like it always did when he thought of her. She'd been the one to dry his eyes when he fell and hurt himself as a small child. She'd held him close when the changes he was going through threatened to make him go mad, never letting the rest of the world or even her closest friends know how difficult being a born vampire was on him.

Only his mother understood what it was like to age so

rapidly. While everyone else marveled at his growth spurts that happened literally overnight, they didn't know that moving from a toddler to a teenager in the span of months instead of years took its toll not only on his body but on his mind and his spirit. She knew, though, and when it became too much for him, she wrapped her arms around him and in that gentle voice of hers told him how much she knew what he was going through and how she was there to comfort him.

*I know this feels like you're going to explode, and you don't know what to do with all the thoughts and emotions swirling around inside you, Theron. I know because I went through it just like you did. If I could take away the pain you're going through, I would, but I can't. What I can do is promise that I'll always be here, and I'll always be someone you can trust to share your pain with, honey.*

That was three nights before she disappeared.

As his emotions threatened to overwhelm him, Theron shook his head to rid himself of the memories of his mother. He couldn't think about her now. It hurt too much and made him feel lost without her.

Instead, he needed to focus on his father. Finding him was his first priority. Then he'd join him in killing as many Archons as possible this night. His blood yearned for vengeance for what they'd taken from him.

From them.

He struggled to sense his father's location, likely because he wasn't a born vampire like his mother. Theron pushed everything else out of his mind and focused solely on the image of his father he carried around with him in his thoughts. The hulking vampire who'd protected him from the rest of the world so eager to take advantage of his gifts stood over him in his memories, his somber expression hiding how genuinely loving he always was.

Slowly, where his father was right then came to him, and Theron quickly moved to join him. They had work to do this night, work that only the two of them had responsibility for.

THERON LOOKED around what he sensed must be a big city. The sounds of cars and the whine of an ambulance siren a few streets away filtered into his brain as he scanned the area around him. A tower in the distance stood lit up against the dark night sky. He had a feeling he'd seen pictures of it before at some point, but he didn't take the time to give it much thought.

More important than his location was if his father was nearby. He'd sensed his presence back at the Order's headquarters, but after following his thoughts, he wondered if he'd made a mistake. Theron had only recently begun using this ability, so perhaps he'd misjudged. Or maybe his emotions about his mother had muddled his thoughts as he tried to pinpoint his father's location.

Looking up, he saw he'd transported to a spot next to a six-story building. Bushes dotted the landscape around him, thankfully giving him some cover since he had no idea where he was or who might show up while he figured that out. In the moonlight, he could see the street name on a sign a few yards away.

Avenue du President Kennedy

He walked around the front of the building and gazed

up at it. Awnings on some of the windows made it look like a residence, but he had a feeling this wasn't just some house.

The sound of footsteps startled him, and he quickly looked around to see who was there with him. One look and he knew he'd come to the right place.

The large figure of a male crouched near the front door didn't see him as he walked up to join him, but when Theron stopped a few feet away from him, he turned his head. His eyes flashed a wildness he hadn't expected, but the male was his father.

"Dad, it's me," he said quietly as he moved toward him.

But the response he got wasn't what he expected.

"Go away," Ramiel growled. "Whoever you are, go before I make you go."

His words so full of rage stopped Theron in his tracks. He understood his anger and shared in it. He just thought when he finally found him again that he'd be happier to see his own son.

Gingerly, he took another step and stopped. "Dad, it's me. Theron. Your son. I'm here to fight with you and kill those bastards who took my mother."

His father said nothing, but after a few moments, he leaned forward and stared at him. It had been a few weeks, so undoubtedly he'd changed since the last time they saw one another. Theron had gotten used to how fast his appearance transformed from one day to the next, but he suspected his father didn't recognize him now.

"Theron?" he asked in his usual gruff voice, now tinged with a kindness few heard from the Visigoth vampire.

Nodding, Theron smiled. "Dad, it's me. I know I probably look different. I'm still growing and changing, but it's me, your son. I've come to fight with you."

Ramiel walked toward him shaking his head. "I wouldn't know you if you hadn't said your name. You look so different."

He stopped in front of Theron and nodded. "But now up close and I see your eyes, I can't believe I didn't know you instantly. You always did have your mother's eyes."

"I thought I had your eyes," the young vampire answered, unable to let himself think about her at that moment for fear he might be overwhelmed by emotion.

"No. Never my eyes. Your mother's, though, definitely. I can't believe you're here. How did you find me?"

"I just focused on the image of you in my mind and it brought me here," Theron explained. "It feels like it should have been easier since you're my father, but maybe this power is just new."

Ramiel opened his mouth to speak but only shook his head. "I guess Kali didn't get a chance to mention that power before I left." He hesitated for a moment and then continued. "How are the rest of the Sons?"

"They're fine, Dad. They have their assignments, and now that you've begun the war, they're ready, just like me."

"Did that son of a bitch Nico force you into service already?" his father asked in disgust.

Theron smiled, happy to tell him the truth of what happened. "He didn't have to. I'm the head of the Sons of Navarus now, Dad. As for Nico, he was a spy for the Archons the whole time. A traitor. He's gone over to their side, and the first chance I get to stake that bastard, I'm going to."

His news made his father step back into the shadows. Shaking his head, Ramiel sighed. "A spy? For how long?"

"We have no idea. His sire is with the Archons and has been for a while. Kali told us because he's her sire too. Some guy named Consera. He's a magistrate who's behind the whole Archon takeover."

Ramiel blew the air out of his lungs. "Jesus Christ. Nico a traitor. Now I've heard everything. I had my problems with him, but I would have never thought he'd turn on the Sons."

"We don't need him. I've taken over, and everyone has their assignments in this war," Theron said proudly, happy to give that piece of news to the man who had worked so hard to protect him until he was ready.

But now he was, and he didn't want to waste any more time waiting.

Ramiel looked at him and smiled. "I guess I didn't have to worry about you, after all."

"I guess not. Now I can fight alongside you and get those bastards who took Mom from us. I want to kill them all, Dad. Every last one of them."

"We will." Ramiel hung his head and sighed. "I just want to tell you I'm sorry, Theron."

"For what?"

His father let out another sigh, this one deeper than the first. "A lot of things. Mostly, for not finding her in time." He looked up at Theron and continued, "But I tried. I loved your mother more than life itself. And when I lost her, I thought I lost everything. But now I know I shouldn't have left you and your sister. You needed me, and I wasn't there. I'm sorry for that too."

Theron patted his father's shoulder in sympathy for what he knew he was going through. Of all the things that were odd about his life, the one part that had always made him feel normal was how much his parents loved one another.

"I know, Dad. I know you would have saved her if you could. Her death isn't your fault. It's theirs. And when they're eliminated from this world, there better not be anyone who says it wasn't the right thing to do because I'll have something to say about that. And don't worry about Leta and me. Terek and Ilona are the best stand-in parents around. She was happy and healthy the last time I saw her, and when this war is over, you can go back and bring her home. She's growing like a weed, so you won't have a baby to look after either."

"Let's just hope she's not a teenager by the time this war ends," his father said in a sad voice.

"Well, she's not growing like I did, so at least there's that. She looks a lot like Mom, too."

"She must be beautiful."

The two vampires said nothing else because all they could think of was Noele. Theron read his father's mind and knew how much sadness he was hiding. He understood why. He didn't let the rest of the world know how much it hurt to not have her around anymore either.

Ramiel's face grew stony, and he shook his head as if to rid himself of all that emotion he kept bottled up. "Time to get these fucks for what they did."

Looking up at building in front of them, Theron nodded. "I'm ready. Who's here?"

"The Archon of Paris. He's the last of the French Archons. You like the way he lives in this palatial estate? Six floors of luxury when he's supposed to be working for the vampires he rules over. Time for him to see what life on the other side looks like."

"How many vampires are in there with him?"

"Half a dozen maybe. They've been leaving in droves since they got the news of what I was doing around the country. He's still in there, though, with a handful of staff. I don't care about them. They didn't do anything to deserve what he does, so don't bother with them unless they come at you. So far, I haven't had anyone do that at any Archon office I've hit."

As they walked around the back of the building, Theron thought about how easy those vampires who worked for the Archons were getting off. They made the choice to work for a bureaucracy that did nothing to help their fellow vampires. Bliss ravaged their populations, and still they worked for these fuckers. The Archons wanted a war with the only vampires who had ever tried to help all their kind, and still they stayed loyal to their bosses.

No, he wouldn't be letting them go like his father chose to. That was his right, but Theron had no patience for vampires whose greatest excuse was they were only doing what they were told. Nope. That didn't work for him, so if he had the chance to send any of them on to the Underworld, he'd take it willingly.

War had come, and there were only two sides. Too bad they had chosen the wrong one.

Moments later, Ramiel and Theron walked into the building that had looked so plain from the outside. The inside, however, was far different. White marble floors ran throughout, and gold fixtures more ornate than anything Theron had ever seen even in books were everywhere. In the corner of each room stood white marble columns that resembled those in the Order's headquarters.

"These Archons are supposed to be working for all vampires' benefit and they live like this?" he asked as his father checked his hip for his stake.

"It looks like someone's been working for himself for a long time," Ramiel mumbled as they walked down a main hallway.

They passed a conference room with a table and chairs for twenty-five and two crystal chandeliers hanging from the ceiling. Three gold candelabras positioned around the room were the only light in that room and gave it a spooky feel.

"Are you sure he's still here?" Theron whispered as they made their way down the passageway.

Ramiel nodded. "He's here. I can practically smell his fear. Like others of his kind, he's not a fighter, so he's scared. He's heard about my travels in the past few nights and knows he's next."

They came upon a room with the door locked, and Theron knew they'd found him. He searched the minds of the four vampires inside and read their thoughts. Everything but regret for who they chose to support in their world raced through their heads.

If even one of them other than the Archon had just considered what they'd done to the rest of the vampire world a mistake, he would have let them go. But not a single one did.

So they'd be turned to dust, too, like their boss.

Turning to look at his father, he mouthed the words, "They're inside."

And with that, Ramiel lifted his foot and knocked down the door. Theron had never seen his father so physically imposing before. The man who let him place bugs on his toes when he was a little boy now marched through a door into the offices of the Paris Archon like he'd been moving through the hedges outside.

He said nothing but let out a low growl when the four vampires huddling in the corner of the room put up their hands in surrender. As if that was a possibility now.

Theron wanted to let them know exactly why they were about to meet their fate, though. As his father pulled the Archon up onto his feet and across the room to the opposite corner, he stood over the three females cowering before him and looked down at them with nothing but disgust.

"You think because you're not an Archon that you shouldn't have to suffer like he will in the next few seconds. You're wrong."

The youngest looking of the females began to cry when behind him Ramiel staked the Archon. "Why are you blaming us? We're just like everyone else. We never had a choice."

Shaking his head, Theron refused to let that excuse go. "At some point along the way, you had a choice to make, and you made the wrong one. You had a choice to stand by your fellow vampires and help them instead of working in a place like this that puts the lives of most of us to shame for a vampire like your boss."

"That's not true," she sobbed. "You don't understand

what it's like to be a female vampire. Working for an Archon is the best job we can get."

Fuck her and her bullshit excuses. "They've let loose that shit Bliss, and everyone knows it. I can read your minds and I see what you're thinking. 'It's not my fault. I never had control of anything. I was just doing my job.' The problem with that is you knew what he and his kind were doing and still you turned your head and looked away."

The female next to her raised her hands higher in the air and said in a tiny voice, "We did know something, but what could we do? How could we stop it? You know as well as we do how powerful Archons are in our world. What would you do if you knew what they were doing?"

Theron turned around and pointed his stake at where his father stood next to a pile of dust that used to be the Paris Archon. "I'd fucking stake them just as we plan to do tonight and every night after until there are none of them left."

"We aren't like you, though. You're warriors. We're just females," she said in a trembling voice.

He thought back to what he'd seen in Dante's mind about how his mother looked after the Archons tortured her and left her for dead. As strong as she'd been, she still was just a female up against a group of males who chose to hurt her instead of protecting her. Were these three terrified female vampires any different?

As much as he wanted to punish them for making the wrong choice, he could hear his mother's voice in his head telling him being the vampire he was came with responsibilities. If she saw him now, she'd warn him he would be no better than the Archons he hated for killing her if he hurt these females.

She'd remind him that of all the things the Prophecy of Idolas claimed he'd be, the savior of the vampire world was the most important.

He looked into their eyes and saw the utter terror in them. In their minds, they were sure he would kill them like they'd always believed would happen if they disobeyed the Archon. To them, no matter what he wanted to think, he was as bad as the ones he sought to destroy.

His father walked up behind him and patted him on the shoulder. "Leave them be, Theron. They aren't our enemies. They're as much victims of the way Archons have terrorized our world as your mother."

As his emotions swirled around inside him, Theron knew what his father said was right. Whatever he'd been born to do, it wasn't to slaughter defenseless females like the Archons had done to his mother. Her memory deserved better than that.

Finally, he lowered his stake and looked over at Ramiel. "Fine, but I want to take out the next Archon."

His father nodded and turned to walk away. "That's fine with me. When we're done with the local offices, we can go to headquarters, and you can stake as many as you like. There I won't stop you from taking out anyone."

As he backed away from the three females, they began to cry and thanked him for sparing them. It should have made him feel good about what he'd done, but all it made him want to do was find another Archon fast. His vengeance hadn't been sated in the least yet that night, and if it didn't happen soon, he couldn't promise he wouldn't take out his anger on the next group of innocent victims.

That's not the kind of vampire he wanted to be. However, he wouldn't be able to contain his rage at what he'd lost for much longer. Archon or not, someone would help him take the edge off his need for revenge that night.

When he caught up with his father outside, Theron thought he saw more sadness in his eyes than before. Confused, he asked, "What's wrong?"

Ramiel sighed. "I thought killing Archons would make me feel better, would make me miss your mother less. I'd hoped getting my revenge would help get rid of the empty feeling I've had since I lost her."

"We'll make them pay, Dad. Every last one of them. They'll pay for what they took away from us."

He nodded and forced a smile. "She'd be proud of you, Theron. I know what you wanted to do back there, but she'd be proud that you didn't."

"Are you proud, Dad?"

"I've always been proud of you, son. Next up is Germany. Are you ready?"

Theron nodded. "Let's get them."

He didn't care where they went next. He just wanted his revenge on the Archons, and even though he didn't know it before tonight, he cared about fighting next to his father in this war he was born for.

## 5

---

Vasilije pulled Sasa close to him as they walked across the threshold of the Dracos' castle. In a few hours, he, Terek, and the dragons would go to war, so he wanted to have her next to him every minute until then. He'd lost too many moments with her already, moments he'd never get back.

Every time he thought about those nights he spent without her, he couldn't stop the rage inside him from bubbling up to the surface. He didn't want to always react that way. Fuck, part of him wished he could just be the vampire everyone thought he was—uncaring, thoughtless, and cold.

He wasn't, though. At least not when it came to Sasa. Everything else could go fuck itself for as much as he cared. The Archons and this goddamned war could fade away into nothingness, and he wouldn't bat an eyelash. Fuck them all.

But Sasa was different. Maybe it took losing her to see that so clearly, but now that he did, he wouldn't let a moment go by without enjoying what she brought to his world.

Tapping him on the arm, she whispered, "What's wrong? You look like you want to kill someone. Is there something going on here I don't know about?"

Clearly, he wasn't as good at hiding his feelings about what happened even now.

He shook his head and smiled. "Nothing, love. I can't think of another place in the world I'd want to be than right here with the dragons, Terek and his family, and you. Maybe this whole war will be cancelled once Ramiel and Theron get together, and we can all live in peace right here. I'm sure the Draco brothers wouldn't mind. It's a big castle."

Sasa's dark eyes opened wide, as if even the possibility of that made her excited. "I wish. I'm afraid of what's coming, so if those two could handle the entire war, I'd be all for that."

For a moment, Vasilije considered how possible that outcome may be. Ramiel was nothing less than hell bent on avenging the loss of Noele and had already taken out half of the Archons on the Continent. Not that he blamed him. They deserved nothing less than a stake to the heart, every single one of them.

And Theron had rage enough to level a city. Without his mother around to tamp down his reckless tendencies, that vampire seemed hell bent himself, but Vasilije had a feeling it wasn't just to get revenge on those Archon fucks for what they did to Noele.

His rapid aging was clearly affecting him in ways other than his becoming a man in less than two years. His overconfidence had blown up into dangerous cockiness.

He looked like an adult, but in reality, he was little more than a child with enormous power, and that power might get them all killed.

But Vasilije had seen another side to him that he wasn't sure the other Sons had yet. Theron's rapid ascension to leader of the Sons of Navarus seemed to be what the Prophecy of Idolas indicated, but beneath all his anger and bluster seemed to be a vampire who didn't know where he fit in. While the rest of the Sons saw the group as their family, Theron had shown he had no issue with treating them as useful pawns in a war he saw destined to prove his own value.

As much as he'd been brought up by Ramiel as his father, Vasilije had a sense there was an unhealthy dose of Thane inside him that could endanger them all just as he had when he betrayed them. He'd paid for that with his life.

Vasilije just hoped they all wouldn't pay for Theron's quest for greatness with their lives.

"Did you hear me?" a male's voice asked, tearing the Romanian out of his thoughts about their immediate future.

He turned to look at Terek and shook his head. "Sorry, no. What's up?"

With a smile, he answered, "I don't usually consider you a deep thinker, but lately you seem to always be lost in thought. Anything you want to share with your old friend?"

"Nothing other than thinking about what's coming at us. What did you want?"

"I thought we should sit down with the dragons and discuss the plan. Kerik said he and his brothers would be available in about an hour and for us to get comfortable while we wait. I'm going to take Ilona and Leta upstairs to the room where they'll be staying while they're here, so what do you think of us getting together when the dragons come back? The sooner we're all on the same page, the better, as far as I'm concerned."

Vasilije knew Terek had hoped the war could be put off, but Ramiel's attacks on the Archons throughout Europe had crushed that pipe dream. He saw by the worry in his friend's green eyes that he wasn't as sure as their new leader that this fight would end up as wonderfully as planned. True, Theron had been smart when he assigned each of them to the respective allies, but war had a way of being all too unpredictable and rarely in a good way.

"That sounds good. I'm going to take Sasa up to her room, so we can meet in the main hall in an hour?"

"Okay. See you then."

Even though Terek flashed a smile, Vasilije saw how worried Ilona looked standing just behind him with Leta in her arms. A born vampire like her mother, the child wasn't a baby anymore. Thankfully for her adoptive parents, she wasn't growing as fast as her brother, but she had her own challenges as a young girl left practically orphaned at such a young age. Although Ilona had never said anything, he knew she wished Terek could just turn his back on the Sons and this entire war and stay with her and their child for the rest of their lives.

Little Leta had already basically lost her first parents. She didn't need to lose a second set of them in her lifetime. But that was exactly what might lay in her future because of the war with the Archons.

He didn't envy any of them for what they were going through.

"Let's go relax for a few minutes before you have to leave for the meeting, okay?" Sasa whispered as she tugged him by the arm toward the stairs.

"I'm all for relaxing, as you well know, but I'm not going to that meeting alone. You're going to be right there by my side."

She stopped on the third step and stared at him in confusion. "What? Why? I'm not able to fight in this war, Vasilije."

Cradling her face, he bent down to kiss her softly on the lips. "I'm not letting a minute go by without having you at my side as long as I can. No, you won't be fighting, so you'll be safe here while I am, but until then, I want you close to me. I don't want any regrets this time."

He expected her to question what he meant by that, but she didn't, thankfully. He didn't want to discuss the past anymore. Back there was littered with mistakes he couldn't change, but he never intended on making them again, that was for sure.

Plus, the plain truth was that he enjoyed having Sasa with him concerning Sons matters. As an empath, she read others far better than he ever could, and even though he knew a lot of what they had to discuss at this meeting in an hour might upset her, she was tough and could handle it.

Squeezing his hand tightly as he pushed the door to her room open, she gasped when she looked in. He'd gotten used to the castle's accommodations since he'd been a guest of the dragons' for so many years, but he had to admit the place did pack a punch, especially when it came to the bedrooms.

She released his hand and rushed into the center of the bedroom to spin around with her arms at her side. All smiles, she cooed, "This is the biggest bedroom I've ever seen! It's even bigger than the one back at the monastery, and I thought that was huge. They could move another bed in here and I could have Ilona and Leta stay with me it's so big."

With a quick glance, he judged another bed could fit, along with a child's bed, if necessary. "If that's what you want, we can ask Kerik if it's okay. I'm sure he'll be fine with it."

Sasa stopped twirling and sat down on the edge of the bed. "I know I should be somber because all hell is about to break loose, but this just made me so happy. I bet you think it's silly, but I feel like if I don't find some kind of happiness in all of this, I'm going to spend the entire time you're gone crying."

He lifted her chin with his finger and smiled down at her, loving how genuinely happy she'd been for that short time. "We don't need any more somber. We have more of that than we need. I'm happy you like it here. You'll be safe. It's a little drafty and the castle can make you feel like you're getting lost in it sometimes, but you'll be protected here. The Dracos will put their enchantments on it so no one will be able to get to you, Ilona, or Leta. I promise."

Her smile faded, and she asked, "What about you? Will they be able to put their enchantments on you so you'll be safe when the battle starts?"

Since lying to her had never worked in the past,

Vasilije took a deep breath and tried to find the words to make the truth sound better than it actually was. Sitting down next to her on the bed, he took her hand in his and brought it to his lips in a kiss.

"War is never safe, but I'm far less worried about Terek and me than I am about Saint. Those werewolves are going to have a hard time fighting the witches' spells. They aren't elemental beings like the dragons, so that hocus pocus nonsense the witches dish out will work on them."

That didn't come out as positive as he'd intended, but it was the truth. He saw by the worry etching itself into her expression that she'd understood exactly what he'd said, though.

"Do you think Saint and Solenne are going to be okay?"

In all honesty, he had no idea. Vasilije wouldn't have been happy to hear Theron say he had to fight with the weres, but that had more to do with his sour feelings about what that damn Hadrian had done in Rome than anything else.

"Saint's tough, and Solenne is a descendant of Idolas, who was the child of two gods. That has to count for something."

Sasa rested her head on Vasilije's shoulder and sighed. "I hope they come out of this safe and sound. I hope all of us do. Then I just want to live a peaceful life somewhere just the two of us. Maybe we can go back to Romania."

"Or maybe New Orleans," he said quietly. "I liked that place. As long as we can avoid the voodoo ladies, I think we'd be okay."

For a moment, he wasn't sure Sasa had heard what he said because she didn't say a word or even move. He listened for the sound of her breathing and heard it, though, so he waited for her response.

And when it came a few seconds later, he couldn't help but smile and be genuinely happy.

She turned to face him with a look of pure shock. Never before had he suggested the two of them return to New Orleans before this, so her surprise was understandable. But he hoped beneath that would be a reaction far happier.

"Did you just say maybe we could go back to New Orleans?"

Nodding, he shrugged. "It was just a thought. We don't have to, if you don't want to."

That's all it took. She threw herself against him, wrapping her arms around his neck, and began crying. "Oh, Vasilije, I'd love that! I know how much you love being here, but I miss where I grew up."

"Well, then it's settled. After this war is finished, we'll go to New Orleans."

She sat back and wiped her tear-stained cheeks. "We can get one of those old mansions if you want. You seem to like big homes, and they're huge. Maybe it will come with ancient trees that have Spanish moss hanging off them. Oh, it's going to be so great!"

"It will be great. Just the two of us, Sasa."

His news thrilled her more than he imagined it would, and she jumped up from the bed. Pacing across the floor, she began planning their life after the Archon War right there in front of him. "First, we'll get one of those big houses. I remember when I was a little girl growing up I always wanted one of them. Mama and I never could afford anything bigger than the tiny places we lived in, but now I'll finally have a home in New Orleans like I've always wanted. Can we get one in the Garden District? They have the most beautiful homes there, Vasilije. I know you've gotten used to living away from humans, but can we?"

She stopped in front of him and gave him a look with her big brown eyes wide open, like she was pleading for him to say yes. How could he give her any other answer when this house of hers made her so happy?

He reached out and took her hands in his to pull her to him. "Yes. Whatever you want, it's yours."

With a gentle smile, she corrected him. "You mean it will be ours."

As he leaned in to kiss her, he whispered against her lips, "Ours. Vasilije and Sasa's big house in the Big Easy."

Sasa closed her eyes and smiled as he pressed his mouth to hers. She wrapped her arms around his neck and softly trailed her fingers across his shoulders, making his body come alive. In a few hours, this time they had together would be the sweet memory he'd carry into battle, but for now, it was the most important moments in his entire existence.

"I love you, Sasa."

Opening her eyes, she looked at him and sighed. "And I love you, Vasilije."

With a wave of his hand, she stood in front of him naked and more beautiful than any other woman on Earth. She giggled and began to unbutton his shirt.

"Someday, I'm going to get the hang of that trick and

use it on you," she said sweetly as she carefully made her way down his chest, button after button.

"No need, love," he said, and with a second wave of his hand his clothes disappeared too.

Her gaze roamed over his torso as a wicked glint in her eyes appeared. "I still want to learn it. I think it might come in handy with you some night."

Vasilije moved his hands over her body, worshipping every precious inch of her as he kissed the soft spot just under her ear where he first drank from her. Against her skin, he said, "As if there would be any night that I wouldn't willingly remove my clothes for you."

She pulled him into her, holding his head against her neck as he leaned back onto the bed and then pulled her on top of him. No matter what his future held in only a few hours, at that moment with the woman he loved staring down at him with a mixture of desire and love in her eyes, he couldn't imagine ever being more content.

Sasa rolled her hips, taking him into her, and as he sank into the depths of her body, he let himself revel in the simple feel of fucking her. He held her hard at her hips to set the pace of their lovemaking, and as always, she frowned down at him because she wanted to set her own pace.

He may have changed in many ways for her in the recent months, but he was as he'd always been when it came to sex. Not that he thought she really wanted him to change. For all that pouting she did, the moaning that came shortly after the pout disappeared each time he fucked her the way he wanted to told him she wouldn't want him to be anything but what he'd always been in those moments when he was inside her.

"Mmmm...you're driving me crazy," she said sweetly in that pleading way that let him know she loved how he made her feel.

"We have time. There's no need to hurry."

As he watched her ride his cock, he knew he hadn't spoken the truth there. They didn't have time anymore. Tonight may be their last night together for a while. Or forever. There were no guarantees.

Knowing this, he rolled her over onto her back and silently promised her if this was the last time they'd ever be together, she'd always know he wanted no one other than her in the moment when it counted the most.

He cradled her face and kissed her long and deep while his cock filled her completely. He took her breath away, but she did the same to him, leaving him desperate for more of her. Rearing his hips back, he began fucking her in earnest, needing her release as much as he needed his own.

Sasa clung to him, her nails tearing his back and shoulders as the two of them raced toward that place they could only find in one another. He felt the first squeeze of her cunt around his cock telling him she reached it before he had. But his body had become so in tune with hers that it would only take feeling her come to push him over the edge.

Arching her back, she moaned his name in his ear and then she came apart beneath him, just as he felt the first twitch of his release. With one last thrust into her cunt, he flooded her body with all he had and groaned in sweet relief.

Vasilije didn't know how long they lay there in each other's arms, their bodies joined in the most intimate way possible. If he had his choice, he'd never leave that very bed and the only female who had bewitched him in all his years as a vampire.

"Promise me you'll stay safe and come back to me."

Her voice was small and shaky, and each word felt like someone squeezing his heart. He swore he never wanted to lie to her now that they had this second chance together, but at that moment, he couldn't bear to force the truth into what they'd shared.

"I promise, Sasa. I promise."

It was only a partial lie. He hoped someday when he confessed the truth to her as they sat in that big house in New Orleans that she'd forgive him.

## 6

For the past five minutes, Terek had watched Ilona press her lips onto Leta's little belly and blow raspberries against her skin, and he honestly couldn't imagine anything else in the entire world more enjoyable. The little girl giggled so sweetly, completely unaware that the world she'd been born into was about to set itself on fire. Ilona seemed utterly able to push away that reality too, and as he watched the pure happiness the two of them shared, he wished he possessed the ability to ignore the truth of what lay ahead of them all in the near future.

"Who's a beautiful little girl?" Ilona cooed before blowing on Leta's skin again. Lifting her head, she smiled and repeated the question. "Who's my beautiful baby girl?"

That Leta wasn't their daughter had gradually become a fact neither one of them brought up anymore. Terek had thought they needed to keep that in mind to avoid the pain of having to give her back when Ramiel returned to be her father again, but that hadn't happened and slowly Leta became part of their family so much that Terek had a hard time remembering what life was like without her.

Turning her head, Ilona smiled at him. "She's so beautiful. Sometimes I find myself just staring at her when I didn't even realize I was doing it. This little doll is a dream come true."

Now that the war had officially begun and Terek knew he had to leave to fight against the Archons and their allies, he wondered what their life would be like when peace returned to their world. He hadn't realized it before, but now that every night could be his last, he felt the need to live his life more fully than ever before. No more worrying about what might happen when it came time to give Leta back. No more wishing he could give Ilona what she so wanted.

No. With the outbreak of war, he felt surer about what he needed to do for the ones he loved. When Ramiel returned, it would be hard, but there were other born vampires in the world who needed parents to love them. There had to be. He'd scour the Earth if it was necessary, but he'd find one. After watching Ilona fall in love with Leta, he had to.

Exhausted from playing, Leta closed her eyes and drifted off to sleep under the watchful eye of her adoptive mother. He'd wanted to spend some time with her before he left, but even a warrior's plans had to take a backseat to a child's sleep schedule.

After covering her with a pink blanket, Ilona quietly walked around to where he sat on the opposite side of the bed. "I think I wore her out," she whispered as she looked over at the little girl. "I probably dote on her too much, don't I?"

Terek eased her down onto his lap and kissed her softly on the cheek. "You dote on her as much as a loving mother would. I don't think it's possible to love a child too much."

"I know she's not ours, but I'm so happy I'm going to have her with me while you're gone. Sasa's going to be here with me, but I feel like Leta is one of us, so it's like you won't be really gone," Ilona said, forcing a smile.

He cradled her face in his hands and pressed a kiss onto the center of her lips. "When I get back and we don't have to worry about war anymore, I want to spend a few weeks just with the two of you, Ilona. We'll take turns making her giggle, and when she's older, I'll get her a swing set so she can play outside."

For a moment, he stopped, and then he said the words he should have said years ago. "I also think we should get married."

Even though the mere thought of that thrilled him more than he thought it could, his words came out so calmly that at first they didn't register with Ilona. She continued to look over at Leta as she slept, smiling and nodding as he spoke.

But then her smile faded, and she tilted her head to look at him. "What did you say?"

"I said I think we should get married."

"Really? Why? I thought you decided a long time ago that you didn't like the idea of marriage."

"I'm seeing things a little differently lately. So you still haven't said yes or no."

Ilona wrinkled her nose. "You didn't ask me anything that required a yes or no answer, Terek."

"Will you marry me after all this war business is over?" he asked, calmer than he thought he would be when those words left his mouth.

As tears filled her eyes, she nodded. "I will marry you. Can I ask what changed your mind about marriage now?"

He kissed her and tried to think of a way to explain how much had changed in him in the recent months. Finally, he just said, "I was afraid that if we married that I'd lose you, but I'm not afraid of that anymore."

She threw her arms around his neck and hugged him as she quietly sobbed. "I love you, Terek. You've made me happier than I ever imagined I could be. Now my life is perfect. The perfect male, a beautiful little girl, and a future I can't wait to get started on."

Terek held her to him and closed his eyes. He couldn't wait for that future to begin either. As soon as the Sons and their allies ended this damn war, he'd have that life he'd always dreamed of but feared he didn't deserve. He'd done his time as a Son of Navarus. Now he just wanted to be a husband and father like he'd planned to be all those centuries before.

Quietly, he broached the reality of what the two of them may face concerning Leta. Smoothing Ilona's long blond hair down her back, he said, "When Ramiel comes to take her, I promise I'll find us another child who needs a family."

Leaning back away from him, Ilona grimaced for a moment and then nodded. "I know he very well may come back like you say. I'm not blind, Terek. I know Leta has a father. But even if I do have to give her up, I want to help another born vampire child. I've learned so much about them because of her. Like how fast they age. I guess I expected her to age like Theron, but it's slower. And born vampires age until they find their mate. I love that. And they only drink blood, like Noele used to. I continue to learn things about her every day, too, and although you don't show it, I know you love having her around."

"I do," he admitted, not ashamed of the truth now. "Having her in our life has made me see things I didn't want to acknowledge were true. She's part of the reason I want to get married. Seeing you with her opened my eyes to how much I was taking you for granted. I don't want to do that anymore."

Ilona looked over at Leta still sleeping soundly on the other side of the bed and smiled. "I thought she was an angel from the moment she came to us. Now I know she is."

"Whatever happens with her, we'll have a child, Ilona. I promise. We'll have that family the two of us want."

She turned back to face him and kissed him. "Thank you, Terek. Thank you for understanding how much this means to me. I can't explain it, but being a mother is something I've felt destined to be all my life. I've never been happier than these past weeks with Leta and us together. I finally feel like I'm who I've always been meant to be."

"Then I'm happy. That's all I've wanted is to make you happy, Ilona."

He'd never wanted anything else, but for so long Terek felt like something had been missing in their life. He showed her he loved her all the time, and she showed him too, but there always seemed to be a space left empty between them. He'd fought against believing a child was what would make them complete, but now he knew his hunch had been right.

Having Leta to take care of had filled that gap between them, and now he didn't want to go back to how it used to be between them. So once this stupid war was over and he could return to her, they'd be three again, no matter if Ramiel took his daughter back or not.

"I need to go meet with Vasilije and the dragons before we leave. I wish I didn't have to go..."

He couldn't bring himself to say the rest of his sentence. She knew he had to leave. The two of them had known for far too long this night would come eventually.

Closing her eyes, she whispered against his lips, "Be sure to say goodbye to Leta before you leave. Come back to us, Terek. Come back so we can be happy again."

One last kiss filled with all the hopes and wishes the two of them had for that life in their future and he pulled her close for a final embrace. He walked around the bed to where Leta lay and bent down to kiss her softly on the forehead.

Stroking her soft cheek, he whispered to her, "I love you, little one. Be good for your mommy and I'll see you soon."

Ilona stood by the door, and he stopped before leaving, hating how his responsibilities to the rest of the world had to take precedence over the ones he loved. Her eyes filled with tears, and she turned away, swallowing hard to hold in her emotions.

"Look at me," he said as he gently turned her head to face him. She hadn't succeeded in controlling her feelings, and a single tear rolled down her cheek.

"I'll be back. I promise. I've fought in wars before with nastier enemies than the Archons. Wait for me and kiss Leta for me every night. I love you both more than you can know."

Pulling him to her, she cried even as she tried to remain strong. "I love you, Terek. Please make sure you come back to us, okay? We need you."

He took a deep breath in and inhaled the scent of her shampoo into his nose. He wanted to remember the soft scent of vanilla that always surrounded her while he had to be away from her side.

"I love you. Stay here with Sasa and don't let anyone into the castle."

As he backed away from her, he struggled to keep his emotions in check. He'd left for war before as a vampire and never before had any problem.

He didn't have a family that loved him then, though. This time, it mattered if he didn't return.

Ilona held his hand until she had to let go, and the last thing he saw as the bedroom door slowly closed was the tearful look in her eyes as she said goodbye one last time.


VASILIJE and the dragons were already downstairs when he got to the main hall, and Terek was surprised to see Sasa there too. Did his friend intend on having her fight with them?

As if he read his mind, he turned to look at Terek and smiled. "I didn't want to have to say goodbye yet, so Sasa is sitting in on the meeting."

"I just left Ilona and Leta upstairs," he said, nodding

his understanding of how Vasilije felt. He hated that he had to say goodbye already and he'd just left them moments ago.

"Ever think of just turning your back on it all and living happily ever after?" the Romanian asked with more than a hint of suggestion in his voice.

As they walked toward the table where the dragons sat talking with Sasa, Terek answered, "Never more than tonight."

They took their seats around the large table in the castle's main hall, and Vasilije took the lead in explaining Theron's plans. Terek gladly let him since he wasn't sure he believed in them enough to be promoting them to anyone else.

"Okay, the seven of us are tasked with handling every Archon in the east here. We expect some blowback from the witches, especially those from this area. They know the lay of the land, and they've made their choice to come in on the Archons' side. That said, I don't think they'll be as successful with their spells and potions on us. We should all just be thankful we aren't fighting with the weres. That's likely to be a shit show of the first order."

Sasa frowned at her mate's flippant way of describing what Saint and Solenne would be up against in the southern areas of the continent. For his part, Terek may not have termed things exactly as Vasilije had, but he didn't disagree with the general sentiment. Witches had powers that would work on weres since they were on the same level in the supernatural world because they retained so much of their human nature. Vampires relinquished their humanity when they became vampire, and dragons were born supernatural. That they looked like ordinary men was a result of their ability to use enchantments to fool the rest of the world.

The earth dragon, Stefan Draco, grimaced and shook his head. "That's too bad. I like those werewolves. They have a great way of knowing how to make any situation fun. Many a night I've partied with them and saw firsthand how much they enjoy that whole wolf thing they've got going on. As for those witches, fuck them and their potions and curses. Bitches. I'll be happy if they're all wiped off the face of the earth."

"Any reason we can't do just that?" Nevar Draco asked. "Not that I'm saying shirk our job to get rid of the Archons, but if their allies are in the vicinity, can we take them out too?"

Terek had always liked the youngest dragon brother. Even though he hadn't come into his powers yet, he had a confidence that sat quietly under the surface at most times, unlike the cockiness of his brothers, especially Victor, the air dragon.

Vasilije leaned over and patted Nevar on the back. "I like the way you think. Feel free to take out as many witches as you like, assuming you get the chance. I've got no love for them, and I think I can safely say that since they've decided to come in on the Archons' side, they're fair game."

"Then it's settled," Stefan said. "Kill 'em all. When do we start?"

Kerik held up his hand as if to slow down his overeager brothers. "Wait a second. I'm sure our vampire friends have more to say. Vasilije, please continue."

He shrugged and looked down the table at Terek. "Actually, that's about it. Our job is to clear this entire eastern area of Archons, and if we do the same with the witches, I don't think that would be a bad thing. Ramiel has already begun clearing the rest of the Continent out, assisted by his son by now, so whenever you're ready to go, let's do this."

Everyone began to stand from the table, but once more, the eldest Draco held up his hand to stop them. "Not so fast. I've been thinking of how we should approach this, and I've come to a decision. Nevar, you'll stay here at the castle."

The youngest dragon's mouth dropped open in shock. "Why? Kerik, I'm more than able to fight with you all. What good will I do here?"

"You're the only hope for our kind to remain in the world if we all fall in battle, little brother. We can't afford to lose all of us."

But still Nevar protested his brother's decision. "Why are you assuming you'll all die in battle? You're going up against vampires who aren't even a tenth as powerful as the ones sitting at this table and witches. They aren't enemies dragons can't handle."

"You haven't even come into your powers yet, Nevar. That leaves you with only your physical fighting skills, and that may not be enough."

"I've been training with Ivan. Tell him I've gotten good with the swords. Tell him, Ivan," the youngest dragon brother pleaded with the dragon who ruled water.

"He has been getting pretty good, Kerik. I mean, he's not my level, but he could probably defeat any of you with a sword."

But none of this changed the oldest Draco brother's

mind. Shaking his head, he said in a low voice, "I've made my decision. You'll stay here with Sasa, Ilona, and Leta. You are to defend this castle and stay alive. We need you as the final line of defense so there can be at least one dragon left in the world."

Nevar angrily shoved his chair away from the table and stood up. "This is bullshit, Kerik. This castle is impenetrable, so why the hell do these women need me? I know vampire abilities. If someone breached this place, they could just disappear. They don't need me for that."

Everyone sat quietly as his pleas made no difference with the one brother who mattered. Finally, after a few moments more, he realized arguing was futile and stormed out of the room, slamming the door behind him.

Gently, Sasa said to Kerik, "Ilona and I would be okay here without him, if you want to let him go with you. What he said is right. Only another vampire would be able to force us to stay here if we wanted to leave."

"Thank you for that, Sasa, but my mind is made up. If we all fall in battle, no matter what the circumstances or what being we're fighting, we need Nevar to be able to continue the dragon bloodline. Of all of us, he's probably the most important, and I can't risk him dying in this war."

The table fell silent once more. Much like Theron, the youngest dragon had a lot to lose by fighting before he was ready. Terek wondered if things would have turned out differently if the Sons had made a similar decision regarding Theron.

Not that they could. As much as he wished this war could have been postponed for a while longer, the vampire foretold to save their world in the Prophecy of

Idolas grew too strong and too fast for any of them to be able to make decisions regarding when he would be ready for battle.

And then his father began attacking the Archons, sealing Theron's fate for good or for bad, and now they were all at war.

"Say your final goodbyes, gentlemen. We'll be ready when you are," Kerik said as he stood from the table.

Terek looked over at Vasilije and saw worry in his eyes. He knew his friend too well and for too long not to understand what he was going through.

"Let's go upstairs so you can say goodbye to Ilona one more time," Sasa suggested as she and Vasilije began to make their way toward the door.

He didn't know if he could handle leaving her another time that night, but he couldn't turn down a chance to see her and the baby one last time. Terek knew Sasa was doing all she could to delay the inevitable, and he didn't blame her one bit.

Opening the door to Ilona's room, he saw the hopeful look on her face before she jumped up from the bed. "What's going on? Is the war over? Are we going home?"

Sadly, he shook his head and forced himself to smile so she couldn't see how much he wished those things were true. "No. The meeting with the dragons is over, and we're going to be leaving now, so I wanted to see you and Leta one more time."

Ilona's eyes filled with tears. "Oh. I guess that sounded naïve, but I just thought maybe there was a possibility something had happened so you wouldn't have to go."

"I wish that was the case, too, but they have to go,"

Sasa said as she walked over to stand next to Ilona in the middle of the room. "I figured it would be nice for the two of us to have each other to help us get through tonight."

She reached down and took her hand, but Terek saw tears in Sasa's eyes too. For all her bravado, she was as torn up about them leaving as his mate.

Vasilije kissed Sasa and whispered, "Until we're together again, remember I love you. This castle is safe for you, so don't worry. And when this is all over, we'll get that house with the mossy tree out front in the yard."

"I love you too, Vasilije. Stay safe. Please."

Terek gave Leta one last kiss and then turned toward Ilona. Her tears now rolled down her cheeks, so he made his goodbye a quick one. Cradling her face in his hands, he pressed a kiss to her forehead and whispered against her skin, "Remember what I said. No matter what happens, we'll have our family just like we want. I love you, Ilona. Stay here and I'll be back. I promise."

She threw her arms around him and hugged him tightly as she sobbed. "I love you, Terek. Come back to me alive."

This goodbye nearly tore his heart out, and as Terek stepped back, he struggled to fulfill his responsibility to the Sons and the vampire world. He knew he had to leave the two most important souls in his world there without him, but he'd never wanted to turn his back on everything as much as at that moment.

As he and Vasilije left that room, he said to him, "For the first time in all my centuries as a vampire, I fear leaving my family."

With a chuckle, his friend nodded. "That's what being

happy does to a male. Do you wish you hadn't fallen in love with her?"

Terek shook his head. "Not for a second. She and that little girl are what I'm fighting for. More than justice and more than making our world safe again, I'm going to war for them."

"Then let's get those fucking Archons and their allies so we can come back to the ones we love," Vasilije said as they started down the stairs to meet the dragons.

May they all come back to the ones they loved.

## 7

Dante scanned the growing group of clytens arriving at the Order's training center and nodded with satisfaction. The call had gone out for his kind to join in the fight against the Archons, but he didn't know how many would actually come. Clytens weren't exactly common, and their unique nature made them very independent. Nobody knew that better than he did.

But so far, they'd heeded the call and turned up. Nobody knew exactly how many clytens existed in the world. Actually, the Archons were supposed to know since they were the ones running the vampire bureaucracy that would be involved in those kinds of things, but they'd long ago abdicated that responsibility in favor of their plans for tyranny. As a result, a proper census of all vampires hadn't taken place in hundreds of years, so the clyten population remained mostly a mystery.

For his part, Dante had only run into a handful in his relatively short time as a vampire since the 1980s. They viewed the world differently because of their gift. There was a freedom and a real sense of superiority that came from not having to fear sunlight and yet still getting to enjoy all the other benefits of being a vampire. They felt as if they'd conquered nature in some way, and it never failed to be reflected in their attitude toward life.

"I didn't realize there were so many of you," Sion said as he watched with Dante the continual stream of clytens enter the training center building.

Dante turned to look at him and smiled with pride. "I don't think I knew there were so many either, but the more we have of us, the better off we'll be in the fight. We bring a special level of ability to any battle against the Archons since we don't have to run for cover when the sun comes up."

His friend rolled his eyes. "So I've heard a few million times."

"Nothing wrong with being proud of who you are, dude. Nobody has a problem when you go around building an entire fleet of drones. They act like you've created a new life, like you're fucking Frankenstein. The clytens get a sideways glance, like we're some kind of redheaded stepchildren in the vampire world, but wait until you see how they fight."

Sion gave him a pat on the shoulder Dante knew was meant to let him know he hadn't intended to offend. "It's Doctor Frankenstein, but I get your point. Clytens do have an edge regular vampires don't, and I think we're going to need it against those damn witches."

Immediately, he apologized. "I didn't mean anything by that, Dante. Sorry."

The clyten laughed off the comment. "No worries. I know you didn't mean Scarlett and her coven. Man, do you hear me? A few months ago, I wasn't even sure I knew what a coven was, and I certainly didn't like witches. Now I'm like their PR guy."

"You went and grew up on us," Sion said with a chuckle. "Settled down with one woman, and she's a human and a witch. Leave it to you to buck the system."

"Well, since you took the woman I was looking at, I had to move on, dude. How is Kali doing, by the way?"

He sighed and rolled his eyes. "Hard at work, as usual. She seems to think there's more to find out about Theron."

Surprised to hear that, Dante took his focus off the growing crowd of clyten in front of him and looked at Sion. "More? Like what? Is he getting more powers than the ones he already has?"

"I don't know. She can't say. All she keeps telling me is she's looking for more about Theron, and then she buries her nose back in those books of hers. I don't think she's left the apartment in three nights. When I go to sleep, she's still working, and when I wake up, there she is at the table reading page after page looking for whatever she thinks she's supposed to find."

Dante didn't say anything, but he heard the frustration clinging to every word. Kali did tend to be an intellectual, much like Sion, so it didn't surprise him that the two of them together resulted in issues. He'd always thought they were too much alike. That's why he'd been so sure he and Kali would have gone well together. He could bring out her lighter side, which Sion had a hard time doing. Even though he'd found a mate, he was still very much the Ice Man.

Oh well. They'd figure it out. Or maybe they'd just

read a book about what they were going through. For Dante, that sounded incredibly sterile, but then again, no one had ever accused him of being an intellectual.

He turned his attention back to the crowd of clytens in front of him when suddenly he sensed Scarlett was in danger. He heard her faint call for help, and she sounded terrified. His witch didn't sound like that normally.

"Sion, I have to go for a while. Do me a favor and keep an eye on things here for a few. I'll be back as soon as I can, okay?"

"Okay. Anything wrong?"

"Scarlett just called out for my help. That's not like her, so I'm worried something's happening. I just want to check, and then I'll be right back. If the group starts to get antsy, show them your drones. Everybody loves those things."

Sion laughed and nodded. "Okay. Hope she's fine."

"Me too."

The problem was he knew she wasn't. He felt her fear in every cell of his body.

———

DANTE RUSHED into Scarlett's house and began searching for her. Her calls had stopped, and he worried the worst had happened to her. Storming from room to room, he reminded himself that he shouldn't think the worst. She may be just fine.

"Scarlett! I'm here! Where are you?" he called out once he checked the living room and kitchen on the main floor.

"Dante, we're up here," she said just barely loud enough for him to hear.

She definitely wasn't fine if she sounded like that.

He tore up the stairs and ran to her room. As he threw open the door, for a split second he hesitated, unsure if he wanted to see what awaited him. Stepping into the room, he stopped dead at the sight in front of him.

Scarlett and her sister lay bleeding from their necks. Someone had attacked them with a knife and slit their throats. One glance at Ivy and he knew he couldn't help her.

Crouching down beside Scarlett, he quickly assessed the situation. If he didn't do something immediately, she'd end up like her sister.

"Help Ivy first. She's worse, Dante," she pleaded with tears in her eyes.

He shook his head, unable to say the words he knew would break her heart.

"No! Ivy, no!" she cried.

His eyes scanned her wound. Whoever had done this to them had cut Ivy nearly clear to the bone, practically taking her head off, but Scarlett's laceration was far shallower. She wouldn't live if he didn't do something soon, though.

Pushing her hair off her face, he leaned down and kissed her on the lips. "Scarlett, I can save you, but only if I make you vampire."

"Vampires did this to us. They attacked us. Why would I want to become one of them after that?" she said softly in a voice that told him he was running out of time.

"I can't lose you. I won't. Let me turn you and everything will be okay."

Scarlett turned her head to look at her dead sister just inches away. "Nothing will be okay," she said sadly. "I've lost my sister. I don't want to lose you too."

He kissed her again and whispered against her lips, "Then let me do this. We can be together if I do."

She didn't answer for a few seconds but then closed her eyes and turned her head away from him. "Do it then."

His fangs snapped into his mouth with a click, and he sank them into her neck, drinking her blood. They'd fooled around with this a few times, but now he truly took her into himself before slicing his wrist and holding it out for her to drink from.

"Take my blood. You have to in order for me to turn you. Take it and drink as much as you can."

When she didn't move, he pressed his wrist to her mouth and held her head to him. "Drink, Scarlett! If you don't, you'll die."

Slowly, she began to suck the blood from his wrist, but Dante worried it wouldn't be fast enough to stop her from dying. She needed to have more and soon before he lost her.

Releasing her head, he reached up and slid his fingernail over the spot in his neck where she could get blood and enough of it. It began to pour out of his body, so he ripped his wrist away from her mouth and pulled her up to him.

"Drink! If you don't, you're going to die!"

He held her head fast to his neck and felt her begin to draw from his wound. His heart raced at the thought that he hadn't worked fast enough to save her. All she needed was enough of his blood to change her and she'd be fine.

But was it too late?

Slowly, she stirred in his arms as she became strong again, and finally, he pulled away from her to see Scarlett gazing dreamily at him. Had it worked? He closed the hole in his neck and hoped it had.

"How do you feel?" he asked as he carefully lay her back down on the floor.

She took a deep breath and sighed. "I can't explain it. I've never felt like this before. I feel strong even though I feel weak. I'm tired, but all I want to do is run outside. I feel like one huge contradiction."

Touching her neck, she felt her injury as it healed itself, the slash across her throat closing against her fingers. "It's like I was never cut. I can't believe it."

Then she looked over at her sister lying on the floor near her. As she began to cry, she reached out to take her hand in hers. "You couldn't do that for her? Isn't there some way? I give you permission, if that's what it takes. Anything to save her, Dante."

"She was gone by the time I got here. I'm sorry. I would do anything to help, but I can't. It's not a matter of permission. The window to turn her had closed already when I found you two."

"I can't leave her here like this. We have to bury her properly. She deserves a proper Wiccan burial."

Dante hung his head. "Whatever you want me to do, I'll do it. Just tell me."

"We need to take her to the woods. I'll do the rest," she answered sadly.

Scarlett sat up and wrapped her arms around his neck. "Thank you for saving me. I know you would have done the same for Ivy if you could."

He gently ran his hand over her back and sighed. Already, this war had taken too much, and it had barely begun.

"Let's get you cleaned up and then do what's right for your sister. We can take all the time we need."

She leaned back and studied his face for a moment. "The war has started, Dante. Those Archons didn't attack us just by chance. I don't know how the rest of the coven has fared, but we don't have a lot of time. They could come back."

"And they'll be dealing with two vampires instead of two witches this go round. We'll take as much time as we need to for Ivy. She deserves it."

Overcome by sadness, all Scarlett could do was nod. She looked over at her sister, the two of them still joined at their hands, and she began to cry as she released her hold on her.

## 8

After saying their final goodbyes to Ivy, the clyten and his new vampire headed to the only place Dante believed they could get answers as to why Scarlett and her sister had been attacked. He'd had a good meeting with the Archon of New York before, so he hoped this time would be just as helpful.

They arrived at Salvatore Nero's office to find the front door open and the receptionist area empty. Not a good sign.

"Where is everybody?" Scarlett asked as he took her hand and held it tightly. "Who's supposed to be at this place?"

He scanned the room as they walked through and down the hallway to Nero's office. "The Archon of New York."

At hearing that, she stopped dead and shook her head defiantly. "I'm not going to talk to the son of a bitch who probably ordered my sister and me killed. I'd sooner kill him myself."

Dante shook his head, wishing he didn't have to deal with this right now. "This one's not a bad guy. I promise. At least he wasn't the last time I spoke with him. I know you want your revenge for Ivy, and I swear to you with all that I am that you'll get it, but right now we need to talk to him."

Scarlett's mouth shrunk to a thin line as she shook her head no. "You can't make me go in there to see him. I'll wait out here."

"Actually, I can. You see, I'm your sire since I'm the one who made you vampire. I can control whatever I want in your life. It's how the whole sire thing goes."

Her eyes opened wide and flashed with anger. "Forget it. I don't give a damn what you vampires think you can do to others. I won't be ordered around by any man, including you."

Dante had fantasized about making Scarlett a vampire so many times, and none of those dreams had included anything like the scene he was stuck playing out with her at that moment. He needed to get answers from this Archon, and he didn't have time to be fucking around with explaining how the rules of the vampire world were structured.

"First of all, you can't say you vampires anymore because you're one of us now. And second, I'm not a man. I'm a vampire. So I will be ordering you to come with me into this Archon's office because I can't let you stay out here alone. It's too dangerous. Now take my hand and walk with me down this hallway."

For a long moment, Scarlett fought her sire's orders, clenching her teeth and glaring at him. But it was no use.

Angry or not, she had no choice. As his vampire, she must do what he demanded.

He had a feeling he'd regret that demand in the near future, though.

No matter. He needed to speak to Nero, and he wanted Scarlett with him when he did, so with him she'd be.

She said nothing as they walked toward the back office, but Dante could feel the rage coming off her in waves. She'd been angry with him before, but never to this extent. Not exactly what he'd planned in all those fantasies of the night he would turn her into one of his own. Those dreams had been full of sexy times, not angry glares.

They reached Nero's office and found him sitting alone in his office chair behind his desk. The room looked as opulent as it had the last time Dante visited him, but now it felt abandoned since the Archon was the only soul left in the building.

"Nero, where is everyone?" he asked as they walked in.

"Dante, how nice to see you. I didn't think we'd have the chance to enjoy that glass of wine I promised you. Would you like it now?" Nero asked as he turned in his chair to reach for a decanter on the bookshelf behind him.

"No, thanks. Another time. Right now, I need some answers. First, where is your entire staff?" he asked as he offered Scarlett a seat in one of the leather chairs in front of the desk.

Of course, she refused, shaking her head and glaring

at him again, so he forced her to sit down and directed his attention back to the Archon.

"You seem to be having a hard time with your vampire tonight, Dante," Nero said with a smile as he nudged the glass of red wine toward the front of his desk. "Maybe a drink will settle her down."

"I'll settle down when I have reason to settle down," she snapped.

"Enough! Scarlett, I have to talk with him. Sit there silently until I tell you to speak again," Dante barked.

Her shock at being yelled at stopped her glaring for just a moment, and then she opened her mouth to tell him exactly what she thought of his order. The problem was she couldn't speak. He had control of her, so she found her ability to say even a single word gone.

She stared up at him with a look of betrayed shock that made his chest hurt, but he had no choice.

"I promise you can say whatever you want to me after he and I get finished here."

Not that saying those words would make his future with her any better. He'd have to deal with that later, though. For now, he had to get some damn answers.

Turning his attention back to Nero, he sighed. "Maybe I will take that glass of wine now. I feel like I need something to take the edge off this night. So once again, where is the rest of your staff?"

"Gone," he answered before taking a sip of wine. "Gone, gone, gone. And I suspect that I'll be gone, albeit in a different fashion, any moment now. If I were you, I'd leave as soon as I could."

"Why are they gone? What happened?"

The Archon smiled and shrugged like any of this was amusing. "I told you I wasn't following orders when it comes to that Bliss garbage. Well, I disobeyed orders again on a different directive that came down from the very top, and once my staff found out, they abandoned me. Not that I blame them. They'd probably be punished for my behavior too, so why would they stay?"

"What was the order?" Dante asked, almost afraid to find out. He had a feeling he already knew.

"We American Archons were given orders to exterminate every witch we could find in our regions," he answered flatly before lifting his glass to his lips to take another drink.

In a flash, Scarlett leapt from her chair and rushed around the desk to lunge at Nero. With her hands around his throat, she shook him as tears rolled down her cheeks. She couldn't speak a word, but she didn't have to. Dante knew exactly what she felt at hearing Nero's news.

He pulled her off him, and she fought him every inch of the way as he forced her back to her seat. Looking up at him with pure hurt in her eyes, she opened her mouth to speak once more. But nothing could come out until he let her speak.

Dante leaned down and wiped her tears from her cheeks as she silently sobbed. "Just let me get this over with, Scarlett. I have to ask him some questions."

Rarely before in his life as a human or vampire had he felt like such a piece of shit. Stuffing his emotions down deep inside, he turned his attention back to Nero.

"I'm sorry for that, but my vampire was a witch as a human, and you just admitted you all set out to exterminate her kind. One of you succeeded and killed her sister tonight."

Nero shook his head as a look of horror washed over him. "I didn't follow that order. Many American Archons did, but not me. I never signed on to become an exterminator of anyone. I swear whoever killed witches in this region wasn't ordered to do so by me."

"And that's why you expect your bosses to arrive and do what they do best at any minute?"

The Archon took a deep breath and let it out slowly as he nodded. "What I expect is they'll be here to stake me momentarily. I've become a problem, and you know how they deal with problems."

What Dante was about to say sounded insane, but he'd given Nero his word at their last meeting. He didn't know why, but he trusted this Archon. His gut told him he wasn't like the rest of them.

"You're coming with us. Let's get going before your former co-workers get here to turn you to dust."

Both Nero and Scarlett stared at him like he'd grown a second head in the past few seconds. He had to admit he always did like surprising others, but at that specific moment, he hadn't been going for shock value. Not only had he promised Nero help the last time, but he could possibly help the Sons if he had any information to give them. He'd been an Archon for centuries. He had to know something useful.

"I have to admit I never thought that was a bona fide offer," Nero said with a smile.

"Well, it's a limited time offer, so what do you say?"

It didn't take the New York Archon long to figure out

the deal he was being given was better than any other choice he had at the moment, and he agreed. "How will your bosses feel about you bringing someone like me along?"

"My bosses are dickbags like yours, so it will be fine. Just prepare yourself for a million questions. It isn't every day the Order of Macaria and the Sons get to have an Archon over."

As Nero came around his desk, he chuckled. "Guess who's coming to dinner, everyone."

Dante wanted to laugh, but he had to deal with Scarlett first before they left. Crouching down in front of her, he tried to make her smile, but she did nothing but glare at him. She had a right to be angry, but he couldn't fight her and the rest of the world. He needed her on his side.

"I'm sorry I had to take your ability to speak away. I didn't want to, but I had to get the answers to my questions. You can talk again and say anything you want. I deserve it."

Scarlett said nothing for a few moments, and then she slapped him hard across the face. "If you ever do that to me again, I swear to God I will kill myself before I let you touch me or even speak to me again. Am I being clear enough for you?"

"I understand. We can talk more later, but for now, I get it and we have to leave this place before someone arrives to stake all three of us."

They stood up and walked over to where Nero stood. Taking both their hands, he focused on the Order's headquarters and closed his eyes.

And then seconds later, the three of them left New

York. Dante just hoped the reception Nero would receive would be as pleasant as he'd promised.

---

THEY ARRIVED to a place in chaos. Elders rushed through the hallways with worried expressions etched into their grizzled faces. Dante didn't know what the hell was wrong, but he knew better than to ask any of them. They only seemed to know how to speak in riddles.

He spied Sion in the doorway of the Order's training center, so he directed Scarlett and Nero to follow him, and they hurried through more elders to reach him. As calm as ever, the Ice Man seemed unfazed by all the madness.

"What the hell is going on here?" Dante asked as Sion smiled at him like it was any other ordinary night in the vampire world.

"Well, I think all the clytens that will be coming have arrived. It's a bigger group than I thought. You seem to have picked up some travelers along the way."

Flustered, Dante threw up his hands. How could this guy be so fucking relaxed while the world went crazy around him?

Pointing to all the people running to and fro, he asked, "Anything you want to tell me about them and what the hell is going on here? The place looks like a mad house."

Sion's smile faded, and the serious guy he usually was returned, finally. Hopefully, now they'd get some damn answers.

"Oh, yeah. Things are a little crazy because the news

of the fight between the weres and the witches in the countryside outside Rome came in and it's bad. Those European witches are routing our allies."

"What about Saint and Solenne? They're down there fighting with them. Any news on how they are?"

"So far, so good, but they need reinforcements now. They're at Hadrian's place. We've been waiting for you to get back to activate the clyten regiment in the hopes that they'll be able to give the edge to our side down there."

"Then let's go! I'll get them ready, so Scarlett come with me," Dante said as he grabbed her hand. "Sion, this is Nero. He was the Archon of New York until a few minutes ago. He's a good guy and not like the rest of them. Treat him with respect because he's an ally now. Don't let the elders go all official on him. Maybe take him with you to see Kali and see what he has to say."

Sion's eyes grew wide, and he turned to look at Nero. "An Archon? Here?"

Extending his hand, the former Archon shook Sion's hand and smiled. "Retired. Just in time not to be killed by my bosses, actually. Nice to meet you."

Dante had a feeling he'd be fine, but still he gave Nero a chuck on the shoulder and said, "This guy's okay. A little machine-like, but you'll get used to it. His girlfriend has been deciphering the Prophecy of Idolas. They're a pretty brainy couple, but don't hold that against them. Tell them everything you can think of that might help us defeat the Archons."

Sion grabbed his arm just as he was about to leave. "I think you should let Theron know what you plan to do with the clytens. Better to all be on the same page."

Damn. He'd all but forgotten about the newest Son

since he left to join his father attacking Archons. Sion was right. He needed to talk to Theron first.

Grabbing his phone, he pressed the number two on his speed dial, and in an instant, Theron answered. He didn't have time for a long conversation, so he launched into the issue headlong.

"Hey, Saint and Solenne and the weres are taking a beating from the European witches down in Rome. I want to take the clytens who've volunteered and go down there to help them."

Theron didn't answer, and then a second later he was standing in front of Dante right there in the Order's head-quarters. "How bad is it?"

"Bad. Sion says they're getting slaughtered down there."

"How many clytens do you have to fight with you?" Theron asked, leaving Dante speechless.

He hadn't gotten into the training center to see how many clyten had shown up. Hesitating, he said, "Well, I don't know yet. I was busy saving Scarlett from the attack on her and her sister and then dealing with the New York Archon. I just got back."

Theron's dark eyes lit up with excitement. "Did you get him?"

Dante's gaze moved over to where Nero stood. "Yes, but not in the way you think. Theron, meet the Archon of New York. Nero, meet Theron."

The newest Son spun around and glared at him for a long moment. "Okay, I don't see anything in his mind to tell me he's going to be a problem."

Quickly, Dante jumped back into the conversation. "I told Sion and Kali to work with him."

"I'll tell you everything I know. Just let me stay. They're going to turn me to dust if I go back out there," Nero pleaded.

"He refused to allow Bliss into his region, and tonight he refused to exterminate the witches in his area," Dante said, coming to Nero's defense.

"Fine. He can go with Sion and Kali, and you can go with the clytens to Italy to help Saint, Solenne, and the weres."

As Theron turned to leave, he stopped and looked at Scarlett for a long moment. Taking her hand, he said, "I'm sorry about your sister. I promise she and everyone else who's been hurt by them will have their deaths avenged."

Scarlett smiled and thanked him, and then he disappeared again, likely to continue attacking Archons with Ramiel in their effort to rid the entire western half of the Continent of them.

With the permission he needed, Dante hurried Scarlett into the training center to get his clytens ready. He wasn't thrilled with taking the woman he loved into a battle zone, but he had a feeling leaving her behind would result in even more pain for both of them.

"We don't have much time, so just stay with me and you'll be fine."

Scarlett nodded, but she looked worried. She had every reason to be. The time had come for him to get off the bench and into the game. Unfortunately, she had no choice but to do the same.

Dante jumped up on a table and raised his hands in the air. "Fellow clytens, the time has come for us to help all vampires defeat the Archons. You're the most unique of our race, and now our race can't do without you. Witches siding with our enemies are slaughtering our friends the weres in Italy. We need to defeat them and save our allies because these battles have only just begun. Are you with me?"

The thousands of clytens in front of him cheered, so now he had his warriors.

"Focus on the area around the city of Rome, and look for the weres. I'll be there leading the fight, but your goal is simple. Save our allies while defeating those witches. Now, go!"

One by one, they vanished from inside the training center until all that were left were him and Scarlett. He jumped down off the table and took her by the hand.

"Don't worry. You'll be fine. You're a clyten like me and all of them."

Looking up at him with eyes full of worry, she shook her head. "But I'm brand new as a vampire. I've never fought anything in my life, except your advances when we first met. How am I going to help?"

"Don't worry. I'm going to find Saint and Solenne first and then get you settled. You'll be helping the weres who get hurt and anything you can to stop the European witches. You can do that, right?"

"Dante, I'm not a very good nurse. What if I can't help?"

He pulled her to him and kissed her words away. Cradling her face, he smiled. "You'll be great. I know you will."

Scarlett nodded, but she looked scared. He didn't show it, but part of him was too.

"Ready?" he asked as he squeezed his hand in hers. "Just hold on and we'll be there in a flash."

Moments later, they appeared in the yard behind Hadrian's villa just outside of Rome. The area felt oddly quiet, and Dante didn't want to take a chance that some witch might attack before he got Scarlett to safety, so he hurried her into the house.

What they found was worse than he'd imagined.

## 9

Saint watched as yet another group of weres were carted past him, some in pieces from the battle with the witches that raged on around the countryside. His stomach roiled from the smell of death that had permeated Hadrian's villa. In just one day, the place had gone from being command headquarters for the battle to a hospital and mortuary.

They were losing, and he didn't know what to do to stop the hemorrhaging. The witches and their spells were too strong for the weres to fend off, and now that some vampires had joined the Archons to fight on their side, they were outnumbered.

Solenne sat down behind him and slid her arms around his chest. Leaning against him, she whispered the words he knew he'd hear tonight.

"There was nothing more we could do. It was just too bad."

Fuck. Hadrian, one of the leaders of the weres, was now gone, along with hundreds and hundreds of his kind. They'd willingly volunteered to fight on the side of the Sons, and now they'd been routed.

More like slaughtered.

Saint didn't even know how many weres still remained to fight. Every inch of Hadrian's home had been filled with the injured, some in human form and some in wolf form, but all in bad shape. Those fucking witches with their spells immobilized the weres, and then it was like shooting fish in a barrel. All the witches had to do once the spells worked was attack, and they came in droves.

He wondered if there would be anyone to fight once this night ended.

The comforting feel of Solenne behind him disappeared, and then a second later she exclaimed, "Dante! What are you doing here?"

Spinning around, Saint saw the clyten and his girlfriend standing there looking fresh and full of hope. They'd come to the wrong place, for sure, if that's what they were looking for here.

"The cavalry has arrived! I've brought thousands of clytens who answered the Order's call, and they're all in this area hunting down your European witches. Even better, I have a former witch right here who I'm sure will be more than happy to do whatever she can to stop those bitches in their tracks."

Solenne looked back at Saint in as much confusion as he felt. Thousands of clytens were in Rome, and why was he calling his girlfriend a former witch? Had something happened with the alliance between the Sons and the American witches?

"What are the clytens doing, Dante?" Solenne asked.

"They're tracking down our enemies as we speak. I just came to drop off Scarlett here because she's not ready to fight."

"Why did he say former witch?" Saint asked, hoping beyond hope they hadn't lost another ally in her coven.

Quietly, Scarlett explained, "My sister and I were attacked by the Archons tonight. They slit our throats and left us for dead. Ivy didn't make it, but Dante was able to turn me vampire before I was too far gone like her. My coven's been wiped out. There's really no more American witches to speak of because of last night's attack."

Solenne pulled Scarlett into an embrace. "Oh, I'm so sorry. The loss of your sister and so many of your kind in only one night. It's so much to endure."

"Thank you. Unfortunately, that means all my witches and I planned to do is gone now, but I can help with the European witches. I know the spells they know, and I know how to counteract them. I just need to get myself situated and I should be able to help," Scarlett said as she struggled not to cry at all she'd gone through that night. "First thing I'll do is cast a spell to show a witch. That way, you can easily find them. I'll let you know when I'm finished."

"And I'm going to rally my clyten troops and see what kind of damage we can do," Dante said proudly.

For the first time since the battle started, Saint felt a sense of hope. It wasn't strong and he suspected it might be snuffed out at any time, but for the moment, perhaps they could turn the tide and not be completely slaughtered in this battle.

"I'll be right behind you," he said, jumping up from his chair. "Solenne, I'll be back. You'll be okay here?"

She nodded and reached out to hold his hand. "I'll be fine. You keep yourself out of trouble. Scarlett and I will do what we can from here to take care of our allies and give you a chance to defeat those witches."

"Don't worry about him, Solenne," Dante said with his usual cockiness. "Their spells can't affect vampires, and with the clytens fighting for us, we'll give them a battle they won't soon forget, assuming any of them live through the night."

He followed the clyten out of the villa and hoped he was right. However, Dante had always had a way of seeing life a bit too much on the sunny side.

"So what's your plan?" Saint asked as he looked around for all of the clytens the fellow Son had been bragging about. "Where are your troops?"

"Scattered around the area," he answered with a smile that seemed completely out of place for their present situation.

All of a sudden, Saint questioned his earlier flash of hope. He also worried about the two of them standing outside alone while there were witches all around.

"Do you have a way of getting them to know we need them, or is that a stupid question?"

Dante turned toward him and gave him a look that said he thought it was a stupid question. "You have no faith, dude. Give me a second and they'll show. Hang on."

"Do you have some kind of call or something?" Saint asked just before Dante let out a howl that sent him stumbling back a few steps. "What the hell was that?"

"The way to let them know I'm here and they need to come to this spot. You off your game tonight, Saint?"

He rolled his eyes and then stepped forward where

Dante stood waiting for his kind to answer his howl. "I'm fine, so fuck off, thank you."

"There's the grouchiest Son," Dante said with a chuckle, patting him on the back. "I knew you were in there somewhere."

As he considered heading back into the villa to call Vasilije and Terek for reinforcements since these fabled clytens didn't seem to be showing, Saint looked out over the countryside and saw them appear one by one. In seconds, thousands of them blanketed the nearby hillside.

"Holy fuck!"

Dante puffed out his chest and nodded in satisfaction. "See? Ye of little faith."

From inside the villa, Scarlett called out, "I completed the spell, so you shouldn't have any trouble finding them. They'll have a glow around them. And I'm putting a protection spell on you and your clyten troops right now."

"Thanks!" Dante yelled back. Far too cocky, he said, "Now watch this."

He took a step forward and said in a booming voice to his fellow clyten, "Find the witches and kill every one of them. You'll have no trouble locating them. They'll be glowing. And don't worry about their spells. They can't hurt you. Now go and when you can't find any more, come back here!"

Saint watched as the thousands of male and female clyten in front of them raised their hands and yelled something that sounded like a battle cry before disappearing. Stunned and actually impressed by Dante's legions, he mumbled, "Amazing. I never thought you had it in you."

"That's because you have no faith, dude."

"Do you guys have meetings you attend to practice that thing they did there, or is that just part of the clyten package?" Saint asked with a chuckle.

Now it was Dante's turn to get testy. Turning to look at him, he sneered. "Fuck you. If you're finished busting my ass about being a superior vampire, maybe you're interested in getting in some fighting tonight, or are you planning on standing here and acting like a bitch until the sun comes up?"

"Damn. Okay, let's go find those witches and end this battle."

They set out on foot to clear the area around the villa, and by the time they reached the back of the building, they saw a pale-yellow glow behind the wide trunk of an olive tree. Saint tapped Dante on the shoulder and pointed toward it, and the clyten gestured his plan to come around the left side of the tree while Saint took the right.

Pulling out his knife, he readied himself to avenge all the weres who'd suffered at the hands of these European witches, and then he and Dante took off toward the tree. As they rushed at it, the light grew brighter, telling Saint they may find more than one enemy.

He came around the right side as Dante came around the left, and they found two witches reciting a spell Saint suspected was meant to do some harm to them. Since Scarlett and the American coven had put a strong protection spell on all the Sons, their hocus pocus nonsense wasn't going to work tonight.

"Time's up, witchy poo," Dante said with a wicked laugh before driving his blade into the first witch's heart.

Saint didn't feel the need to tell his what he planned to do, so he simply stabbed her, but a second later, half a dozen more witches appeared behind them, all chanting their fucking spell.

"I know this sounds bizarre, but I think I hate witches," Dante yelled over their voices.

"Not exactly the thing your girlfriend would want to hear," Saint said as he chose which one to go after first.

Just then, the six women threw bottles of liquid at them that landed at their feet and began smoking. Were they for real? That shit may have worked with the weres because they still possessed some humanity left in them, but it wouldn't work on vampires.

Dante looked down at the ground where the bottle ended up after bouncing off his leg and then up at Saint. "Are they serious?"

With a shrug, he laughed. "I think they are."

The witches began to chant their spell again, so Dante yelled over them, "Ladies, normally I'd just explain to you why this bullshit of yours doesn't work on us, but we don't have time."

They didn't respond, so Saint added, "And for what you did to our allies the weres, we're going to kill you, so fair warning."

He expected them to run or do something to protect themselves other than repeat those words over and over and toss bottles of shit at them, but they didn't. They just stood there saying the same thing again and again.

How the Archons thought this would defeat them he had no idea, but there wasn't time to consider that. They had European witches to kill tonight, so with a look over at Dante to tell him he'd had enough of this crap, Saint lunged at the witch closest to him and sliced through her neck. Dante did the same, and even though the remaining ones could have run, they still stood chanting while the Sons killed all six of them.

That continued for the next four hours. Saint and Dante marched around the countryside looking for witches, along with the clyten troops, and they killed every one they found. When it was over, Saint looked around and couldn't help but think it looked like the battlefields he'd spent his youth on in France. Bodies of witches lay everywhere.

"I hadn't thought about what this would look like when we defeated them," he said quietly as he and Dante walked back to the villa.

For his part, the clyten didn't seem affected much by the hundreds and hundreds of dead witches everywhere they looked. "Yeah, they don't turn to dust or blood like us. The people in this area are going to wake up and think Jack the Ripper came through time and went on a fucking rampage here tonight."

Saint stepped around two in front of him on the ground and shrugged. "Should we do something? I imagine the humans around here are going to be pretty freaked out by all these women."

"Any less freaked out by all the naked men and women who used to be werewolves lying around in the hills up there?" Dante asked, making the point all too clearly for Saint.

This war was between the Archons and the Sons, but so far, only each side's allies had paid the price. While he mourned for the weres and Scarlett's sister, he had nothing for the witches who sided with the Archons. They'd chosen those vampires for a reason, and while he didn't understand it, he knew it wasn't for anything good for their fellow humans.

"I wouldn't want to be a cop on duty when the sun comes up this morning," Dante said with a chuckle.

"Real gallows humor guy, huh?"

The clyten rolled his eyes. "It's my thing. I know you're all about the misery and feeling guilty thing, so I'll let you get all sad for these witches."

As they reached Hadrian's villa, Saint reminded Dante of the reality that both sides had suffered heavy losses tonight. "We lost a lot of our were friends here, you know. I feel bad for them."

Dante stopped and hung his head. "I do too. They put themselves on the line for us, and they suffered at the hands of those bitches. Maybe that we killed them in turn avenged the weres deaths."

He didn't know if that was true or not, but Saint wanted no more of this war already. He just hoped their fellow Sons were faring better with their allies in the east.

They walked up the stairs where Solenne and Scarlett waited. When they reached them, Dante said, "Let's get the hell out of here. I'll tell the clytens to go back to the Order's headquarters, and I need to get Scarlett somewhere safe. This is her first night as a vampire, after all."

Solenne looked up at Saint with sadness in her eyes. "We can't just leave Hadrian here like he is. It's not right."

"I know. We'll take him out back and give him a proper burial for a hero," Saint said. "He deserves at least that. They all do. I wish we could give them all that honor."

After Dante gathered his clyten troops and congratulated them, he ordered them back to the training center at the Order's headquarters and he and Saint dug Hadrian's grave in a corner of his property away from the villa. They carefully lowered his body wrapped in white cloth into the earth before covering him, and Saint quietly said a prayer he'd heard his mother say at family funerals when he was a boy back in Ireland.

"May the earth hold you in its loving arms while letting your soul fly. Your time has come to an end here, but you won't be forgotten, Hadrian. Godspeed, our friend."

Each one of them repeated those last words to the leader of the weres who'd given his life to help the Sons defeat the Archons. His death and that of all his kind who perished that night hadn't been for nothing, though. This first battle had seen both sides of the war lose warriors, and it wouldn't be the last time before fighting ended.

Stepping forward, Scarlett looked up toward the sky. "For Ivy and my sister witches in my coven, Godspeed to you all. You're joined by the weres who lost their battle tonight. Until we meet again, you'll remain in our hearts, and we will miss you."

For now, though, the witches' and the weres' part in the fight between the Archons and the Sons of Navarus had ended. Now the battle would come closer to home for all of them.

## 10

For an Olympian god, Hades had always wondered why he didn't get the kind of existence his brothers got. He wasn't a huge fan of all that fucking water, but he would have taken even Poseidon's life over his on any day of the week. For fuck's sake, he didn't even get to have the title of Olympian god in many mortals' minds.

Assholes. He made sure to put those particular humans who insisted on publishing their work on the gods and not including him in the group of twelve Olympians into Tartarus straight away. No reprieve. No chance to plead their case. No opportunity to revise their opinion. Nope. Straight to the depths of the Underworld for those know-it-all motherfuckers.

And for those ultimate fuckheads who insisted on drawing him to look like some decrepit old man barely able to shuffle his pathetic ass around his own kingdom, he made sure Cerberus was extra hungry when it was time for the decision on their fate. Zeus and Poseidon got to look like fucking supermodels with six pack abs in art of them, and he had to look like some wrinkly old geezer?

Fuck them all. It made him almost want to pay each one of those supposed artists a visit and fuck their wives and girlfriends right in front of them. Then they'd see how off the mark all those ridiculous drawings and paintings were.

Recently, though, he had decided he rather liked being the god of the Underworld, even if he didn't get the damn Olympian title. His wife Persephone had gotten used to his dalliances with other goddesses, mainly Nyx, and now he had a genuine born vampire to play with whenever the urge overtook him.

Which happened as often as he could arrange since living in the depths of the fucking Earth left him little else to do other than torture souls. Oh, and playing games with those asshole Archons in their little war with the Sons of Navarus.

It had all become quite a drain on him, if he was being honest (which he rarely was). This war and Consera's constant calling for help bored him even more than doling out torment and agony.

That's why Noele enchanted him so much. She was a perfect distraction to the rest of his miserable existence. Beautiful, with a body that pleased him unlike many others in the past, he enjoyed everything about her. If he had known vampires were so delicious, he would have gotten himself one ages ago.

The whole thing with Noele had caused a fair share of problems for him with Nyx, though, who at the moment stood in his chamber staring daggers at him. Hades found that confusing. He was, after all, married when the two of them started getting together for their daytime meetings, so why would she be bothered that he liked playing with the born vampire?

Women could be so baffling. So Persephone was okay for him to fuck, but Noele wasn't? Who made that rule, and an even more important question was, why should he give a damn? True, Nyx was an ancient goddess, and even his brother Zeus was afraid of her, but that was because he planned to punish one of her kids for something concerning that ridiculous wife of his, Hera.

All of which meant not a fucking damn to him. His brother's inability to conduct his sex life like a god and instead like a sixteen-year-old punk ass in some high in the sky school wasn't his concern. Nyx and her jealousy were sort of his concern, but he hated the fact that he had to deal with that at all.

They had a nice thing going. Why did she have to ruin it with this latest hissy fit? His last meeting with her had been anything but sexy. He waited for her once her nightly duties were over, and she showed up with an attitude that could make his dick limp for eternity.

"I don't like playing second fiddle, Hades. I am a goddess, and I don't appreciate being forced to stand in line behind one of those fucking creatures."

Stretching his long legs in front of him, he tried to think of something to say that would make her forget all this jealousy nonsense so they could get down to business. Unfortunately, her glaring at him made coming up with something clever and sexy next to impossible, and his mind drew a blank.

"It's just a preoccupation of mine for the moment, Nyx. It means nothing," he said as he beckoned her to step up in front of him. Maybe if she got close she'd forget all this silliness.

She did as he wanted and moved toward him until they were mere inches away from one another. Her long black hair nearly touched his leg, making him think back to all the times she'd ridden him and that hair of hers teased against his skin. He did enjoy long hair on the females he fucked.

Leaning down, she gave him a look at the goods down the front of her black dress with that deep V and smiled. "I won't be toyed with, Hades. I am the daughter of Chaos, and if you want to see what your world will look like when I'm truly unhappy, keep doing exactly what you've been doing with your vampire toy. This is your final warning, love."

Now Hades was torn. On the one hand, he liked what he saw beneath that dress she wore and would have loved to have her on his cock at that very moment. But on the other hand, he didn't like threats and ultimatums. He was a god, after all, so it wasn't like she was better than he was. True, she was a primordial goddess, which meant she was one of the deities everything came from, but he was a fucking Olympian god (regardless of what those jackass humans thought). He didn't have to sit there and be threatened.

He folded his arms behind his head and stared into her jet-black eyes. She was truly stunning, no doubt. But he simply wouldn't allow himself to be ordered around like that. He hadn't tolerated it when he was told he couldn't have a wife, so why would he allow it now when it came to a very pleasing distraction that hurt no one?

No, he would continue just as he desired for as long as he desired. It was time Nyx understood that.

Tracing his fingertip down her neck and between her gorgeous breasts, he smiled up at her as she waited for his response. "The born vampire is something I enjoy for the time being. Do I ever complain about you spending time with that ridiculous god of wine, love? No. I've never once mentioned that bore of husband of yours either, and Erebus never fails to give me the side eye whenever I go down to Tartarus. So you see, we're all just having a good time. Don't ruin the good thing we have for something that shouldn't bother you."

Her dark eyes grew wide, and Hades saw the rage swirling in them. So be it. He wouldn't have his life dictated to him by anyone, least of all her.

Nyx spun on her heels and stormed out of his chamber, her long black dress slinking behind her even after she disappeared from his sight. He shrugged, not particularly happy about how that had gone. Oh, well. She'd get over it.

And if she didn't, what was she going to do to him? He was a god.

The faint echo of Consera's voice calling out to him added another layer of irritation to his day. Closing his eyes, he tilted his head back and took a deep breath in, letting it out slowly. Did other gods have to deal with this kind of shit all the time?

Hades stood from his throne and groaned. Another trip up there to visit Archon headquarters. No doubt that clusterfuck of a group would want his daemons to help more now.

He snapped his fingers at a young male standing

nearby. "Have the born vampire ready when I get back. I don't want to have to wait again like before, so she better be here when I call for her. Got it?"

The frightened daemon with the great pecs nodded quickly and bowed. "Yes, my lord. I will see that it's done."

A smile crept onto Hades' mouth. Now how hard was that? Why couldn't everything be that easy?

When he returned and after he enjoyed some time with Noele, he planned to do something nice for that male daemon. As he took one last glance at his muscular body, Hades thought of about half a dozen things he would do for him.

Being a god had its upsides after all.

And then a second later as he stood in Consera's office with the magistrate staring at him with nothing but desperation in his beady eyes, Hades was reminded of all the downsides. All the time with this guy and all he could do was ask for more.

Fuck.

He looked around and saw no one but Consera. "Did you send everyone out on errands today?" Hades joked.

"No, sire. I mean, my lord. Things have gotten a bit crazy here, so I have everyone out taking care of business." Consera stopped and tilted his head. "I guess they are out on errands, my lord."

Damn, this guy was tedious. He had to give up time with a sexy female at his beck and call whenever he desired for this?

If he didn't hate vampires so fucking much, Hades would have chucked the whole agreement he had with this officious asshole and left the entire Archon problem behind him. That was the problem, though. He did hate vampires and how their very existence flouted everything about him and his power in the Underworld, so that meant he had to stick with the plan he'd made with the Archons.

Even if it pissed him off.

"What did you call me for, Consera? It certainly wasn't to give me a rundown on what you're doing with your underlings today."

More subservient than usual, the magistrate nodded like the young male Hades had just been admiring and quickly explained, "We need your help. Your daemons are needed now, my lord. Our alliance with the witches has fallen apart. They hurt the weres, thankfully, so that helped, but the Sons and their clytens were too much for the witches, and they were slaughtered a few nights ago."

"Slaughtered, huh?" Hades repeated with a chuckle. He never liked being around witches. They were always quite disgusting, especially that Lucinda creature Consera seemed to so often have around.

"Yes, my lord. And then the American witches, well, what was left of them after my hunters killed off most of the coven, they used their powers to help defeat the European witches. Between their spells and the clytens' powers, the witches never stood a chance. They killed a fair number of weres, but in the end, it was a bloodbath."

Hades tried to remember what it was about the clytens that made them so powerful. Was it that they could shapeshift into other creatures? Or was he thinking of other beings?

Fuck, it was hard to keep track of all these damn things.

"Clytens. Remind me again why they would be too

much for witches?" he asked as he leaned against the wall close to the doorway.

"They are vampires who can walk in the sunlight. There aren't that many of them, so they're quite unique, but the one in the Sons of Navarus sent out a call for them to join him, and they came ready to fight."

Consera's shoulders sagged as he finished his explanation. Clearly, vampires who weren't afraid of sunlight could be a significant problem for vampires fighting them who had to run for cover once the sun came up.

"Interesting. Your kind has all manner of freaks, don't you? Archons don't sire and seem to have some kind of ridiculous affinity for the color white and all the sterility it conveys. These clytens get to enjoy the sunlight yet still get to be vampires. And born vampires aren't made at all but are more like humans."

His brief exposition on the various types of vampires didn't seem to amuse or impress Consera. The man fidgeted the entire time, like he couldn't wait for Hades to finish so he could say something.

"Yes, my lord. Interesting. Now, could we discuss bringing your daemons into the war? We've got vampires, including clytens, and dragons preparing for a battle in the east, and your daemons would help tremendously since all we have are our hunters we've impressed into service for this war. On top of that, we've got two of the Sons tearing through the other side of the Continent staking Archons like there's no tomorrow. Your daemons would be a huge help there too."

He hated having to send his minions into battle to help these corrupt vampires, but given that the only other choice was to stand back and let the Sons win this war, Hades knew he had to do as he'd promised. All the vampires—Archons, magistrates, and Sons, along with all those ordinary ones—would all end up the same anyway.

Eliminated from the Earth by him and imprisoned for the rest of time so no creature could ever deny him his right to have them in front of him when they died. Consera thought he and his ilk would be spared. They wouldn't. None would. That had been Hades' plan all along.

But to get to that point, he needed to pretend to back this jackass and his side.

"Fine. I'll send daemons to battle the dragons and the Sons in the east, and I'll send two of my best to kill those Sons who've been giving you such a hard time. No wonder I've seen a steady stream of Archons coming before me in the past few nights on top of all those dead werewolves and witches. I thought maybe the war had gone badly and they were all killing themselves."

"Will two be enough, my lord? These two are unlike the others. One in particular should interest you since he's the born vampire's son who figures so prominently in the Prophecy of Idolas, and the other is her husband."

Perhaps this meeting hadn't been just one giant pain in the ass, after all.

"Really? Well, I still think two of my daemons will be able to handle the job, but I'll make sure to instruct them to make their last moments particularly difficult. Sound good?" Hades asked with a smile, liking how this meeting had turned around.

"That sounds great. Thank you, my lord."

Consera performed his best bow and acted in the way

he suspected Hades wanted him to, supplicating himself all over the place. The god of the Underworld didn't mind a little subservience. In fact, he rather enjoyed it. The problem with the magistrate's willingness to show deference is it now bored Hades.

Time for a little excitement.

"I'll be sending them tonight. I'll tell them to check in with you first so you can tell them exactly where to go," he said with a chuckle.

"Oh, okay. I'll be sure to be here all night then," Consera said in a trembling voice.

The idea of him shaking in his boots as daemons stood in front of him again delighted the god more than he thought it would. As much as he had grown weary of tormenting souls, ruining this one's evening pleased Hades a great deal.

He didn't bother to say goodbye before disappearing from Archon headquarters to head back to his throne room, and seconds later, he was met by the male servant who had so successfully impressed him earlier. Before he could run off to fetch Noele, Hades stopped him.

"Wait! I want the leader of the daemons before the born vampire. And tell him to make it quick," he barked out as he sat back down and stretched his legs out in front of him.

Too much work and not enough play made the god of the Underworld feel like shit. He'd done enough for one day. Now it was time for some fun. Well, after he gave the daemon commander his orders.

The very being appeared before him a moment later and bowed. "You summoned me?"

"Yes. It's time to join the vampire fight up above, so I

want a legion of your best to go fight some dragons and the Sons of Navarus. Go see Consera at Archon head-quarters to find out the exact location. I also want you to choose your best fighter to join you to find the two Sons who've been terrorizing the Archons throughout Western Europe. Talk to Consera about that too. And be sure to make their deaths extra painful. Feel free to torture them for as long as you want. Enjoy yourself."

"As you wish, my lord."

The daemon leader turned to leave, and Hades added, "Feel free to scare the hell out of him when you go see him. Better to have him always remember just what we're capable of down here."

With a simple nod and another bow, the daemon agreed and then disappeared, leaving the god of the Underworld to finally have some fun for the first time that day. Snapping his fingers, he summoned the male who'd pleased him earlier and ordered him to bring Noele to him immediately.

Then he sat back on his throne, but lurking in the corner of the room as she often did lately was Layla. Hades suspected she had been directed to spy on him for Nyx since she was one of her handmaidens, and he didn't need her around seeing what he planned to do with Noele.

"Layla, come here. I have a job for you."

She hurried over to stand in front of him, bowing her head so as not to look directly at him. Such deference. He appreciated that.

"Find the goddess of the night and tell her I'm sorry we disagreed. Tell her I will come to see her tomorrow morning as she ends her nightly duties around the world."

"Yes, my lord," Layla said quietly, and Hades thought he heard a hint of disbelief in her tone.

Not that what a minor daemon he'd given to Nyx to be her handmaiden thought meant anything to him.

Thankfully, she left before the servant returned with Noele in tow. Guiding her to where he sat, the young male kept his gaze to the ground while the born vampire brazenly looked directly at the god. If he didn't enjoy her so much, he'd crush her under his heel for that.

"My lord, the one you desired to see."

"Thank you, boy. Stay close. I'll want to see you again tonight."

The servant backed away, leaving Noele standing in front of Hades. Still not dropping her gaze, she smiled at him like she enjoyed all of this.

"I have interesting news for you. Come, sit on my lap and let me tell you," he said, patting his black leather clad thigh.

She obeyed and perched herself across his legs. "I can't wait to hear this news, my lord."

The way she said that had a faint echo of disrespect he recognized from Layla's answer to him a minute earlier. Women. What a fucking hassle they were.

Hades ran his fingertip along her jaw before leaning forward to kiss her soft lips. She didn't flinch as she had when he first began playing with her, and when he leaned back and opened his eyes, he saw her smiling at him again. Perhaps she did enjoy their games as much as he did.

Not that it mattered. She was his plaything, his whore. What she enjoyed or didn't enjoy mattered none to him.

"You'll soon be joined by your family, Noele. But I don't expect it to be a happy reunion. Imagine what your husband and son will think of what you've become here in my kingdom. I'm sure they didn't expect you'd so willingly take on the role of concubine to the god of the Underworld, now did they?"

He watched her expression for any sign of unhappiness because of his news and his taunting her, but he saw none. Not even the tiniest flinch at what he'd called her, even though he knew she'd never grown accustomed to that name.

"They are from my previous life, my lord. What they think of who I am now doesn't matter. I am, as you said, yours."

As she spoke, Noele ran her hand down over his stomach and let her palm come to rest over his quickly stiffening cock. He hadn't expected her to succumb to her fate in the Underworld so easily and in such a short time, but no matter.

He had better things to do than wonder about how she really felt. All he wanted now was to feel far more carnal pleasures and leave the stress of his day behind, and what better to do that with than his own person born vampire whore?

## 11

––––––––––

Theron took a deep breath and relaxed, the first time he'd been able to do that in what felt like weeks. Not that he didn't enjoy killing every Archon in Europe, but it was exhausting moving around to find the bastards night after night. He looked over at his father as he slept for the final minutes before the sun disappeared behind the horizon and night came upon them again.

He could have gone ahead and cleared out the last few Archons while the sun was still up, but doing it with the one soul he admired most in the world was better. Plus, he knew killing Archons was therapeutic for him. Not a night passed when he didn't mention how much he hated those fucks for what they did to Theron's mother, so why take that small bit of happiness away from him?

They only had one more left in Berlin, so tonight the first phase of their own personal war would end. After that, Theron planned to gather the rest of the Sons and have them all descend on the Archons' headquarters in Corsica with one blunt attack. He didn't know if the dragons would be necessary, but maybe they could join them just in case those daemons showed up to make things interesting.

What did daemons do, he wondered as he felt the last of the sun's rays fade away. Nobody seemed to have a firm grasp on exactly what they even were. Hades was a god, so did that make them like his followers? Or were they more like his army?

If that were the case, Theron had a feeling he would have heard about some war or at least a battle they'd fought. But he hadn't. Even the elders who spent all their time researching everything under the sun didn't seem to know exactly what powers daemons had.

It wouldn't matter. He and his father had handled dozens of Archons and even more vampires, so he had a hard time imagining they couldn't take care of whatever Hades minions were.

Chuckling, Theron imagined maybe they were like that heat miser guy from that Christmas show he'd watched with his mother that one time. If so, then no one had to worry about them as long as they didn't shoot fire from their fingers like that guy. Well, unless they carried pitchforks or something like that. Getting stabbed by those might hurt a whole hell of a lot.

"Something funny?"

Theron looked over at his father as he pushed himself up to sitting position against the cave wall where they'd spent the day away from the sun's rays. Ramiel scrubbed the sleep from his face and stretched before looking out to check it was night.

"Nothing much. I was just thinking about what a daemon looks like and wondered if they're like that little guy in that Christmas cartoon Mom watched with me. The heat miser? You know, the one with the spikey red hair who shoots flames from his fingers?"

His father screwed his face into a confused expression and shook his head. "The what?" Then suddenly, he seemed to understand the description and smiled. "Oh, yeah. She loved that cartoon. Your mother loved sitting with you and your sister and watching them. I guess I never saw the appeal, but she could watch them for hours."

The gentle tone that crept into his voice when he talked about her made Theron smile. Ramiel seemed to get a faraway look in his eyes whenever they said anything about that life they used to have. They were happy. He didn't know everything his father had gone through in his life, but at least for the time he got to spend with his parents, they looked happy.

And then everything good about their lives was ripped away by the bastards who took his mother. In that one horrible night, he'd lost so much. Now that he had his father back, part of that life had returned, but neither one of them could replace what she brought to their lives.

As much as he loved spending this time with Ramiel, it wasn't the same as when his mother was with them. Now his father was hard and full of hate, not the vampire who had smiled down at him when he put caterpillars on the top of his feet or secretly patted him on the back when he learned something new his mother disapproved of. Theron missed that part of him, but he knew why it could never come back. He felt the same way. When she left the world, so did a kindness he'd only felt because of her, and it would never return again.

"Only one more left," Ramiel said in a voice full of satisfaction. "One more and then all we have left is Archon headquarters."

"We'll join up with the rest of the Sons for that. Once we wipe out all of them there, it'll just be a matter of wrangling the magistrates, but I don't see them being a problem. They've always been followers anyway, so they'll just have to follow us," Theron said as he stood to leave.

His father let out a disgusted sigh. "Magistrates. Archons. That's the problem with our world. Too many in charge who have no reason to care about the millions of vampires out there."

"Then things are about to get a lot better for all of them once we get rid of the problem."

Ramiel groaned and stood up, stretching the sleep from his limbs one more time. "That's the plan. Any news on how the other Sons are doing?"

"Saint and Solenne were joined by Dante and his clyten regiment in Rome, but the weres got pretty much wiped out by those witches the Archons have fighting for them. Dante says the clytens crushed the witches, though."

"Always bragging," his father said with a smile. "That Dante is a piece of work. I'll have to make sure to ask him about how the clytens did so he can tell me everything blow by blow."

"You better make sure you have something to eat and drink before you ask him because it's going to be an all-night thing. He has every reason to be proud, though. The clytens did a great job down there. From what Saint said, things would have turned out much worse if they weren't there. Oh, but he did say to tell you the leader of the weres didn't make it."

Shaking his head, Ramiel blew the air out of his lungs. "Hadrian. I'm sorry to hear that. He turned out to be one of the good ones."

Curious what he meant by that, Theron asked, "What do you mean turned out to be good? Was he bad at some time?"

His father let out a hearty laugh. "No, but I thought he was. I was all ready to rip his throat out one night because I thought he was hitting on your mother. This was before you were born and before we'd gotten together. I guess I was a little jealous."

"Mom with a were. Now I've heard everything."

Ramiel smiled and shook his head. "It was nothing. I was just being stupid. He was a good guy."

The two of them stopped talking, but in the silence, Theron wished he had been able to meet Hadrian, if only to know someone else who had cared about his mother. The Archons had taken yet something else good from the world, giving him another reason to annihilate those fuckers.

"Ready to go? We have one final Archon to get," his father said with a smile. "And then we get to go home."

Theron nodded as the idea of home filtered through his brain. Home. Until recently, it had meant where his family surrounded him with love and security. Now home simply meant a different location than the one he stood in. All the warmth he'd associated with that word had vanished.

Gone when they took his mother from him.

"Let's go," he said as the rage that never went away bubbled up inside him.

The Berlin Archon's office looked almost identical to every other Archon's office they'd attacked. White walls gave the place its sterile look that seemed so important to them and had begun to give Theron another reason to hate those bastards. Vampires weren't meant to be so boring. It wasn't in their nature. Perhaps that's what happened to Archons.

These thoughts ambled through his mind as the two of them silently walked from room to room searching for the Archon and his staff. Like in every other instance, they'd be hiding behind some piece of furniture somewhere, cowering and begging for their lives as all the others had.

It wouldn't matter. The same stakes that had turned everyone else like them to dust would do the same to them.

Ramiel silently pointed toward a room with two white doors to give the signal that they'd check that one next. Theron nodded and waited as he slowly turned the handle and opened one of them, his blood racing at what they'd encounter next.

But unlike in the other Archons' offices, no pleas came from anyone. This was the last room to check, so they had to be in there, yet the room remained eerily silent.

He looked over at his father and mouthed the words, "Where are they?"

His answer was a shrug, and the two slowly walked into the room with their stakes in their hands, ready to send each and every one of them on their way to the

Underworld. Seconds later, they finished searching the room and found no one.

"There are no more offices in this building. Any chance they all fled to their headquarters?" Theron asked.

"I don't know. Maybe. It's not like we've been trying to keep what we've been up to for the past few nights a secret. It just seems strange that this is the only one where no one is left."

Looking around the room, Theron saw a closet and pointed at it. "Maybe they all decided to hide in there. Seems a little small, but you never know."

Ramiel shrugged. "Might as well check it before we go."

He opened the door and stepped back, clearly surprised at what he found. Inside, the bodies of the Archon and his four assistants lay stacked up like wood on the floor. Looking back at Theron, he shook his head before reaching down to touch the body on the top of the pile.

"They're dead, but they obviously weren't staked. What the hell happened here?"

Theron walked over to where he stood and looked down at the bodies. Each vampire's expression showed a look of shock at whatever had been done to them, and their skin was a terrible pale grey color.

"I don't know, but they weren't expecting it. That's for sure. Maybe witches killed them?" he said, unsure what could have happened to these five vampires.

"I have no idea. All I care about is they're dead, but it is strange. It's like all the blood's been drained out of them, but where is it? I didn't see a drop of blood anywhere in this room or in this building."

"Maybe they killed themselves with that Bliss stuff," Theron suggested, remembering what he heard from Sion and Kali about the effects of that drug on vampires. "I hear that shit is bad."

"That might make sense if they weren't stacked up like books on a shelf. Someone did this to them."

"Damn. I didn't think about that. I was too busy being surprised that we don't get to kill tonight," Theron joked.

Looking around the room, Ramiel's gaze darted left and right as he slammed the closet door shut. "Keep your wits about you. Something's wrong here, and I'm not sure it's witches. Let's go."

They took two steps toward the door and then slowly it began to open. They raised their arms, clutching their stakes in their hands, and watched as a woman appeared in front of them. Theron looked closely at her, unable to clearly see her face in the darkness of the room only broken by the faint moonlight coming in through a window on the far wall. Was this one of the Archons' staff who had been fortunate enough to escape the fate her co-workers and boss had met?

Ramiel flicked on the light switch and Theron's breath caught in his chest. There in front of him stood his mother just as she'd looked the last time he saw her alive.

But it was impossible. Whatever this was, whatever trick someone was playing on them, she wasn't there. She couldn't be.

His father stepped forward closer to her as she said his name in a soft voice Theron struggled to believe wasn't hers. "Ramiel, I've waited for you."

"Dad, don't touch her. I don't know what this is, but she's not Mom."

It seemed like he didn't hear his warning at all. Ramiel smiled, and whatever this was reached out to touch his face like Noele used to. Again, she repeated his name.

"Ramiel, have you missed me?"

"Dad, back up! That's not Mom. Don't let her get too close!" Theron shouted, but his father didn't pay attention to anything he said. He seemed mesmerized, like whatever this was controlled his mind.

"I've missed you so much, Noele," he whispered and then closed his eyes.

Instantly, the woman changed from the beautiful image of his mother to a monstrous creature with horrible black eyes and claws at the end of its arms. From behind its body, it pulled a stake and held it high above its head.

"Courtesy of Hades."

Theron lunged toward the thing as he yelled, "Get back, Dad! It's a daemon! Back away!" But he didn't reach his father in time.

The stake ripped through his chest toward its goal, and Ramiel turned to face his son, his eyes wide in surprise and his expression contorted into one of agony. He looked at Theron and said in a low voice, "I'll tell her about you. She'll be so proud."

And then he disappeared into dust, gone from the room as Theron stood in shock at how quickly it happened.

Another daemon appeared beside the first and looking much like its twin. They both held stakes in their hands and rushed Theron as he stood stunned at what had happened. Pushing them away, he tore their weapons from their hold and threw them onto the desk behind him. The daemons seemed stunned for a moment, looking at each other like they couldn't believe he'd over-powered them.

"Why isn't he in agony?" one asked as the other shook its head. "He should be in pain after touching us."

Theron didn't know what they meant and didn't care. Inside him, a toxic blend of sadness and loss at watching his father die in front of him mixed with the rage that never seemed too far from the surface for him. He hated the Archons for taking his mother, so he killed Archons. Now he hated daemons for taking his father, so he'd kill them all too.

Pure fury erupted in him, and he lunged at the daemon closest to him. He ripped its head off and threw it aside, and then he tore it limb from limb until there was nothing left but pieces of the fucking creature. It all happened so fast even he didn't know what to make of it.

The other daemon watched in horror but didn't move. Theron grabbed hold of it and repeated his massacre of the creature just as he had its partner. Arms, legs, fingers, toes, eyes, ears flew around him as he tore the thing to pieces.

When he finished, the anger and hatred he felt hadn't subsided. It had actually grown from his murder of the two daemons. His emotions churned inside him, threatening to overwhelm the young vampire. He'd lost his mother, and now his father was gone too.

And all he could think about was avenging their deaths with as much rage as he could hold inside him.

Theron looked around at the bloodbath that filled the floor near him. Pieces of those fucking creatures hung off his clothes and skin, sickening him. Dropping to his knees, he closed his eyes and let out a cry of agony that shook the windowpanes. His body began to grow numb as he replayed Ramiel's death over and over in his mind.

"You fucks! I swear I'll find every one of you and rip you apart with my bare hands. Hades! I'm coming for you!"

He hadn't been able to save his father. Ever since his mother died, Theron had been convinced that if he had been with her, he could have protected her from the Archons. Now he knew that wasn't true. Even with all the powers he possessed, he couldn't stop that daemon from staking his father.

His hands shook uncontrollably from the anger that coursed through his body. Killing Ramiel's murderer wasn't enough. Killing the other daemon who tried to stake him wasn't enough. He doubted anything would ever be enough to assuage his need to avenge what had been done to his family.

For all his strength and power, he had no control over his emotions and there in that Archon's office where he and his father had come to eliminate yet another of the vampires responsible for his mother's death, he broke down and cried. Covered in daemon blood and the remnants of their bodies that clung to his skin, he sobbed until there were no more tears left to cry.

He was as he'd always been—the child the prophecy said would defeat the Archons and rule the vampire world. What that meant to him now he didn't know. All he knew was he had no one left. His enemies had taken everyone he loved from him.

Now all that existed in him was pure, unadulterated hate. Every part of him, every nook and cranny of his being, filled with the need to kill everything Archon and daemon.

And he would end his murder spree by killing the one who sent the creature who killed his father.

Hades.

# 12

---

The image of his son's eyes full of pain remained in Ramiel's mind, seared there for eternity. He'd spend the rest of time there in the Underworld, but his heart would forever be in the world above with Theron.

Regret filled him. He hadn't even been given the chance to see Leta before that daemon took his life. Not that he didn't bear the responsibility for that. It's just that he always thought he'd have more time. More chances to see his daughter after the war ended and he could give her a home again.

More time to do all the things a father should do for his daughter.

Now that would never happen. She'd stay with Ilona and Terek for good, their child to raise from this point on. It gave him little happiness to admit she couldn't have better surrogate parents.

So finally he'd come to the place where all vampires eventually ended up. The Underworld, the realm of Hades. One of his daemons had killed Ramiel, so he assumed it wouldn't be long now before he met the ruler of this dark place and found out his ultimate fate.

He didn't know what to expect. What he knew of the god of the Underworld came from a smattering of memories from his time as a slave in the Roman Empire. Hades didn't have a dedicated following like other gods and goddesses, so most of what Ramiel thought of him had more to do with the threats those in authority used to terrorize those they ruled. The fear of meeting that god was real for children and slaves back then.

His feet seemed to know the way through the dark passageway, even if he didn't. He suspected that had something to do with Hades' power in this place. Trying to focus his eyes in the pitch black that surrounded him, Ramiel saw nothing but sensed he wouldn't spend the rest of eternity simply walking in the darkness. That didn't seem like much of a punishment, and if there was anything waiting for him, he knew full well it would involve the god of this place making him pay for being vampire and denying him his due all these centuries.

As the fog in his brain cleared with every step, Ramiel's heart began to beat faster. Noele was already here. He'd get to see her again, finally. For as much as the memory of the last vision of Theron made him sad, seeing the only female he'd ever loved made his spirit soar.

He didn't allow himself to think of how she'd been treated in her time in the Underworld. A hint of doubt crept into his mind, but he quickly pushed it out. Noele was the strongest female he'd ever encountered in hundreds of years of being alive. No matter what Hades had done to punish her, she was okay. He'd see her again, and she'd be just like she was when they were happy in their life above.

She had to be okay. He couldn't go on if she wasn't.

As if this place could read his mind, he suddenly saw a light that illuminated the rocky tunnel he walked in and saw a figure at the end. Was that Noele? Ramiel strained to see that far, but with each step the being seemed to fade a little more until finally he reached the light, but no one waited for him.

"This way, vampire."

He turned to see who'd spoken and found himself standing next to a young male dressed only in what looked like a loincloth. Quickly, he looked down his body to see if that's how he was dressed, but he saw he still wore the clothes he'd died in, thankfully. Being dead was bad enough. Having to wear a fucking loincloth would be insult to injury.

A voice inside his head whispered, "Clothes, like much around you, are an illusion you create here. Pay little attention to things like that."

Ramiel stopped dead at those words. Who was that speaking to him? Was it loincloth boy?

He waited for him to say something, but the young male just kept walking. So if it wasn't him who said that, who was it?

Already, Ramiel hated this place. Fucking mind games from nearly the moment he arrived didn't impress him. He just hoped this wouldn't be how he'd spend the rest of time. That would be just his luck.

Eternity dealing with high school bullshit.

"Where am I going?" he asked loincloth boy.

"Where you belong," he answered in a low voice but didn't bother to look at him when he spoke.

So now they had moved on from mind games to riddles. Just wonderful. If there was one thing Ramiel hated, it was fucking riddles.

He sized up the boy escorting him and thought he could take him. Not even half his size, the kid would probably beg for mercy and tell him anything he wanted to know if he even laid a finger on him.

Just as that thought settled into his brain, the voice from earlier returned. "The boy doesn't know anything. Hurting him would be a futile effort and would only anger me."

This time, the voice spoke in an ominous tone, and Ramiel had a feeling he was being threatened. "Then just have him tell me where the hell I'm walking to and there won't be any problems."

He expected the boy to at least look over to see if he was speaking to him, but he just kept walking as if Ramiel hadn't just announced to whoever was in his damn head that he had ideas about hurting the kid.

All of this only served to piss the Son off, bringing out the Visigoth in him that he had a feeling would be front and center for all his time in this place. Having Hades chat him up in his head already bored him. Mind games seemed to be beneath a god, but then again, what did he know? He hadn't exactly spent his existence around them. Maybe this was what they did to have fun.

Ramiel didn't care. All he cared about was seeing Noele again. He hoped that Hades with his mind reading bullshit was listening loud and clear at that moment and would have her waiting for him when he finally got to wherever the hell loincloth boy was taking him.

"So how much further?" he asked the kid, relatively sure he wouldn't get an answer or even a riddle this time.

And he was right. He remained silent and just continued walking down the rocky path surrounded by stone walls on each side.

Then, he suddenly turned and the two of them were standing outside a wooden door. It reminded Ramiel of the kind of doors Vasilije's monastery had. Heavy and old. That sort of fit, actually. The Romanian and Hades did remind him of one another.

His mind began to race with thoughts of the past, but he didn't want that. He needed to focus. Soon he'd see Noele, and he wanted all his attention to be exclusively on her.

"You'll stay here until you're summoned. Don't bother trying to leave this room. You can't," loincloth boy said before walking away, leaving Ramiel standing in front of the closed door.

Was this his room alone, or was it someone else's and now he was being added? Was this Noele's room? His heart began pounding in his chest. He imagined the Underworld had millions of occupants, so they probably had to share rooms. He hung his head and chuckled at how stupid that sounded. None of this was real anyway. The voice had told him that.

He looked down at his clothes once again to make sure they hadn't changed into a ridiculous loincloth like the boy's. The last thing he wanted his wife to see him wearing was something like that.

Ramiel lifted his hand to knock on the door but then

let it fall to his side. He didn't have to knock on his wife's door.

Turning the handle, he slowly pushed the door open and looked in. The room looked like some old English castle with wood beams across the ceiling. The walls didn't look like the craggy stone ones from the hallway. Instead, they were made of stone blocks cut uniformly. If he didn't know better, Ramiel would have said this place looked perfectly medieval.

Why did Noele stay in a room that looked like this? If the voice was right, then she could have made it look like anything she desired. Or was this his doing? No. Ramiel wouldn't construct this reality for her. His wife had never been a fan of medieval architecture either. That sounded more like...

And then he saw the reason why this place looked like it did.

Standing in front of him next to a large table perfect for the castle he'd created was his old partner, Thane. He wasn't Noele, but he was a sight for sore eyes.

"Ramiel," he said sadly, shaking his head.

"Thane."

He opened his arms and walked toward Ramiel, clearly emotional about this reunion. "I'm so happy to see you and so unhappy at the same time because of what this means."

As he embraced his old friend, Ramiel felt the loss of what he'd been in life all too well suddenly. He'd been able to push it down as he walked with the loincloth kid and focused on everything else happening to him, but now as another Son of Navarus long gone from their ranks stood there with him in the Underworld, it all became too real.

His time in the world of the living had ended, and now he was in the Underworld for the rest of eternity.

Thane stepped back and forced a smile. "You look good."

"I'm told this is all an illusion," he answered, unsure what his friend was seeing. Hopefully, it wasn't that fucking loincloth or anything else as stupid.

"It is and it isn't," Thane said with a shrug. "You'll get used to it. What did you think of the big guy himself?" he asked with a wide-eyed look.

"Hades? I didn't see him. The guy brought me directly here. And not that I don't love seeing you again, Thane, but I really want to see Noele. Where is she?"

Instead of immediately telling him where his wife was, Thane winced and turned away to walk back to the table. Lifting a bottle of wine, he looked back and asked, "Want a drink? This is one of those illusion things, so if you'd rather have something other than wine, just say it. It's one of the few perks around here that are really great."

Perks? What the fuck was he talking about? Ramiel didn't care that there was a great selection of alcoholic beverages in the Underworld. He asked about Noele and the answer he got from Thane was an offer to have a drink together? What was going on?

Ramiel took a step toward the table and stopped as his friend sat down in a chair that looked like an old English throne. The Son had gotten pretty fucking comfortable in this place, it seemed.

"I don't want a drink. I want Noele. Where is she?

Why are you acting like that wouldn't be the first goddamned thing I'd ask when I arrived here? I want to see her."

"I'm not in charge of that. Hades is. If he wants you to see her, you'll get to. Just relax. Everything will be fine."

What the fuck had happened to Thane? Everything will be fine? He was a Son of Navarus, not some loincloth wearing boy who did Hades' bidding and relaxed until it was his time.

Ramiel planted his palms on the table in front of his friend and looked down at him. "You seem to be pretty cozy here. Having a good time? Maybe we could get you some fucking minstrels to come in and perform a tune for you. What the fuck has happened to you, man? You were a Son—are a Son—and you sit here like you're some bird in a cage."

Thane sighed and took a sip of wine. "This place changes you. I know you won't understand that for a while since it takes some time, but you'll get used to it. Figure out the rules and play by them and this place isn't too bad. You'll probably do even better than I have since it took me a while to get the hang of the place."

What the hell was he talking about?

"Play by the rules? Get the hang of the place? You were a goddamned warrior of your race, and now you're what? A nobleman living a make-believe life of leisure in the Underworld? I want to see my wife, and I know you know where she is, so once more I'm going to ask, where is Noele, Thane?"

He looked away and refused to make eye contact with Ramiel. Fidgeting with his shirt collar, he said, "You have to understand. This place can be very difficult for some.

She's tough, but even the toughest of us have to do things we don't want to do."

Terror tore through Ramiel. Had something horrible happened to her? What could Hades do to someone down there? They were already dead, so what was worse? He didn't want to think about that. All he wanted was to see her.

"I know how tough my wife is. Remember, I married her? We had two children together. We had a fucking life together, so I know all about Noele. I want some straight answers, Thane. Is she okay? Is she hurt? Where is she?"

The silence that followed his questions threatened to crush him. As he waited, every muscle in his body began to ache. Noele hadn't fared well in that place, and Thane didn't want to tell him the truth.

But he had to know.

Finally, after what felt like an eternity, Thane answered, "Noele is as okay as anyone else down here. She's still in love with you. I know that. I want you to keep that in mind for when you see her. She's never stopped loving you, Ramiel."

That sounded cryptic. Why would he have to remember that when he saw her?

"And I've never stopped loving her, so we'll be fine on that point. I don't like the way you sound, though. Why are you talking like this? Why would I need to keep in mind that she loves me?"

Thane opened his mouth to explain, or at least Ramiel hoped so, but someone walked in behind him and interrupted their conversation. He spun around to see not the woman he loved but a fucking daemon like the one who'd taken his life.

Without saying a word, he rushed her and set his hands around her neck. He had no idea if they could be strangled, but he damn well wanted to test it out. Squeezing his fingers into her flesh, he felt her throat begin to crush under his strength and her eyes grow wider and wider, filled with fear.

Good. That's for your friend staking me.

Behind him, Thane pulled hard on his arms to stop him, screaming, "Let her go! Ramiel, let her go!"

Let her go? Why? She was a fucking daemon!

Ramiel looked back and saw worry written all over his friend's face. What the fuck would he be worried about the likes of this thing?

"Let her go. She's a friend of mine and Noele's."

His words ricocheted around Ramiel's brain for a few seconds before he released her and staggered back in shock. A friend? Now the two people he cared about most in this place were friends with a fucking daemon, the same kind of creature that wanted to wipe the Sons of Navarus and their allies off the face of the earth?

Thane helped her up off the floor and gently eased her into a chair as Ramiel watched in horror. What the fuck had happened to him since they'd last seen one another?

"Are you okay?" he whispered softly as he smoothed her short blond hair and she morphed into a beautiful young female. "I'm sorry that happened. I didn't get a chance to explain things to my friend."

"Why don't you try now?" Ramiel said as his stomach roiled. He felt like he was going to be sick watching this scene playing out in front of him. Did he even know who Thane was anymore?

Taking the daemon's hand in his, Thane brought it to his lips and kissed it. "This is Layla. She's a friend to both Noele and me."

"She looks like way more than a friend. You just make yourself at home with the ladies no matter where you go, don't you?" he asked as flashes of Thane with Sasa rushed through his head.

No wonder this guy hadn't been unhappy to be in this fucking place. He got himself a little daemon piece of ass action. Nice.

"It's not like that, Ramiel. Layla was the first one to make me not hate this place. She kept me from going crazy when I first got here. Until Noele arrived, Layla was all I had."

Suddenly Thane's reluctance to tell him about Noele made sense. He'd gotten together with her since she came to the Underworld!

Ramiel tightened his hand into a fist and cocked his arm back. He finally knew how Vasilije had felt when Thane stole Sasa from him. What the fuck was with this guy?

He didn't care to know the answer to that question. All he wanted to do at that moment was pound the fuck out of him.

Thane saw him move to swing at him and ran around the table. "What are you doing? Why are you trying to hit me?"

"You're a traitorous son of a bitch! I stood by you when you pulled that stunt with Sasa, and now I come to this fucking place to find out you've done the same thing with Noele. Stop fucking running like a little girl and stand up to me so I can beat the hell out of you for being a shitty friend!"

"What are you talking about? I didn't do anything with Noele. I just told you I'm with Layla. Calm down, will you? Maybe go over and sit down on the couch for a little bit. I wouldn't do that to you, Ramiel."

This place made his head fucking pound. If it wasn't head games and riddles, he had to deal with the reality that the vampire he thought he knew in Thane had changed to something that hung out with daemons and couldn't give him a straight answer about his wife. Eternity in the Underworld was going to be pure shit based on the way it had begun.

He slowly backed away and sat down on the couch on the other side of the room as Thane suggested. Not that any amount of calming down was going to make him feel any better. The only thing that would do that would be seeing Noele.

As he tried to make the pounding in his head stop, he heard the door open. How many of them were going to have to stay in that tiny room?

"Thane, I've got news! The witches fighting on the Archons' side have been defeated. That's good news, but the bad news is that means the daemons are getting into the war. Layla, we need you to go tip off the Sons. They need to be prepared for Hades' legions."

Instead of answering her, Thane simply looked over to where Ramiel sat in shock staring at Noele. Now he understood why his friend had been so hesitant to explain what she'd been doing in the Underworld.

Dressed in barely enough fabric to cover her breasts and private parts, she looked like some kind of sex toy

Ramiel had once seen in Dante's apartment. He had no idea why she would choose to look like that, but as he tried to find an answer that didn't involve her being with another male, the voice returned.

"Isn't my favorite whore delightful? She's been the perfect distraction for me," it said with a chuckle.

Ramiel's heart sank. Instantly, he hated this place more than he thought possible. Noele had been made to be Hades' sex slave. His wife was the god of the Underworld's favorite whore.

## 13

---

Noele followed Thane's gaze to the other side of his room. Ramiel. Her breath caught in her chest, and she instinctively ran to him. They were finally together again!

"Oh, Ramiel! I've missed you so much," she said as wrapped her arms around him and began to cry.

She waited for him to envelop her in his strong arms like he always did, but he stood still, his coldness instantly noticeable. Why wasn't he happy to see her? What had changed in the time between when they were last together and now?

Lifting her head off his chest to look up at him, she saw a sternness in his eyes she hadn't seen since the first night they met. He stared down at her like she disgusted him. Without saying a single word, he made her feel like she wanted to cry.

What had happened to the man she loved?

"Ramiel, what's wrong? Why aren't you happy to see mc?" she asked, fighting back a sob.

His gaze traveled down from her face to her body, and

she understood immediately. Not that she blamed him. Noele knew what kind of male Ramiel was, and seeing the woman he loved dressed like some kind of whore would never make him happy, even if it was the first time they'd seen each other since her death.

She took his hands in hers and kissed them. "I did what I had to so I could help you and the Sons. Our son."

"You became Hades' whore to help me? How does that work?" he asked in an icy voice that chilled her to the bone.

He tugged on his hands, but Noele refused to let go. "Didn't you just hear what I told Thane and Layla? She can warn the Sons so they can be ready to fight against Hades' daemons."

"Thane and Layla? So you're fine with hanging out with daemons too? How nice for all of you. Curious how I got here? A fucking daemon, Noele! But what does that matter when you've been fucking Hades the whole time?" he barked as he yanked his hands from her hold.

She hated seeing him so unhappy. Somehow, she needed to reach him, but she knew her husband. When he got a thought into his head, it was hard to get it out. So she did the only thing that had ever worked with him.

Tilting her chin up so she could meet his gaze, she took a deep breath and gave him the truth he sorely needed. "Well, I'm sorry a daemon staked you, dear, but we've got the fate of the entire vampire world we're working with down here, so you'll forgive me if I'm happy to see my husband again. And yes, I have had to do some things I'm not particularly pleased about, but I wasn't just going to let my family and friends I love fight this war on their own."

Ramiel's mouth dropped open just like it always did when she let him know how things really were. He could be a very stubborn male, so sometimes he needed a reality check. She understood he wouldn't be happy with what she'd had to do with Hades, but desperate times called for desperate measures.

In a far softer tone, she added, "I've never been the kind of female to just sit on the sidelines and not do whatever I had to for those I love, Ramiel. Tell me you understand. Please?"

"That you've been sleeping with Hades? That's what you want me to understand, Noele?" he asked in a voice full of hurt.

And still she needed him to understand.

"Yes. Tell me you know I have never stopped loving you and only did that because I wanted to help you and the rest of the Sons."

Ramiel hung his head and sighed. "I want to understand. I do. It's just a bit much to find out the woman you love has been with someone else when you're not around."

"I know, baby, but it means nothing to me. This body has done things, but he's never been in my heart. You are the one who claimed that a long time ago."

He sighed again and finally looked up at her. "I'm going to be honest here, Noele. I'm pretty fucking tired of the woman I love having to sleep with other guys."

She knew her husband well enough to understand that was his attempt at humor. He needed that to start to get past the reality of what she'd done and would have to continue to do to help the Sons win this war.

Standing on her tip toes, she cradled his face in her

hands and kissed him for the first time in far too long. "I've missed you so much, Ramiel. I love you, and that hasn't changed since we've been apart. It never will."

For the first time since she lay eyes on him that night, he smiled in that way that never failed to melt her heart. Her Visigoth she'd fallen in love with, that hard man the rest of the world feared, had come back to her.

"I've missed you, Noele. I didn't want to go on when I lost you. I couldn't be around anyone without feeling like I wanted to die. The only thing that kept me going was my hate for the vampires who took you away from me. I killed as many as I could, but it didn't take away the pain of not having you with me anymore."

She took him in her arms and held him as the thought of him alone made her want to cry. For all his strength, he was a male who needed love to remain with the world. Without her, she knew what he'd become. The same kind of vampire he'd been before her.

A loner who saw the world through eyes filled with loathing.

"You're not alone anymore. We're together again, Ramiel," she said against his chest.

He pulled her close to him and sighed. "I'm sorry for what I said, Noele."

Looking up at him, she smiled at how silly he could be. "You're the only one for me. How could you ever doubt that? I love you, Ramiel. I have from the moment I realized you were exactly the mate I wished for all those starry nights. We were happy before, and we can be happy here. I know that sounds impossible, but it's not. Love stays, no matter where we have to be."

"I was with him when I got staked. Theron. He's all

grown up now and a Son like me. You'd be so proud of him, Noele. He's grown into the kind of vampire we hoped he would."

She tried to hide the sadness at hearing her baby boy had been forced to become a man too soon, but it was impossible. "Is he happy? I just want him to be happy."

Ramiel smiled. "Leta is safe too. Terek and Ilona are taking care of her, so don't worry."

Her baby girl. She hadn't let herself think of her in so long because it hurt too much to know she'd miss her entire life, and now that Ramiel had said her name, Noele couldn't stop herself from crying. She'd never see her children until they ended up in the Underworld, never see them enjoy life.

Covering her face, she sobbed harder than she had since she arrived in that place. When she thought she was doing something useful there, she could at least tolerate being in the Underworld, but the thought of never seeing Theron or Leta again made being there nothing but misery.

"I know how hard it is. I wish we could be there with them too," Ramiel said as he wrapped his strong arms around her shoulders and held her to him.

"I've missed you all so much. I had so many plans, and they were all just stolen away that night."

"We'll make the Archons pay for that and everything else. I promise, Noele."

That's all she wanted now that she had Ramiel back and could believe her children were happy. Every Archon in the world dead.

"Theron found me, Noele. He found me, and for the first time since you died, I smiled. I wish I could have had more time with him. He's the leader of the Sons of Navarus now, and we were wrong. He was ready."

She sighed at that reality. "So Nico did get to him after all?" she asked as she wiped the tears away.

"No. Nico turned traitor. He's on the Archons' side now."

His news stunned her. "Traitor? I can't believe it."

Behind her, Thane interrupted. "Nico a traitor? No way. I won't believe that."

Ramiel nodded. "Believe it. His sire is some important vampire and on the Archons' side. He's been selling the Sons out for a while."

Suddenly, Noele wondered something terrible. "Did he have anything to do with the night they found me? I thought it was strange that he insisted on you going to see Hadrian and the weres that particular night."

He shook his head slowly, but she could tell he was now thinking the same thing. "I don't know. If he did…"

Thane didn't give him a chance to finish his sentence. "How is everyone? I mean, other than Nico. Like Sasa?"

The room felt silent as Ramiel hesitated for a long moment before answering, "She and Vasilije are back together and happier than ever."

Noele watched Thane struggle to keep the emotion from showing on his face, but she knew how he felt. Even though he and Layla spent time together, it wasn't what he felt for Sasa. Hearing that she and her sire were back together no doubt was devastating to him.

Quickly, she changed the subject and got back to the business that brought her to his room in the first place. "Layla needs to go to Theron right now. He needs to know what he and the Sons face with the daemons getting into the war."

"He already knows. It was a daemon who got me. That left him with two against just him. I wouldn't be surprised if we saw him with us before long," he said sadly.

"That's just another reason for Layla to go right now. Warn my son about what Hades plans to do. The Sons need to know."

Thane nodded his agreement and leaned down to kiss Layla. "Yes, you should go. Find Theron and tell him everything. They may have been able to handle witches, but daemons are an entirely different story."

A second later, she disappeared from the room and Noele turned back to face Ramiel. "Again, we're forced to do things we don't want to, but Theron needs my help. I know how hard this is going to be on you, but always remember I love you."

Wincing in pain, he shook his head. "You don't have to do anything with Hades now, Noele. She's warning Theron and the Sons about his plans. That's all they need."

Noele brought his hand to her mouth and pressed a gentle kiss onto his fingers. "I've been doing more than that. Because of how close he's let me get, I know where Macaria, Navarus, and their sons are here. If we get the chance, we can set them free from their cells in Tartarus, the prison beneath the Underworld. That could tip the scales in our side's favor even more."

Ramiel's eyes opened wide in surprise. "The original vampires Macaria and Navarus from the stories?"

"Yes. I spoke to Nikator, Idolas's brother and the son

my bloodline is descended from. They're all down there, Ramiel. If we can figure out a way to get them out of there, they might be able to help defeat Hades and his daemons. And I'm still trying to find out more from him. He likes to brag a lot, so all I have to do is listen."

"And sleep with him," Ramiel grumbled. "It's not worth it to do what he wants."

Pressing her cheek into the palm of his hand, she looked up at him and hoped he saw in her eyes how much she loved him. "Trust me. I hate every minute I'm anywhere near him, but if it means I can help Theron and the Sons, how can I not do everything I can?"

"That sounds vaguely familiar to the last time I had to watch you go sleep with another male. I'm sick and tired of this. Let someone else have to do it."

"I know, but we have to do everything we can to help our son and our friends. We can't give up now, Ramiel."

He hung his head and kissed her softly on the lips. "Will we ever just get to be together and happy again?"

She kissed him back and smiled. "I guarantee it. I just need you to have faith, okay?"

Noele didn't know what she would have done if the prophecy required her to see Ramiel sleep with another female and then with a goddess. She couldn't understand what he was going through, but she needed him to believe in her, and in that she knew Ramiel wouldn't let her down.

## 14

Everywhere he looked, Theron saw another memory of another time he'd been happy in the only home he'd ever known. The cardboard caterpillar book his mother used to read him each morning before bed. The chair his father used to sit in when he'd bounce him on his knee. The scrapbook his mother loved to explain to him so he knew the history of born vampires.

He wandered through the house from room to room, lost in the past and all he had then. They had been happy. That he never doubted. He didn't know so much then, but it didn't matter. What he knew was they loved him.

Theron stopped in the doorway of his parents' room and stared in. He could almost imagine her smiling at him long before the last of the sun's rays set below the horizon. Never an angry expression for waking her up before he was supposed to. No, she just smiled and waved him over to where she lay next to his father still asleep.

Her long brown hair lay across the pillow, spread out

like an angel's behind her as she looked up at him standing next to her. "Did you have a nightmare, honey?" she would ask with true concern in her voice.

Nightmares never woke him up. He was a clyten, so his body never wanted to sleep during the day. He didn't know how to stop that then. But she never scolded him for that. He didn't realize it until later how much she sacrificed for him, even in things like waking before she had to.

The memories of this place made his emotions run amok. He had a loving family and a home, and those fuckers took it away. They killed his mother, and then they killed his father. Now he had only his sister, but she was just a child. They were orphans because of the Archons.

How could he be expected to know what to do now? Without the parents who helped him understand the world and his place in it, how would he win this battle against the bastards who ruined his life and a god with unlimited power?

The future threatened to overwhelm him. He couldn't do this. Not alone. Not without the two vampires who had always made him feel like he had someplace safe in the world.

Theron's legs shook as his emotions unraveled inside him, and he slid down the wall of his parents' bedroom, falling to the floor. He'd cried when Dante finally told him the truth about his mother, but that had been more out of rage than sadness. Barely a vampire with a teenager's mind, he only knew to react with anger then.

Then his father's death at the hands of that daemon made those same feelings surface once more. Again, his rage took over, smothering his sadness, and he tore those fucking things of Hades to pieces. Anger and hatred coursed through him in those moments, but since he'd returned to his childhood home, they'd disappeared, replaced by utter sadness he didn't know how to handle.

And as he sat there on the floor in the only place he'd ever felt safe in his entire life, the tears finally came for all he'd lost. Not out of anger but out of sadness. For the mother taken too soon. For the father he'd gotten a second chance with who'd been taken cruelly in front of him.

For a life lost to his fate that had been destined from the moment he was conceived.

Once they started, he didn't know how to stop them. The tears didn't wash away his sadness. They didn't make him feel better. Nothing he'd ever heard about how they healed a broken heart happened. He merely cried and continued to cry without getting anything from it.

After a while, the lack of any good to come from crying turned his sadness to anger once again. That's all he knew, so he naturally reverted to the rage that filled him from the moment he realized who he was in this world.

The vampire born solely to defeat the Archons and take over the Underworld.

He had no other purpose, no other meaning, except to the two vampires who had lived in this place with him. Now they were gone, ripped from his life when he needed them most, and he again had no other reason for being alive other than to perform as the war machine the Prophecy of Idolas claimed he'd be.

Once, in a time that he only knew of through memories, he thought life would be more. Back when his mother and father loved him and Dante spent his days teaching him about how to be a clyten, Theron had looked forward to a future filled with happiness and fun. He had a way of making females want him, and he felt powerful and protected.

As he thought back to those days down near the sea with his only friend, a hint of sadness once again slipped into his mind. The hours they spent together then had promised so much, but what had they really delivered? Sweet lies wrapped in sun-drenched moments and the smiling faces of beautiful girls.

Theron's hands curled into tight fists at his disappointment that nothing he'd ever believed had come true. He thought his parents would be there for him, and then they were taken away. He thought being a clyten and born vampire would make him something special, but he was nothing now, a being created solely to fulfill some cipher from ages ago. He thought being a Son of Navarus like his father would give him what he sought to be that vampire everyone needed in this war, but it turned out he was only their leader because of his stronger powers.

He couldn't go on like this.

This war needed to be ended tonight. He could do it himself. Fuck everyone else. He'd go to Archon headquarters and wipe all of those motherfuckers out. Hades' daemons didn't have any power over him, so he didn't have to worry about them, and the Archons were just a bunch of sterile fucks who thought they should rule the vampire world. None of them would be able to stop him.

Slowly, he convinced himself he should do it, so he stood and took one last look at his parents' bedroom before leaving. He had nothing to lose now. They'd taken everything he'd loved, so now he'd do that and more.

Out of the corner of his eye, he spied something in the darkness as he walked into the living room. A flash of blond hair alerted him to the fact he wasn't alone, and in a flash, he rushed whoever had made the mistake of coming there.

He clamped his hands around their neck and began to squeeze as they tried to speak to him. The words didn't make any sense, and he ignored them.

Curious to see what he was about to strangle to death, he turned on the light and saw he'd caught himself a daemon. She looked more human than the ones who had found him and his father, but she was daemon, none-theless.

"Another one of you? I'll do to you what I did to the other two, and then maybe Hades will get the hint," he growled as he slowly tightened his hold on her neck.

"Please, Hades didn't send me. Your mother did," she croaked out, barely loud enough for him to hear.

For a moment, his heart skipped a beat at her mention of his mother. But she was a daemon sent to kill him. A creature who would lie to trick him.

"Don't bother with the mother stuff, bitch. I'm not buying it."

His thumbs pressed into the front of her neck, and he felt the tendons strain beneath them. It wouldn't take much more to kill this one either, but he wouldn't do to her what he did to the others. Not in his home. He didn't want that there.

He didn't fucking want her there either, for that

matter. She was a filthy follower of the god of the Underworld.

Her dark eyes opened wide while he pushed harder against her throat. "Please...Noele said to tell you that Hades plans to crush the Sons and their allies with his legions. She wanted you to know."

Lies. It didn't matter that she knew his mother's name. She was still a liar sent by Hades to trick him.

"I don't believe you. My mother would never deal with something like you," he said and then spit in her face.

As if that was a step too far, the daemon lifted her arms and pressed her hands to his face. Too bad for her she didn't know he was immune to whatever daemons could do to other vampires with just their touch. The surprise that her attempt to hurt him didn't work registered on her face, and for a moment, her hands simply hung suspended in the air near his head.

"Sorry. That doesn't work on me. I'd say you should go back and tell your boss that, but you'll be dead in a few seconds."

Her arms began to flail, and she tried to push him away, but it was no use. Whatever power she possessed as a daemon, it was no match for him.

Finally, she squeaked out a word Theron didn't recognize. "Nyx."

Her eyes fluttered closed just as he felt the life begin to leave her body, but then someone touched his arm and he didn't know why, but he had to release the daemon. She fell to the floor in front of him while he looked down in shock.

What the fuck had happened?

Quickly, he turned to his right and saw a woman standing there looking at him. She wore a long black dress that showed off her body nicely, especially her breasts it barely covered. Her black hair hung nearly to her waist, and her dark eyes studied him like she was curious what he could be.

"Who are you? Why did you stop me from killing this thing?"

"Layla, return to the Underworld right now," she said, completely ignoring his questions.

The daemon disappeared from in front of him, irritating Theron more than he had been before. "I don't care who you are. I was going to kill that."

"It's her, not it," she said in a silky voice that rolled over him and seemed to ignite something inside him.

"I was going to kill *her* then."

"And I couldn't let that happen. So now she's gone back to where she belongs."

Who the fuck was this beautiful woman and why did she think she should have any say regarding what he wanted to do with daemons?

As he wondered just that, she reached out and touched his cheek. Theron simply rolled his eyes. "Sorry, but that daemon shit doesn't work on me."

Then just as the last word left his mouth, he felt lighter, like all the sadness and rage inside him disappeared. The woman smiled and then softly sighed as she moved her hand from his face.

"So much emotion in one being."

"What are you? You don't act like the other daemons I've met."

"I'm no daemon. I'm Nyx, the goddess of night."

Theron stood watching her, not understanding what was happening to him. "And that's how you can change how I feel?"

A slow smile spread across her lips. "One of my many powers."

"So you're a goddess? Any relation to the god I'm supposed to overthrow? Hades?"

In a split second, she changed from happy to furious, startling him. Her eyes grew pitch black, and her eyebrows drew in like angry slashes toward her nose. Worst of all, the beautiful smile she'd just given him vanished, replaced by an angry frown.

Clearly, he wasn't the only one with emotions in that room.

"No, he's no one to me."

"Good, because when I'm finished with him, that kingdom of his will be mine."

She ran her fingertips along his jaw and then over his head as her smile returned. "Who are you? A vampire who can overthrow a god? I've never met a creature like you in all my existence. You intrigue me."

Her touch excited him, sending waves of desire along every inch her fingertips glided over. "I'm the one prophesied by Idolas to defeat the Archons and Hades to rule the vampire world and the Underworld. I'm Theron."

Nyx closed her eyes and said his name in a faraway voice that made him feel like he was in a dream. "Theron."

"Are you really a goddess?" he asked, suddenly needing to know the truth as everything inside him churned in a way he'd never experienced.

She opened her eyes and nodded. "I'm one of the

ancients. Before Hades and his brothers and sisters existed the gods and goddesses like me."

"And you control the night?"

"Night, dreams, sleep, darkness, pleasure, and death."

Her mention of death pushed out all the other thoughts out of his mind. "Have you been sent to kill me by the ancients because I plan to take Hades' throne from him?"

Nyx stepped forward until her body touched his and shook her head slowly. "No. They have no interest in the troubles of Hades, the Archons, and the Sons of Navarus. I came because my handmaiden called for my help."

"A daemon is your handmaiden?"

"Yes. And who do you have for you, Theron?"

Sadness returned as he considered his answer to her question. "No one. I am alone in the world."

"But you are a member of the Sons of Navarus. Are they not there for you?"

He shook his head. "I am alone."

Once more, she ran her hand through his hair and every bit of sadness in him disappeared. "You are alone no more, Theron."

His eyes fluttered closed, and then he felt her lips on his. Her kiss was soft and seductive, like the very night itself. The scent of jasmine gently swirled around him, making him feel lightheaded.

And when her tongue slid into his mouth to tease his, Theron felt like he was flying, untethered to the ground he stood on and soaring through the night sky. He had no idea how Nyx made him feel like this, but he didn't care. After what seemed like a lifetime of rage and sadness filling him, now he sensed nothing but pleasure.

"Doesn't that feel better?" she whispered against his lips.

Opening his eyes, he looked at her beautiful face and smiled. "I think I know why you're the goddess of pleasure too. I've never felt like that before."

A wicked smile lit up her face. "I neglected to tell you what kind of pleasure I control, Theron. Sexual pleasure. While other goddesses lay claim to some part of that, it is mine to rule."

He wanted to answer with something, but at that moment as her hand slid down the front of his shirt and under his pants, not a single word formed in his mind. All he could do is focus on where her body touched his and silently pray to any god who may be listening to let this feeling go on forever.

Theron watched as she waved her hand and suddenly her dress disappeared to reveal a body so perfect it could only belong to a goddess. In his short life, he'd enjoyed more than a few females, both vampire and human, and they paled in comparison to Nyx. Full breasts led to a tiny waist that flared to hips that made him want to bend her over and fuck her from behind.

For a moment, he wished he'd figured out that whole making clothes disappear trick other vampires could do, but as if she read his mind, she waved her hand again and removed his for him. Curious to know if his power of mind reading worked on her, he attempted to focus his thoughts as she slowly kissed his neck, sending waves of need coursing through him.

Nyx lifted her head and smiled. "I sense what you're trying to do, but that doesn't work on me. I can, however, read your mind, and I love what you're thinking."

"I just wondered," he admitted as she returned to kissing his neck.

"Don't wonder, Theron. Just enjoy," she murmured against his skin just above his collarbone.

Her words wound their way into his brain and seemed to fill up every inch of his mind. He could think of nothing else but enjoying her and what she offered. Whatever power she had over him, he didn't want to fight it.

He stuffed his hand into her hair and tugged her head back so she had to look at him. Could he control her thoughts even if he couldn't read them? He stared into her eyes and thought about how good her mouth would feel on another part of his body.

With a smile, she shook her head. "I told you. Your powers don't work on me. But if you want me to do that..."

Her sentence faded into nothingness as she moved her mouth down over his chest and abs, finally kneeling before him. Looking down, he watched her palm his rock-hard cock, the feel of her hand sending a shock of pleasure through him like he'd never felt before. His heart slammed into his chest as he waited in wild anticipation for her to slide her mouth over him, and she seemed to delight in making him wait.

"Are you trying to torture me?" he asked before placing his hand on the back of her head and pulling her to him.

Nyx didn't answer and instead sucked his cock into her mouth, taking every inch of him down to his balls. Her tongue teased the underside of his shaft as the head pushed up against the back of her throat, sending Theron's need for far more into overdrive.

She slowly retreated up to the head, but he quickly thrust his hips forward, fucking her mouth hard. Her ability to make him want her combined with his sex drive that usually bordered on intense to make their fucking wild and uninhibited.

Just the way he liked it.

After a few more jabs of his cock into her mouth, she pushed his hand from the back of her head, stood up, and kissed him hard on the mouth. "I've never had a vampire before. Are all of you like this?"

Theron shook his head and grinned. "There's no one like me."

She slid her hand up and down his cock and moaned. "Prove it."

He didn't need to be asked twice with an ordinary female, and Nyx was no ordinary female. Lifting her off the ground, he positioned her over his cock and pushed her down onto him as he spun them around so her back faced the wall. She clung to his neck and stared at him wide-eyed, and with the first hard plunge into her cunt, she cried out in ecstasy.

Theron planted his hands on the wall behind her and let his desire dictate the speed of their fucking. He didn't know if it was because of her powers or because she'd taken away all the sadness and anger inside him, but he felt nothing but pure pleasure like he'd never felt before with anyone.

Her cunt fit like a glove around his cock, and with each thrust, she met his motion with her own, her body begging him to take her harder. In his ear, she moaned sweetly and repeated his name over and over, like some prayer of worship for him.

Scraping her nails across his shoulders, she drew blood that dripped down his chest, igniting his desire for what all vampires craved during sex. Theron dipped his head to taste the soft skin of her neck, and then his fangs snapped into his mouth with a vicious click.

She lifted her head for a moment and looked at them with wonder. She'd never been with a vampire before, and now he'd show her what he could do to her.

Slowly, he ran his tongue over his fangs and smiled. "Let's see if I can make you feel like you're flying too."

Lowering his head to her neck, he grazed the tips of his teeth against her skin and then savagely bit down, sinking into her body as he continued to fuck her hard. Blood rushed into his mouth, and immediately he knew the blood of a goddess was like nothing he'd ever experienced before. Instantly, he became lightheaded, slowing his thrusting into her perfect cunt for a moment as he gained his bearings.

Her blood was immediately addictive, and he felt it rush through his veins. It made him invincible, like nothing in the world could defeat him. He'd thought biting her would give her an incredible sensation, but he hadn't anticipated how her blood would affect him.

Nyx held his mouth to her neck and came hard on his cock while he continued to pull from her vein. The feel of her cunt milking him through her release sent him over the edge, and with one last plunge into her, he came inside her as he sucked her immortal blood into him.

They said nothing for what felt like hours as he held her in his arms, his cock still inside her and his mouth still drawing her blood into him. With any other female, he would have drained her by drinking so ferociously, but finally, Nyx lifted her head and smiled.

"That was out of this world. Now let me give you something in return. I'll help you defeat Hades, Theron."

"How can you help?" he asked, barely able to form the question through the haze of what her blood did to him.

"I live in the Underworld. I have my ways."

He didn't care to ask any more about how she'd help. At that moment, he didn't give a damn about Hades, the Archons, the Sons, the war, or anything else in the world.

All he cared about was her.

## 15

The buzz of Sion's drones flying overhead signaled to Vasilije the time had come for their final push. The dragons waited high in the hills, while Terek stood with Dante and his clyten forces on the plains waiting for the battle cry to let them know to attack. In the distance, daemons waited, as exhausted as the Sons and their allies from the battle that had dragged on into its third night. Vasilije suspected even they prayed for it to end tonight, one way or another.

As for him, he intended to do everything in his power to make that happen. So far, their side had held while the Archons' allies had found fighting vampires and dragons hard enough, but when Sion's drones arrived to attack them relentlessly from the sky, it all became too much for them. They'd fallen back to a safe position that morning, and while Dante wanted to attack with his clytens and the dragons to end them once and for all, everyone needed a rest, so the battle was put on hold until sundown.

The last hint of the sun's rays had fallen below the horizon just seconds ago, and as expected, Sion released his drones right on schedule to begin the attack on Hades' daemons. They filled the sky like a plague descending from the heavens, and the buzzing noise they made drowned out every other sound around them.

The Sons and their allies had funneled the daemons into this valley between two mountains just east of the dragons' home. For three nights, they'd fought them with every means possible, but as tired as he knew the daemons must be, they continued to throw themselves at them. The first night, Vasilije himself knew hundreds had died at his hands alone, and Terek had slayed over twice as many since he was far more experienced in battle. The clytens had taken over the next morning and killed even more, yet that night Vasilije could have sworn there were as many as the night before.

They just seemed to keep coming, like Hades had an infinite number of daemons to sacrifice. The problem was the Sons and their allies didn't have that many troops on their side. Some vampires from the population around the dragons' castle had joined up when they heard they were fighting the Archons, but that left them with less than half of what the other side had to fight with.

Sion's drones had turned the tide of the battle on the second night, though, and now as Vasilije looked out across the valley, he saw fewer daemons than the night before. He could only hope that with their relentless harassment from the air combined with the vampires and dragons on the ground, the battle could finally be won tonight.

He dreaded the idea of it stretching into a fourth day and night. While Sion had more than enough machines to send into the air, the Sons and their allies were beginning to get worn down. One more night might mean the end of them.

From across the plain, Terek held up his sword and Dante yelled out the cry for the battle to begin. Behind them, the dragons screeched into the night sky, each Draco brother shifting into their true form, their magnificent colored scales shining in the moonlight as they hovered above the nearby hills and prepared to swoop down on the daemons as they attacked.

The sound coming from the opposite side of the plain was nothing less than horrifying. Hades' daemons made a high-pitched shrieking noise when they attacked, and now as they began to rush toward the ground Vasilije and the rest of the vampires held, the sound became deafening, even drowning out the drones.

He took one last look down the line of his kind as they raced toward what would be the end for far too many of them and focused his rage on the enemy. They appeared and disappeared constantly, but that trick didn't work as well as it had the first night. Now they knew that whenever a daemon prepared to blink out, they had to gather their strength first. It seemed disappearing wasn't something easy for them, and they expended a great deal of energy doing it. Thankfully, Terek noticed that little tell in the first hours of the battle, and since then, the Sons and their allies knew to watch the daemons carefully. If they suddenly fell still, even for a few moments, they were about to disappear and that was the perfect time to get them.

The noise of the battle fell away as Vasilije's heartbeat pounded in his ears, and now as he ripped the head off one of the enemy, he heard nothing of its screams of pain or any of the other deafening sounds in the air around him. At his left side, a vampire hacked a daemon to pieces, but on his right, Vasilije saw one of his fellow fighters suffer as a daemon placed its hands on his skin. One touch and a vampire instantly felt intense pain take over their entire body. He sliced the daemon's head off, but it wasn't enough to save the vampire, who fell to the ground writhing in pain.

Kneeling at his side, Vasilije saw his mouth open when he let out the final scream of agony before he died. He deserved a hero's death, not some second-rate death at the hands of Hades' scum, so Vasilije ripped his stake from his belt and drove it into his heart.

"Rest in peace, warrior," he said quietly as the vampire turned to dust there on the battlefield where he'd willingly chosen to help the Sons.

There was no time to mourn him and the hundreds others who would die that night, so the Romanian pushed ahead, determined to kill as many daemons as he could. In the distance, he saw Terek slice and dice dozens of the enemy with precision. He always did have a way of pushing down that whole spiritual side of him when it came to battle.

Dante grabbed a hold of a drone, along with twenty or so of his clyten regiment, and they flew above the enemies' line to come at the daemons from behind. He'd explained his plan to do just that before the rest of the vampires fell asleep that morning, and for his part, Vasilije had made the mistake of doubting he'd actually go through with it. He should have known the clyten better. A stunt like that was just his style.

But as long as it helped them defeat the daemons, he didn't care what tricks Dante wanted to try.

As all of this marched through his mind, he saw a daemon rush toward him, its arms extended and its hands aiming for him. "Not tonight, motherfucker. I don't plan to go to the Underworld because of one of you bastards!" he yelled as he dodged its attempt to grab him and then spun around to bury his knife into its head.

Blood spurted everywhere, covering him with daemon ooze, but thankfully, their innards didn't have the same effect as their outsides. Vasilije spit to get rid of blood that landed on his mouth, disgusted by the very idea of having anything of theirs on him.

And so it went for hours through the night. At one point, he heard the cry of the fire dragon, Kerik, and saw him as a band of daemons attacked him. He held out for what seemed like forever, but the pain they could inflict even penetrated the dragon's hard scaly shell. In a sight that made Vasilije turn away in sadness afterward, he watched the mighty leader of the dragons collapse to the ground and then just before he died, a puff of smoke exited his body before he fell still.

The battle eventually turned in the Sons' favor, but as they killed the last of Hades' daemons and left their discarded bodies on the battlefield, they couldn't say it had been an overwhelming success. The air dragon, Victor, lay mortally wounded and his brothers cried out in pain to see they'd lost nearly half their family. The clyten regiment suffered huge losses, but even as Dante walked the field to give each of them the proper death they'd earned, he had to admit it would have been worse without the drones.

"They were the trick," he admitted sadly before staking yet another of his troops.

Terek nodded, but his sadness over the loss of life he saw all around him made him sigh. "I don't know if the Archons will be able to convince Hades to send more of his daemons to slaughter, but I don't know if we have much more left on our side either."

Even Dante, who had never shied away from any fight as long as Vasilije had known him, had to agree. "I called for Theron a few minutes ago. This can't go on. He's going to have to come up with another plan because this one has run its course. My clyten troops can't go through another battle like this."

Looking across the land at the hundreds of dead, Terek said, "None of us can. Theron will have to understand that."

Just as he said that, the leader of the Sons of Navarus appeared beside them and nodded his agreement, surprising all of them. Theron had been nothing less than hell-bent on war, so his change now seemed odd.

"I agree, Terek. The time for battle between the two sides is over. Now we need more surgical strikes."

"Surgical?" Vasilije asked, unsure what he meant. "As in what?"

"I just came from the Orders' headquarters. I've known all along that at some point we'd have to stop fighting all these allies of the Archons and Hades and instead just fight them. Saint and Solenne have a right to go after that Archon that raped her. Sion and Kali have their own wrongs to avenge with her sire, who's working with the Archons. So they'll be heading to Corsica. Your job is done, gentlemen."

Vasilije looked over at Terek and Dante and saw the shock in their expressions. "Done? You think sending one Son and his mate to handle the Archons at their headquarters, which is likely one big trap, a good idea? Why not send us to fight with them?"

"Because they deserve to do this on their own, especially Saint and Solenne. As for Archon headquarters being a trap, I'll be with them to clear the place out so they can focus on their targets."

"What if Hades sends more daemons? What then?" Dante asked.

Theron smiled. "He's not. He didn't want to in the first place, but because he agreed to come in on the side of the Archons, he had to send some after our side defeated the witches down in Italy. He has no interest in sending more of his troops to be killed."

Still unconvinced, Dante asked, "How do you know this? I get you have all those great powers and things, but are you now able to read a god's mind too?"

Vasilije watched as Theron's smile changed to one he knew all too well. He had no idea what the vampire had been up to, but it hadn't all been battling the enemy.

"We have a spy in the enemy camp. A daemon my parents have been using to get me messages for the past two nights. She assures me Hades is done with this war."

"Your parents?" Terek repeated with surprise. "Noele and Ramiel?"

Theron nodded. "It seems ever since my mother got to the Underworld, she's been working to help us up here. When my father joined her, they began sending me messages to let me know what Hades is up to. Trust me. He's done with the war. He's too busy planning for his next fight with me."

"So the war is over," Dante said with restrained hope in his voice.

"It will be once Saint and Solenne take care of that Archon and Sion and Kali do what they need to with her sire."

"And what about you?" Vasilije asked, still curious about what their young leader had been up to lately.

With a casual shrug of his shoulders, Theron answered, "Well, either I defeat Hades and take over control of the Underworld and the vampire world like the prophecy says, or he defeats me and puts me in his cellar down there. Those are the only two choices. Either way, some of you will be happy and others will be disappointed, if I'm reading your thoughts correctly."

Opening his mouth, Vasilije began to ask what that meant, but suddenly terror struck at his heart. Something was wrong. Very wrong.

Something was wrong with Sasa. She was in danger.

"You look like you've seen a ghost. What's wrong, Vasilije?" Terek asked with fear hanging off every word he spoke.

"Sasa. She's in danger. I have to go."

"I'll come with you."

He didn't argue with his friend and focused on the castle before disappearing. But instead of going to the room where he'd left her, Vasilije found himself outside the castle. Terek joined him a second later, clearly as confused as he was why they hadn't appeared inside.

"There's only one reason why," he explained as

Vasilije began running toward the front door. "Only another vampire could stop us from entering that way."

The front door of the castle didn't budge when he pushed on it, so he called out to Sasa to let her know he'd sensed her danger. "I'm here, Sasa! Hang on. I'm coming!"

He and Terek slammed their bodies against the door, but still it didn't move an inch. With each passing moment, Vasilije grew more and more worried about his vampire's safety. She should have been fine since Navar stayed behind with her, Ilona, and Leta, but he'd felt her fear as surely as he'd been next to her at that moment.

"This isn't working," he said in frustration after the fifth time they tried to bust down the door. "It's too heavy."

"I'll call Dante and tell him to bring some of his troops. We have to get in there. Something's very wrong. I can sense Ilona's terrified. I just don't know why."

Vasilije scanned the castle walls for another way in. "Same with Sasa. I hope I'm mistaken, but something feels very wrong. I need to get to her now!"

Just then, he saw a window above their heads about twenty feet to the right of the doorway. He tried to materialize on the ledge, but he couldn't do it. Something was making his powers ineffective.

Pointing up at the window, he said, "I can't get up there on my own. Something's wrong. If you can hoist me up, I should be able to reach it."

The two hurried over to under the window and Terek lifted Vasilije up on his shoulders so he was standing on them. But they weren't tall enough.

"Let me call Dante."

Vasilije didn't want to wait for more help. If he could

jump, he could probably grab the stone ledge and then pull himself up. He just hoped the window wasn't tempered glass or all of their acrobatics might be for nothing.

"No! I'm going to jump to the ledge. Stand still."

As Sasa's terror grew inside him, Vasilije leaped off Terek's shoulders and stretched his arms out to grab onto the ledge. He barely reached, but after securing his hold on the stone, he pulled himself up. Set back about three feet, the window sat in an alcove that barely held him. With as much power as he could muster, he threw himself at the glass two times, but it refused to break.

He needed to get in there. If his body wouldn't do the job, maybe his foot would. Lifting his leg, he thrust his boot into the window and shattered it. A few seconds later, he crawled through and saw the window was on the stairs up to the second floor.

Terek called out his name, but at that moment, Sasa screamed, so Vasilije forgot about his friend and tore up the stone steps toward her voice. A body lying on a step near the top stopped him dead, and he looked down to see the youngest Draco brother Navar splayed out dead and surrounded in blood, his throat slit from ear to ear.

Who had done this?

He raced up the last few stairs and down the hall toward Sasa's room, calling out for his mate. "Sasa! Where are you? I'm here, Sasa. I'm here!"

All the while, images of her hurt and in pain tore through his brain. What had happened in this place?

Outside the room next to hers, Vasilije saw a body and the telltale blond hair of Ilona. Like Navar, her throat had been slit and she'd bled out. Leta lay on the floor just inside their bedroom unconscious, but she hadn't been hurt in any obvious way.

As much as he wanted to stop to help, he sensed Sasa might suffer the same fate as Ilona and Nevar if he didn't reach her, so he yelled for Terek to come and ran toward Sasa's room. He still sensed her, and that meant she wasn't dead yet.

Throwing open the wooden door, he stopped dead, stunned by the scene in front of him. Sasa stood crying, and behind her, Nico had his arm wrapped around her and in his other hand a knife he held to her throat.

"What is this, Nico? Let her go," he said in his calmest voice, hoping not to scare Sasa.

The eldest Son of Navarus shook his head and frowned. "I can't do that, Vasilije."

"Vasilije!" she cried, her voice trembling from fear.

"Why? She's done nothing to you. Let her go and we can talk out whatever you're dealing with."

"I stayed at the Order for centuries. I watched over everything that was so dear to us. You know that, don't you?" he said, still shaking his head.

Sasa began to cry harder, so Vasilije instinctively stepped forward to help her. Nico pressed the knife to her throat, so hard the point drew blood that began to drip down her neck.

"Not any closer or she gets what the other two got," he said in a low voice Vasilije didn't even know now.

"Okay. Nico, it's okay. We all know what you've been through for the Sons. You spent your entire life at the Order. I get it."

His response to Vasilije's attempt to placate him told the Romanian his friend was long gone, replaced by someone he barely recognized after all their years of knowing one another.

"The Archons don't want to ruin our world. We had it all wrong. We were fed a pack of lies. Because of it, we let ourselves get deluded. We shouldn't be fighting this war. They want to make the vampire world better. The Sons can't do that. They don't know how to run it like the Archons do."

Vasilije didn't give a fuck about any of that. The politics of the war with the Archons had ceased to mean a damn thing the second he saw Sasa standing there with a knife to her throat. All he cared about was getting her away from Nico and keeping her safe for the rest of time.

"I agree. This war needs to end. Just let Sasa go. It's going to be okay, Nico."

"No, it won't! You don't get it because your judgment is clouded!" he barked so loudly it startled Vasilije.

Sasa sobbed loudly and reached her hands out for him, but he didn't dare make a move while Nico had that knife to her throat. If only Terek would get there, the two of them would be able to overtake him.

"It's okay, love. It's just Nico. We're all friends here. It will be okay," he said as he looked into her dark eyes and saw nothing but pure fear.

"Love," Nico sneered, shaking his head in disgust. "Everything began to go wrong when females got in the way. Kali fucked everything up. All she had to do was obey her sire, but she couldn't even do that. Same with this one here. Do you know the Archons were content to ignore us until you met her? From that fucking moment, we were on their radar, and my life became a living hell."

He pushed the knife deeper into her skin, and Sasa

screamed in pain. It tore through Vasilije like the knife was cutting him. He had to do something before Nico killed her like he had with Ilona and Navar.

"I don't know what you're talking about, Nico. Sasa didn't do anything. Let her go. If you want to kill someone, then make it me. I've done so fucking much in my life I deserve it. She doesn't. Let her go," Vasilije pleaded, hoping to reach some part of his friend that would never do this to a female.

Nico began rambling about all he'd endured from the Sons and Archons, so Vasilije took that chance to lunge at him. He pushed Sasa out of the way, and she fell to the floor. Whatever happened now, at least she'd be safe.

"Run, Sasa! Get out of here!" he ordered as Nico regained his focus and swung the knife at him.

His eyes flashed a madness that Vasilije had never seen in him, and he flailed his arms like he'd lost his mind, repeatedly trying to cut anything he could. To give himself the chance to subdue him, Vasilije hit him hard, sending him staggering back. He needed to get him on the floor to get that knife away from him, so he took another swing, but Nico jerked in the other direction.

Behind Vasilije, he heard a noise. He turned his head to look for Terek so they could end this, but instead he saw Sasa standing there with a stake. She screamed his name, and he spun around just in time to avoid Nico cutting him. His knife sliced through the air, and then he heard a sound that made his heart stop.

In her attempt to help him and stake Nico, Sasa got in the way. The knife slit her throat.

Vasilije watched in horror as she collapsed to the floor. He rushed to her and dropped to his knees beside her as blood poured from her body. She clutched at her neck, but it was no use. She couldn't stop the blood.

He had to save her. Sinking his teeth into his wrist, he opened a vein and pressed his arm to her mouth. "Drink! Take my blood, Sasa!"

She tried, but Nico's knife had done too much damage. Each time she attempted to drink her sire's blood, she choked and gagged, sending more of her own blood pouring out of her neck.

With each second that passed, he saw her life fade away until he knew there was no more time for them. He cradled her face and stared into her dark eyes, now pleading as she struggled to speak one last time.

"You have to let me go."

"No! This isn't the end. I can save you."

She reached up and touched her bloody hand to his cheek. "I'll be waiting for you. I promise," she said softly.

And then she wasn't there anymore.

Vasilije's eyes filled with tears at the loss of the one soul he loved in the world. Barely able to see, he felt around for the stake and said his final words to Sasa before he let her go.

"I love you. I have always loved you."

He cocked his arm back, and with one swift plunge of the stake into her heart, he gave her the ending she deserved. She turned to dust before his eyes as he slumped onto the floor where a second before she lay mortally wounded.

Behind him, Terek stopped as he entered the bedroom. "Vasilije, he doesn't leave this room."

Rage coursed through Vasilije, replacing the sadness that filled him with the need to avenge Sasa's death.

Jumping to his feet, he stalked Nico around a table and, along with Terek, cornered him.

"The two of you know better than any other vampires the power of a sire. I had no choice," Nico said unapologetically, never once regretting what he'd done to his friends and their loved ones.

Terek grabbed hold of his shoulders and ripped the knife out of his hand as Vasilije tightly clutched the stake he'd just used to send Sasa on her way. This time, though, he wouldn't perform the final act with respect or love.

This time he aimed to send Nico to the Underworld with a promise.

"You'll never find peace. I won't let you. I don't care who you have on your side. I'll make sure you suffer for what you did."

He pulled back his arm and watched Nico stare at him like they were strangers before driving the wooden stake into his heart. The eldest Son disappeared into dust, and Vasilije spit on his remains before turning away in disgust and rage.

Terek stood with his head hung and pointed toward the bed where Leta lay peacefully. "She's all I have left of the life I planned with Ilona," he said sadly.

Overwhelmed by his sadness, Vasilije wished he had that. He'd lost the only soul he loved, and now he wanted nothing to do with anyone.

Fuck the Archons. Fuck the Sons. Fuck the world.

Without Sasa, he was done. He had no reason to stay and fight. The vampire world held nothing for him now.

"Goodbye, my friend," he said quietly without looking back at Terek and then walked out of the castle, disappearing into the night.

## 16

Saint silently padded across the bedroom floor and out to the balcony where Solenne stood looking out over the city. Nighttime always made it look so beautiful, its white buildings set against a backdrop of the dark sky. He looked up as he slid his arms around her waist and saw no stars in the sky tonight.

"Nothing to wish on," he murmured in her ear.

She turned to look at him and smiled. "Maybe we don't need to make any wishes anymore."

"We do have everything we've ever wanted."

He kissed her neck and inhaled the sweet smell of her skin and the vanilla lotion she loved to slather on after a bath. A tiny hint of guilt tugged at him for having so much while his fellow Sons were still fighting in the east.

"I wonder how things are going."

Solenne slid her hand over the back of his head and kissed his cheek. "I know. I've been thinking about them for hours. I'm hoping that since Sion and Kali haven't called that it means things are going well. They do have dragons fighting with them in this battle."

"I would have taken dragons any night of the week," Saint said quietly as he gazed out at the city, instantly regretting his words as the memory of Hadrian's death flashed in his mind.

"We only had witches, Declan. They're up against daemons controlled by the god of the Underworld. I'll take witches any night of the week."

"I'll take none of this ever again and the two of us living peacefully on a farm somewhere. That's what I'll take any night of the week," he whispered as he hugged her tightly to him.

The two of them fell silent, but that was nothing strange for them. Saint had never been much of a talker, and while Solenne had her moments, lately they'd enjoyed the silence for what it offered. After the battle in Italy, the two lay in each other's arms in their bed saying nothing. There was no need to. He knew how relieved she was he didn't get staked, and she knew he wanted to be nowhere else in the world that night.

They'd been through the worst that could happen for two souls in love. Separated by her sire out of jealousy, they spent a century apart. Then she sacrificed herself with Verrater to save Saint, something he planned to avenge on that Archon bastard as soon as he could. Kidnapping, separation, and worse, they'd dealt with it all. Now, they had one more hurdle to clear before they could live out their lives in peace.

As if she knew what he was thinking at that moment, she quietly said, "I'm worried, Declan. I can't help but be anxious about what's going to happen when we go to Corsica."

"I know, but things will be okay."

She trembled against his body, so he slid his fingers over the back of her neck where his mark showed everyone she was his to calm her. Pressing his lips to it, he smiled. "I've never been prouder than when you got this."

"And I've never been prouder to get it," she said, turning in his hold. "But I'm still worried, Declan."

Those beautiful blue eyes that never failed to show her true feelings stared up at him with concern filling them. Gently, he pushed her red hair off her forehead and kissed her softly.

"We've been through too much not to be together at the end of this, Solenne. I believe that."

"That's terribly optimistic of you, isn't it? You're usually the glass half empty guy to my glass half full girl," she said with a chuckle.

None of what she said was wrong. Seeing the bad side of life had been his usual style, but recently he'd begun to appreciate the benefits of looking at the bright side. Things rarely turned out how he hoped, but there was something nice about not always being miserable.

And not having the woman you loved calling you a curmudgeon all the time was pretty great too.

"I thought I'd try being a bit more optimistic. I figure it couldn't hurt."

"Well, then we've flipped because I'm more worried than I've ever been. We're going to be going into Archon headquarters. What if you get staked? I don't know what I'll do," she said with a hitch in her voice on the last words.

"You'll kick all their asses and stake the hell out of the whole bunch, Solenne. That's what you'll do. But I'm not going to get staked. I'm a man on a mission when it comes to those fuckers."

She lowered her head and sighed. "I think you might have more faith in my fighting ability than I do. What if I forget everything in the moment? What if I freeze when it counts the most?"

Saint cradled her face in his hands and gently forced her to look up at him. She needed to see how serious he was when it came to believing in her.

"You've trained for months. You're a descendant of Idolas. Don't worry. Being a warrior is in you."

"But you didn't think that when you first found out."

"I'm an idiot sometimes. This is a well-established fact, honey. I doubt you'd be able to find five vampires I've run across in this lifetime who wouldn't attest to that."

Her beautiful mouth turned down into a frown, disappointing him that his joke hadn't worked. "Don't make light of this, Declan. We're going to hunt that bastard. There's nothing funny about it."

"I know. And what I said was only to make you worry less. I was an idiot when I first found out about your background, though. I let my male ego get in the way. Again. Thankfully, you didn't hold it against me."

Now she rolled her eyes, which at least was an improvement from her being sad.

"I didn't hold it against you, but now that it's almost time for this all to happen, I'm wondering if just having a long-lost relative is that meaningful. Maybe it's not a big deal that my bloodline is descended from Idolas."

"A being who's descended from two gods himself and

who wrote the prophecy that foretold everything that's happened? That sounds like a big deal to me."

"Okay. I'm being stupid. I get it."

After taking a deep breath, she let it out slowly and added, "The most important thing is I'm there when that son of a bitch is turned to dust. I want to look into his eyes as the stake is driven into his chest."

And with just that mention of Marc Verrater, Saint felt all the negative thoughts he had to fight each night creep into his mind. He couldn't even hear her call him a son of a bitch without being overwhelmed by hate.

"Hey, don't do this, Declan. I feel you drifting away and growing distant just because I said that. You and I can't run away from what happened."

His hands fell away from her, and he turned to walk into the bedroom. "I know. It's not like I ever forget, so I get it."

Before he could take another step, she caught the bottom of his shirt and tugged him back toward her. He didn't want to do this now. It didn't have to happen. He knew what that fucker did to her. Why did they always have to use the word to refer to it?

The word he hated.

"Do you even realize you're running away from this?" she asked with hurt covering every word.

Saint shook his head as he avoided looking at her. It wasn't that he was ashamed of her. Never. He wasn't ashamed of what he felt every time he thought about that fuck who hurt her. He just didn't want to rehash it again. They'd done it so many times, and never once did it help him come to grips with the reality of what she went through.

"Honey, I need you to look at me. It's important," Solenne said in a soft voice.

He focused on her eyes and waited for her to say what she needed to. If only it didn't have to be that fucking word.

"I know you struggle with what happened. For a long time, I felt like that meant you didn't love me anymore or you didn't want to be near me because I was dirty."

Before she could go on, he stopped her. "I never thought that. Never for a single moment, Solenne. I'm sorry if you thought that. I never meant to make you feel like I didn't love you. I've loved you for as long as I can remember. I honestly can't think of a time when I didn't love you."

Reaching up, she touched her finger to his lips in that cute way she did when she wanted him to stop talking. "I know. I just need you to understand that for me, the word rape isn't something I'm ashamed of. What he did is the reason I need to be there when his evil ass is sent off to the Underworld, though."

And there was that word again to torture him. Rape. Silently, Saint swore that he would make that bastard's last moments in this world more painful than anyone had ever endured to pay him back for what he did to her.

Quietly, he said what he knew he should have so long ago. "I know, and I swear I'm trying, Solenne. It's just that every time I even think that word, I want to kill someone."

"That's why I need to be there, Declan. You want to avenge me because you love me, and I love you for that. But I'm the one he raped, so it's important I get to show him I survived and I'm the one making sure karma comes for him."

Desperate to change the subject, he hugged her to him and whispered, "What's the first thing you want to do once this whole war is over?"

"I want to go back home to France. I want us to find a house and live a quiet life, just the two of us," she said against his chest. "I want to plant a garden and cook dinner each night after sundown. I want to walk along country roads in the moonlight, just the two of us holding hands and talking about whatever. The weather even. It won't matter. I know that might sound boring, but after all of this, boring sounds perfect."

Boring did sound perfect, and as he closed his eyes and pictured that idyllic life she described for their future, Saint held her close and smiled. If that's what she wanted when their job in this war was finished, then that's what she'd get.

"I think we should get a dog."

Solenne lifted her head off her chest and looked up at him in shock. "A dog? You've never wanted to have a pet. First, you're a brand-new optimist and now this? I'm wondering if I even know you anymore."

He loved when she teased him like that. When they pushed away the rest of the world and got to be playful with one another, those were the best moments between them.

"A big dog, in fact. One who will lay at the foot of our bed during the day taking up too much space. That will mean we'll need a big yard with this house we're getting."

A skeptical look crossed over her face. "Your big dog better not get into my garden and ruin it."

"Don't worry. He won't. I'll train him so he stays away from it."

She rolled her eyes again, so he lowered his head and pressed a soft kiss onto her lips. "I can't wait to live that life with you."

"Me too."

His cell phone rang, breaking up one of the best moments they'd had together in a long time. Fishing it out of his pocket, he saw it was Dante calling.

"Hey, Dante. I'm going to put you on speaker. Solenne's with me, and I want her to hear what you have to say."

Holding it up, he listened as his fellow Son simply sighed. That wasn't a good sign.

"What happened? Did things go bad tonight?" he asked, his heart sinking with every second Dante didn't answer.

Finally, the clyten said, "It went as well as can be expected. We killed thousands of daemons. Two of the dragons died on the battlefield. The Draco brothers are taking it pretty hard. My clyten regiment took on heavy losses, but they did great. I'm proud of them."

But nothing in his voice said any of this was good. Saint and Solenne exchanged worried glances, and she asked, "Dante, what's wrong? You just said our side did well, even if we had losses."

"We did. We won the battle, and we've heard Hades isn't going to be sending any more to fight us. For the most part, the war is over."

"Then why do you sound like something else is wrong?" Saint asked as his stomach tightened into knots.

What was Dante hesitating to tell them? Did they lose Vasilije or Terek?

Quietly, he finally said, "Sasa and Ilona are gone. They died with the youngest dragon at the Dracos' castle where they were staying. Terek is devastated. Leta survived, and he's taking care of her, but I've never seen him like this. He's taking Ilona's death hard. And Vasilije's gone. He's in the wind. Terek said he just left after Sasa died."

Tears began streaming down Solenne's cheeks as Saint struggled to process Dante's news. "Sasa and Ilona dead? How? They weren't fighting with you, so what happened?"

"Nico. He slit the throats of all three of them. I can barely believe it myself, but that's what happened. We knew he turned traitor, but I can't say I ever expected him to do anything like this. Terek says that Vasilije went into a rage after Sasa died and staked him. I say good fucking riddance. I just can't believe she and Ilona are gone."

Dante sounded like he was crying too, and then the phone fell silent as the three friends tried to grapple with the tragedy of losing those they'd loved in such a horrible way. Saint pulled Solenne to him, and as she sobbed against his chest, he felt his rage grow inside him.

All their friends had suffered, and for what? The Archons were to blame for their deaths and all the misery that had befallen the Sons and those they loved.

"I have to go," Dante said sadly. "I just wanted to let you know. Terek has already told Theron he's done. He won't fight anymore. Theron claims all that's going to happen now is you two taking care of that asshole Archon and Sion and Kali going after her sire who's been backing the Archons. Theron's got his thing with Hades, but for the rest of us, we're done. It's over."

"Thanks, Dante."

"Hey, Saint. You two stay safe, okay? We can't afford to lose any more of us. Oh, and make that motherfucker pay for all those son of a bitch Archons have done."

"I will. We'll talk to you when we return. Bye, Dante."

Saint ended the call and tossed his phone onto the nearby table. The news of their friends' deaths had hit Solenne hard, and as she cried against him, he vowed to kill every Archon he saw from this point on.

This wasn't just about getting even with Verrater and making him pay. Now it was about avenging the loss of those they loved, innocents who hadn't been part of the battle.

None of them would be left standing if he had anything to say about it.

Looking up at him, Solenne wiped the tears from her cheeks and tried not to cry any more. "Sasa and Ilona, Declan. Vasilije must be beside himself. They just got back together, and now she's gone. And Terek? He and Ilona had all those plans to bring up that little girl, and now she's dead too? I don't think I can handle this."

Tears began running down her cheeks again, so Saint hugged her tightly to him. This was almost too much bear, but they had a job to do. They'd just have to channel all their sadness into it and take out those who were to blame.

Those fucking Archons. Their time had come. Any of them left in Corsica were about to meet their end, along with Marc Verrater. It was time they paid for what they'd done.

# 17

Sion saw in Kali's eyes the terror she felt for what they had to do tonight. She'd pretended to be okay for the past three hours as they prepared to leave for Archon headquarters in Corsica. He noticed she seemed less talkative than usual, but that wasn't surprising. She'd been tasked with staking her sire. That wasn't something any vampire did lightly.

Hers had tremendous power over her. Or he had in the past. Slowly over the months as the Archons continued to poison more of the vampire population with that garbage Bliss, Kali had come to see only pure evil would do what her sire and the Archons had done with the drug. For some reason, she could understand her sire's tricking her into getting hooked on it, but doing that to other vampires showed her he wasn't the maker she'd thought he was all these centuries.

She'd said little about her sire's actual identity until recently when she explained to Sion just who he truly was. A magistrate, he held a position in the vampire world honored by everyone. While Archons had long turned into officious creatures clearly out to line their own pockets and improve their own lives at the cost of everyone else, magistrates still represented law and order in the vampire world.

That her sire had turned his back on the very values he'd sworn to uphold to act like the Archons made Kali sadder than anything else. Sion didn't understand her sentimental attachment to a sire who had treated her so horribly throughout the centuries, and not only because he tended to think logically whenever he could.

His sire had been just and good, so his only experience with that relationship made him think all sires were like that. True, he'd seen how some tended to treat their vampires as family while others treated them like a harem, but overall, what Sion had mainly seen in his time since being turned were sires who cared for those they made vampire.

Consera was not that type, and exhibits A and B were Kali and Nico.

As he watched her pack her bag full of stakes, Sion leaned against the wall, still shocked about what Dante told him about the eldest Son of Navarus. He'd struggled to believe he'd turned traitor, but killing Sasa and Ilona, along with the youngest Draco brother? The thought of Nico truly being that heinous staggered his mind, and that wasn't an easy task.

Then again, he struggled to understand the emotions and motivations of others more often than not. He didn't see why Kali would feel any allegiance to her sire after all the terrible things he'd done to her, nevermind to the rest of the vampire world. He couldn't comprehend why Nico would have killed his friends' mates, females he'd known for years.

Suddenly, a thought made Sion's breath catch in his throat. Had Consera ordered him to kill them, and had Kali been next on his list of victims? He didn't put it past him. Sion had made sure to keep Kali close by at all times in the past few months. After finding out her sire had given her the dose of Bliss that got her hooked, he knew he couldn't be trusted.

But had he wanted her dead? He didn't know for sure, but he suspected it might be what he planned. She had, after all, disobeyed him by falling in love with a Son.

All he knew was he didn't let her out of his sight ever, not even when he had to conduct the drone strikes in the eastern battle near the dragons' home. Dante had insisted he join them close to the battle, but he refused. Modern technology meant he didn't even need to be on the same continent to attack with his carefully built machines that could be directed from miles away. They could attack just as fine from the Order's headquarters, and he told him that. And that's how his part in the battle had been conducted.

With Kali by his side, her nose stuck in her books, as he directed his drone team from his laptop.

What they had to do tonight couldn't be done that way, unfortunately. Consera hadn't left Archon headquarters since the defeat of the witches in Italy, so Sion's drones couldn't get to him as he sat protected in that building in Corsica.

"Are you okay? Why are you leaning against the wall like that?" Kali asked as she dropped her bag and hurried over to Sion's side.

"I'm fine. Just taking a break for a little bit. Nothing's wrong," he said, forcing himself to smile even though that's the last thing he wanted to do.

She hung her head and sighed. "I was just worried. I've had a few nights where the cravings are really strong, and sometimes that means I just have to sit back and fight with myself until they go away. You know, like those couple times I got all weird a few weeks ago. I thought maybe that's what you were doing."

"No, I'm fine."

He had experienced exactly what she described a few times since kicking his Bliss habit, but he never mentioned those instances to her. Sion didn't want to rehash what that damn drug did to him, so better to remain silent about the aftereffects of it too. Whenever the need for it hit him, and it hit like a ton of bricks, he just found a quiet spot where he could be alone and hung on until the feeling went away, telling himself all the while how the drug had no hold on him.

It's how he got through things. Logic. If there was a better way for him, he hadn't found it yet.

For Kali, though, logic tended to leave her lost. She worked on a different level, one that involved far more emotion, so she needed to talk things out to get through them. The few times she'd opened up about the residual effects of Bliss and how her blood seemed to call to it sometimes, he tried to be helpful and supportive. What he usually ended up doing was sitting silently as she talked herself through it. Not very helpful, in his mind, but he tried.

She lifted her head and stared up at him with pure fear filling her brown eyes. "I hope I can do this tonight."

Pulling her close, he held her to him and gently pressed a kiss to the top of her head. "You will. I'll be right there, and we're going to do this together. You won't be alone, Kali. I promised you that when we got together. You're never alone."

She relaxed in his arms and sighed. "I know. I just worry that I'm not strong enough. He has always had such a hold over me."

Sion ran his hand over the back of her hair, smoothing it down over her shoulders. "I know, but that's over now. His time has come. We need to do this to end this war once and for all."

Kali tilted her head back to look up at him. "I wish I was like Solenne. I bet she's chomping at the bit to go and kill that Archon. Saint is probably having to hold her back from racing down there to stake him."

The way she described Solenne's desire for vengeance made Sion smile. He had no doubt Saint and Solenne couldn't wait to finally give Marc Verrater exactly what he deserved. But that situation was different. It didn't involve the killing of a sire.

"Solenne's got a damn good reason to want that bastard dead and dusted, but you have your own reasons too, so don't forget that."

"I know. I just worry that when the moment comes that I won't be able to do it. He's always known exactly what to say and do to make me weak. I don't want to be that anymore, though. You know that, right?"

Sion took her face in his hands and stared down into those eyes that had read thousands of pages of encrypted text from those ancient tomes full of dust that no one else had been able to figure out. That she worried about being weak showed him she had no idea how much she'd done for the Sons all this time.

"You are not weak. We'd be lost without you. If it wasn't for you, the Sons would still be back at square one and not knowing what the hell was going on with that prophecy, Theron, and this war. Don't ever let your sire or anyone else diminish you and make you think you're anything but a superwoman."

Kali's smile spread across her face and lit up those dark eyes he loved. "I try. I'm just glad I could help."

"Never forget that your sire sent you to infiltrate the Sons just like he had Nico do. The difference is you didn't turn traitor while he did. He was weak. You're anything but."

His mention of her fellow vampire from their sire made her smile fade to nothing, and she shook her head. "How could he have done that, Sion? I can only imagine what Consera did to him to make him kill like he did. He killed women. Do you know that Terek thinks he tried to kill Leta too, but since she's had the ability to heal herself since birth he failed? A baby, Sion. He put his blade to a child's throat. What kind of monster does that? How could the vampire we've known for all these years turn on us like that?"

She stopped talking for a moment as her eyes grew big. "What if he does something like he did to Nico with me? Promise me if he does and he orders me to kill you or anyone else you won't let that happen. I'd rather be staked than kill someone."

"Don't say that! He doesn't control you anymore. You have all the power, Kali. I need you to remember that."

He hugged her tightly and hoped she knew deep

down all the power to fight off that sire of hers resided inside her. As the male who loved her, he would do anything to protect her, including staking that bastard who made her, but for Kali to ever be truly free of her sire, she needed to be the one to kill him.

Time would tell if she could bring herself to take that final step. If she couldn't, he'd do it for her. She'd stood by him when he was lost to Bliss and never gave up on him. He'd do the same for her now, if she needed it.

"I just want this to be over. Promise me when this war ends and we don't have to be who we are now that we can go off and live happily ever after," she whispered against his chest. "I just want it finally to be over."

Sion hated hearing the agony in her voice. If he could give her that happily ever after at that moment, he would move heaven and earth. He couldn't, though, so he'd do the next best thing.

Against the top of her head, he whispered, "I promise. We'll go anywhere you want and forget about all of this."

She let out a heavy sigh and looked up at him. "I love you. I'm sorry I'm such a wreck about this."

"Don't be sorry. You're going to be great. You always are."

Lifting herself onto her toes, she kissed him sweetly on the lips and nodded. "Okay. I'm going to finish and then I'll be ready to go."

Sion gave her a smile and hoped she didn't sense how uneasy he felt about what they were about to do. Killing wasn't something he had a problem with. He'd killed in war before, and he would again. He just didn't know how she'd react to having to become like him, even if for only one night.

Or worse, how she'd react to seeing him as a killer.

---

HOLDING his arm out in front of Kali, Sion stopped her before they walked around the corner to the hallway. Consera's office was just a few doors down from where they stood.

"Hang on. I want to see what's waiting for us," he whispered to her before taking a tiny metal disk out of his pocket.

She looked down at it and shook her head. "What's that?"

"Watch."

Sion placed it on the ground and lifted his hand from it. Instantly, it silently shot around the corner and down the hallway. Three seconds later, it returned to where they stood, and he lifted it off the ground.

Stuffing it back into his pocket, he took his phone out and swiped the screen. Two taps of his fingertip on the screen and then a picture came up clearly showing how many men guarded Consera's office and what weapons they carried.

"Two hunters are standing guard," he whispered to Kali as he sized up the males. They both stood at least six and half feet tall, and they held what looked like machetes. Consera clearly didn't feel at ease in his office tonight.

Another tap on his phone's screen showed a second picture of the magistrate himself alone in his office. Good. That made what they had to do easier.

"I want you to wait here. I'll take out the two guards, and then we'll go in. Got it?" he said quietly in her ear.

She nodded, holding her breath in anticipation of what was to come next.

The two guards were far too large for him to take on physically. Big, hulking beasts, they required something far more advanced to take them down than traditional weapons like swords or knives.

Sion flipped open the pocket on his jacket and grabbed the stun gun he'd brought just in case. He hadn't thought they'd need it, but it paid to be prepared, obviously.

Leaning around the corner of the wall, he aimed at the first guard and pulled the trigger. A jolt of electricity three million volts strong shot into the male, sending him crashing to the ground. The second guard spun around, stunned at his partner's fall, and Sion took advantage of his surprise to shoot him too. In seconds, both guards lay in a giant heap on the floor.

But as satisfying as that had been, he couldn't waste time with self-congratulations. Consera may have heard the noise and could come out at any time, so Sion rushed down the hallway and quickly staked both vampires to dust. Not exactly a fair fight, but then again, nothing the Archons had done was fair, so why should the Sons' attack on them be?

Kali poked her head around the corner and looked down at where he stood amongst piles of dust. Surprised, her mouth dropped open.

He waved her down to where he stood, signaling for her to stay quiet. He wanted to catch Consera unprepared, so they needed to ensure they didn't give him any notice they were there before the two of them appeared before him in his office.

Kali pointed toward the door, and Sion nodded. The time had come.

The doorknob twisted easily, and he pushed the door open to find the magistrate in front of his desk on his knees calling for the only one who could possibly help him now.

"My lord Hades, I ask for your help at this moment. Protect me from all who would seek to harm me."

His eyes remained closed, and Sion waited for the god of the Underworld to answer his summons. He didn't. Consera repeated his plea, but it was no use. Nobody was coming to help him.

"That god has his own problems. He can't help you now," Sion said with a slight chuckle.

The magistrate's eyes flew open as he realized he wasn't alone anymore, and he quickly jumped to his feet. The look of shock on his face pleased Sion more than he thought it could.

"You're all alone for your time of reckoning, sire," Kali said quietly.

Consera's face contorted into an angry grimace, and he instantly ordered his vampire to kneel before him. Even though she struggled to disobey, Kali couldn't, and she fell to her knees.

"I'm not as weak as you and your boyfriend think," he said with a sneer.

Sion took a step toward him, but Consera shook his head. "No, that would be a bad idea. I don't think she has the strength to overpower me, and I can end her life with a snap of my fingers."

A slow smile lit up his hideous face. "On second thought, maybe we should cut to the chase and see how strong she is. Kali, stake him."

Tears filled her eyes, and she stared at Sion, silently pleading with him not to be angry as she reluctantly pulled out a stake from her bag. He couldn't believe she'd kill him, though. Consera hadn't seen her real strength yet.

"You can't control her anymore. You've lost."

"I think Kali on her knees proves that claim wrong."

Shaking, she began to sob as she clearly tried to fight against his control. Her hand trembled as it clutched the stake so hard her knuckles turned white. Sion hoped she saw in the way he looked at her that he believed she could beat her sire. She just had to believe too.

But instead, she cried out, "Why have you treated me so badly ever since you made me your vampire? What have I done that I deserved what you've done to me? You've tortured me, forced me to take drugs and nearly die from them, and used me to do harm to other vampires. Why?"

Consera merely laughed at her obvious pain. "I did what I did because you were weak and I was strong. Nothing more, nothing less."

"I did everything you wanted of me. I never disobeyed for over a millennium. No matter what you commanded me to do, no matter how much it harmed me, I obeyed. And what did I get in return? Nothing but more pain. Why did you do that to me?"

He shrugged as if nothing about the waves of sadness coming off her meant a thing to him. "Because I could."

His answer and his utter disregard for her pain broke

her. Hearing those words come from the one who made her left Kali weak, and Sion watched with a broken heart as she fell to the floor in a heap. Consera had finally hurt her too much.

The magistrate turned to him and laughed. "And that's why I win. I'll win with the Archons too. There's still time for my plan to work. There are supporters still out there who won't let your kind take over our world."

"You're delusional. The Sons and the Order of Macaria won't let that happen. You and the Archons failed. Hades doesn't care anymore, and he's not sending any more of his daemons to support you. It's just vampires versus vampires now, and in that, you'll always lose. Your supporters will either come to see that, or they'll suffer like you and your Archon buddies. It's over."

"Never! The Sons will never rule the world I've spent thousands of years building. You won't be able to handle it without the likes of me and the Archons. We kept order in a world full of madness."

Sion didn't know how Consera had become so lost in his schemes of world domination, but he didn't care enough to ask. He'd come to do a job, and he intended on doing it.

Lifting his stake, he cocked back his arm to let it fly toward the magistrate's chest, but from behind, Kali drove her stake through his heart with a cry of pain that hit Sion deep inside and sent him stumbling backwards. With a last look of utter shock, Consera opened his mouth to say something and then disappeared in a puff of dust.

Kali stood sobbing, her tears streaming down her cheeks and leaving white trails over her skin covered in the remains of the sire who had made her life a living hell for over two thousand years. She began to hyperventilate and shake, so Sion rushed to take her into his arms. She had found the strength when it mattered most.

"I did it! I stopped him finally. I'm so sorry I pulled a stake on you, Sion. I couldn't disobey him at that moment, but I kept telling myself I could do it. I had the strength. I just had to use it. I don't know if I could have done it if he showed me an ounce of kindness, but he didn't, and something inside me snapped."

Sion wiped her cheeks with his thumb and kissed her lips. "You did it. I knew you could."

She rested her head on his chest and let out a sigh. "I did it."

One less enemy existed in their world now. He only hoped Saint and Solenne had success with their villain and Theron defeated his.

## 18

---

The first hint of the sunrise fell over the land, making Theron yearn for something other than solitude. Sitting in the darkness of his childhood home, he waited for the sun to come up. He had chosen to remain alone in the hours before he intended to set out on his mission to the Underworld, but something about night ending made him regret that choice.

Unlike other vampires, he'd always preferred the day. Being a clyten explained that partly, but he never had the sense that Dante would ever choose day over night. Vampires were creatures of the night. This was an accepted fact.

Just not for him.

He'd never truly felt like he should be a vampire anyway. Given the choice, he'd eat and drink like humans instead of drinking blood like vampires. True, only born vampires had to consume blood exclusively, but even the average run-of-the-mill vampire liked blood.

Not Theron. Other than when he was fucking someone, he would happily avoid drinking blood for the rest of his life. It tasted metallic, and he never failed to want to drink gallons of water after having it in his mouth.

Never once had he told anyone about how foreign being a vampire felt to him. They wouldn't understand. Being born into the vampire world meant that's what he was. Vampire. He had no choice, like he'd never had a choice to be anything other than the one prophesied to defeat the Archons and Hades.

Closing his eyes, he thought about the humans he heard when he mingled with them at outdoor cafés on sunny afternoons. They complained about everything from their debts to their homes to the people they slept with, and so many of them wished they didn't have so many choices to make. Each time he heard them say something like that, he wanted to jump up out of his seat and scream at the top of his lungs how stifling life truly felt with no choice. They so desperately didn't want to have to make decisions, and he'd give anything to be able to walk away from who he'd always been and deny the truth, no matter the cost.

But he couldn't. He had a destiny, and he had to follow it. The entire world depended on it.

For a while when he was what others would call a teenager, he resented that destiny. He wanted to rail against it because of how it threatened to smother him at any moment. It terrified him and made him want to die.

Theron didn't know when that feeling disappeared, but at some point, a strange calm came over him and he simply accepted his future. There was no logic to being angry and lashing out. What was to come would come anyway. He could thank Dante for that little nugget of wisdom. The only one who ever seemed to be able to reach him, he explained that simple yet profound idea one day in his usual way that included the word dude far too much, but Theron understood it.

No matter what he did to prevent his destiny from happening, it would happen just as it had been prophesied. There was no choice in that, so he accepted it.

"My vampire is so unhappy," Nyx whispered to him. "What troubles you this morning, Theron?"

He opened his eyes and saw her next to him on the floor. Dressed in that long black gown she wore each night as she traveled the earth, she looked regal beside him.

"No unhappiness. Just waiting for the right time to leave," he answered as she cozied up next to him and rested her head on his shoulder.

"I waited for you. I thought you'd come during the night," he said before kissing her.

"No, I can never be yours at night. Other worldly demands keep me from doing anything at night."

Yet another reason Theron enjoyed the day more.

"So now that your duties are done, you come here for me?"

"You called to me, so I came," she answered, confusing him.

He hadn't called for anyone during the night.

"That wasn't me, Nyx. I didn't summon you," he said as he pulled her onto his lap.

Her hurt feelings registered in her expression, even as she tried not to let him see he'd bruised her ego. "Perhaps I should leave then."

She moved to get off his lap, but he kept her right

where he wanted her. "Maybe you read my mind?" he asked with a smile.

Nyx arched a dark eyebrow and leveled her gaze on his face. "Maybe I can sense when you need me."

Theron didn't like hearing her say he needed her. In fact, it made him inwardly cringe to think he needed anyone after losing so much, but she wasn't entirely incorrect. He did feel a sense of need when it came to her.

Cupping her breasts in his hands, he nodded. "Maybe. Can you figure out what I want now?"

As she thought about his question, he pinched her already excited nipples through her black dress that left no doubt about how perfect her body was. The goddess had everything he'd ever wanted in a female.

Nyx didn't answer him but instead slid off his lap to open his pants. Already rock hard, his cock sprung free the second she lowered the zipper.

"I guessed correctly."

Theron let his knees fall to the sides and leaned back. "Not exactly rocket science. You do have an advantage over me. You can read my thoughts."

She slid her tongue over her lips and smiled. The time for talking had ended, thankfully, and he watched her as she slowly lowered her mouth to his cock. The first touch of her lips against his skin sent a jolt of electricity shooting through his body, making every nerve come alive. He had no idea what special power Nyx possessed when it came to fucking, but something about her sent his body into overdrive like no one had ever been able to before.

A quick flick of her tongue on the underside of his cock made need course through him, and he stuffed his hand into her black hair to push her head down. Now was not the fucking time for teasing.

Moaning against his skin, Nyx took every inch of him into her until the head of his cock bumped up against the back of her throat. She scratched her fingernails across his abs as she sucked hard, just like he wanted, mixing pain and pleasure wherever she touched.

"Fuck...oh, baby, suck that cock."

She obeyed his command and began bobbing up and down on him, slowly retreating all the way up his shaft and then devouring every rock-hard inch until her tongue grazed his balls. Theron felt like the top of his head might blow off if he didn't come soon, but he wanted to relish her blowing him for a bit longer before he let that happen. Prolonging the pleasure made the end so much better.

A few more times up and down his cock delayed it enough, and when she cupped his balls in her hand and gave them a gentle squeeze, that's all it took. He lifted his hips from the floor and drove his cock down into her throat as jets of cum pushed out of him. She swallowed every fucking ounce of it, and when she lifted her head and smiled down at him, Theron wasn't sure who had enjoyed themselves more.

"You're such a base creature," Nyx said as she wiped the sides of her mouth.

"How's that?" he asked, his brain not working at its full capacity after a blow job like that.

"You're sensual and prefer the physical to everything else. I don't think I've met a being like you in centuries."

He had no idea if she was insulting him or compli-menting him, and as he recovered from their sexual romp, he didn't care. She excited him like no one ever had, and he liked fucking her in every way possible. If that was base, so be it. Considering all he had to deal with in this life, he had the right to enjoy something.

"And you suck cock like no female I've ever met. Are all goddesses like that, or is that just one of your talents?"

"I wouldn't know about other goddesses, but I'm glad you enjoyed yourself," she said coolly, her tone telling him she didn't appreciate his compliment as he intended it.

Pulling her against him, he tried to smooth over her hurt feelings. "Come here. I didn't mean that as anything but praise. You'd be surprised at how some women use their teeth when they suck cock. It's like getting a blow job from a paper shredder."

Nyx looked at him and said nothing for a few moments before giggling. "You are the most unique creature, Theron."

"I've heard that. Let's just say I'm one of a kind."

She smiled and reached out for him to run her hands through his hair. "This destiny of yours weighs heavily on your heart."

Sliding his arm around her, he pulled her to him. "I guess there's no point in saying it doesn't. You can read my thoughts, so you know."

"I can sense you plan to kill Hades, but that's impossible, Theron. He's a god. He can't be killed."

Of course not. Killing him would be too easy.

Theron tilted his head left and right to crack his neck in the hopes of relieving the headache that already began to form at the base of his skull. So now this destiny of his had a new wrinkle in it. Why had Kali believed Idolas prophesied he would kill the god of the Underworld if he couldn't?

"Because she's a vampire translating a prophecy thousands of years old. It says his reign will be put to an end by you. She took that to mean you killing him, but Hades cannot die, my love. No god can."

He looked over at her next to him. "So you can never die?"

Nyx smiled. "No. Gods can be forgotten. They can also be imprisoned. But they cannot die."

"Then I'll just have to find a prison strong enough to hold a god."

"I have just the place," she whispered into his ear. "Do to Hades what he's done to so many gods before him. Imprison him in Tartarus."

"Looking for a new neighbor?"

"I was thinking maybe I wouldn't be living there anymore once you're the ruler of the Underworld," Nyx said with a wicked grin.

"So you want to rule the Underworld in addition to the night?" Theron teased, already intrigued enough by the goddess to like the idea of reigning with her by his side.

Slowly, she ran her fingertip down the middle of his chest to the spot just above his pants. "Not rule. Just assist the new ruler."

"You know, I've done a little reading and Hades was put in charge of the Underworld by his brother Zeus. How is he going to feel about a vampire taking over that place and putting a family member into Tartarus?"

The last thing Theron needed was to have to fight through an entire pantheon of gods. Kali had never mentioned anything about that, but then again, she had made the mistake of thinking he could kill Hades. Maybe she'd missed that point about having to fight his way through a godly gauntlet too.

Nyx tilted her chin up proudly and smiled. "First, Zeus will do as I tell him to. He may not be afraid of other goddesses, but he fears me. More importantly, he's imprisoned in Tartarus, along with the rest of his family, except for Aphrodite, so he'll be more than happy to assist you in sending his brother to his just ends."

"The god of the Underworld put all the gods and goddesses in Tartarus? He's a mean one, isn't he? Why not Aphrodite?" Theron wondered, curious as to what made her so special. "Is she someone special to him?"

"I'm not sure, but since she's the goddess of love, I imagine it has something to do with him needing her to be free so he didn't end up alone. He hasn't had much luck with love, poor thing."

Theron sensed some resentment in Nyx when it came to Hades. He'd heard it a few times before when she mentioned him, so it was time to find out what she was really up to.

Pulling her onto his lap, he held her fast to him so she couldn't escape and stared into her nearly pitch-black eyes. "I think you need to tell me truth about why you hate the god of the Underworld so much. Don't bother lying because I can tell. I may not be able to read your thoughts, but your hatred for him is written all over your face and I hear it every time you talk about him."

She hesitated for a moment and then frowned. "If you must know, he and I were together for a time. He decided to break it off in favor of his newest toy, which offends me greatly."

"Why? You don't seem like the lovesick kind of female."

Fury flashed in her eyes. "I most certainly am not."

Nyx turned her head to avoid looking at him, but Theron roughly grabbed her chin to force her back toward him. "Then what's the problem? Who is he with?"

Again, she seemed to not want to tell him the truth. Finally, after a few moments, she answered his question. "A mortal."

"So it's fine for you to be with me, but it's not fine for him to be with this mortal? Why?"

"I don't want to answer any more questions. Let me know when you want to go to the Underworld. I can guide you there."

"Give me a few minutes to clean myself up and I'll be ready to go," he said as he zipped up his pants.

Nyx crouched down beside him and shook her head. "Take your time. This will be your only chance to take over the Underworld, Theron. Do not rush yourself."

"I've been born exactly for this purpose. Well, that and defeating the Archons. I've done all I can with the Sons of Navarus on that, so now all I have left is to over-throw Hades. I'm told it's been prophesied, so why wouldn't I go now?"

A strange look crossed her face. "It has been, but be careful. Hades is a force to be reckoned with. I will help you every way I can when you need it most, but you will have to be the one to defeat him. The Underworld is a very different place from the world you live in, my love. You will be trespassing as you aren't dead, so you don't belong there. What you'll see may chill you to the bone, so I need you to take your time."

"I don't scare easily, Nyx. I've seen those I loved die in front of me. I've had to live a lifetime in a matter of years. I can handle whatever the Underworld has in store for me."

She leaned forward and kissed him sweetly. "I hope that's true, but I suspect what you'll see there will change you forever. Remember why you're there, and don't get lost in everything else and I think you'll be fine."

"You act as if I'm not ready for this. It's my destiny. I have no choice."

Nyx stood and sighed. "Then I'll be ready to escort you to the Underworld when you want to go."

As Theron walked into the bathroom to splash some water on his face and clean himself up, he wondered what she kept referring to when she mentioned things he'd see in the Underworld scaring him. No matter. He'd told her the truth when he said he had no choice but to go. His only choice was when, and there was no point in putting off the inevitable.

Either he would defeat Hades, or the god of the Underworld would defeat him. There was no third possibility.

## 19

The Archon headquarters felt oddly quiet, as if everyone had deserted the place before Solenne and Declan could arrive. She felt a sense of dread that they'd missed their chance at finding Marc Verrater and it grew with every step they took through the building and saw not a soul.

No Archons. No hunters or guards. No one appeared to still be there.

"Where is everyone?" she asked Declan as they reached the second floor.

He shook his head and sighed. "I don't know. There weren't that many Archons left after Ramiel and Theron got to them. He's here, though. I know it."

Solenne could only wish that Marc hadn't disappeared before they could give him exactly what he deserved, but she was losing hope. Office after office sat empty, but there didn't seem to be any hint that a mass attack had occurred. No piles of dust showed as evidence that Sion and Kali had cleared the place out before they arrived.

They finished searching the second floor and headed into the stairwell to move up to the next floor. Declan looked like a man on a mission, his arm cocked with his hand clutching his stake as he prepared to send any vampire they found onto the Underworld. Solenne just hoped they wouldn't suddenly find a pack of Archons who may be able to overpower the two of them. He didn't seem to be worried about that, but as this was her first real battle, she didn't have the kind of confidence he possessed.

He slowly opened the heavy metal door and crept out of the stairwell onto the third floor, his head swiveling left and right to check for any stray vampires. After a few seconds, he waved her on to join him, and they began the tedious job of clearing yet another floor. For all her training, Solenne hadn't been prepared for this part of the fight.

Suddenly, a creaking noise put her on edge, and she looked down the long hallway toward where it came from. At the other end of the floor, another stairwell door opened, and seconds later, two vampires rushed out toward them.

Declan stepped in front of her instinctively to do what he always did when danger presented itself, but she hadn't trained for months to simply be a female who needed to be protected. She pushed her way around him to stand by his side and readied her stake for the attack.

"Solenne, just remember what we did in training!" Declan yelled as the vampires launched at them.

Even as pure terror rushed through her, everything he'd taught her came back instantly, as if her body knew what to do even as her mind filled with fear. The male came at her like a being possessed, his fangs flashing as he lunged at her neck. Before learning how to fight, she would have been yet another victim of his since she was sure he'd killed before. The rabid animal look in his eyes said as much.

But she wasn't going to be a victim this time.

Slashing her weapon through the air, she took aim at his chest and sunk the point of the stake into his heart in one swift motion. The thrill of hitting her mark the first time coursed through her, and she rammed that piece of wood through his body until it came out the other side. A second later, he made a gurgling noise and then exploded into a puff of dust that slowly drifted down toward the floor.

Solenne staggered toward the wall, grasping for anything to hold her up as the reality of what she'd just done settled into her mind. A vampire had come at her to kill her, and she'd defended herself successfully. Even more, she'd killed him. The hand holding the stake shook from a mixture of excitement and shock.

But was Declan safe too?

She turned to look over at where he'd been when the vampires attacked and saw him drive his stake into the chest of his opponent. He didn't seem as surprised as she was that he'd succeeded, and immediately, he turned toward her with a look of concern.

Without saying a word, she looked down at the pile of dust that had been her attacker and smiled. Declan's mouth dropped open, and he shook his head as a smile lit up his face.

"You did good, honey. How did it feel?"

Still shaky, she leaned against the wall for support as she tried to come up with a truthful answer. "That was the scariest thing I've ever done in my entire life."

"He was just an appetizer. The main course is next, so get ready. You okay to get moving again?"

"You don't give a girl much time to rest, do you?" she said before taking a deep breath and pushing herself off the wall.

Her knees knocked together, but after a few moments, her legs felt strong enough to let her walk. She took a step toward Declan, but he met her halfway and pulled her to him.

"I promise there will be all the time in the world to rest once we finish here. I don't want to give you a chance to start thinking about what you just did, or you might lose your nerve," he said, punctuating his words with a kiss on the center of her lips.

Solenne looked up at him and smiled. "Don't worry about me. I'm ready to do what I have to."

"Then let's go. He's here. I know it."

For the first time, she knew it too. Marc Verrater wasn't far away, and when they found him, he wouldn't have much longer to live.

---

AT THE END of the hallway on the fourth floor, Solenne stood next to Declan in front of the only door they hadn't checked yet. A sense of calm washed over her, and she knew the time had come.

He was in there.

Declan turned to look at her and nodded before pushing the door open and rushing in. She followed close behind, and when they reached Verrater's office, she finally saw the face of the monster who had terrorized her mind and body for so long.

Marc sat behind his desk and looked at them with a stunned expression, like he was oblivious to the fact that the rest of his fellow Archons had abandoned their head-quarters or had been killed. Half a dozen glass vials sat empty and strewn around his otherwise empty desk. Solenne knew what that meant.

"You bastard. The vampire world is burning down around you, and here you sit doping yourself up with that Bliss shit," she said as disgust filled her once more over the garbage he'd created from her own blood.

"Lena," he said in a faraway voice. "Are you for real or am I just dreaming?"

She looked over at Declan, who didn't seem impressed by Marc's drug-induced stupidity. Something about killing him while he was like this disappointed her, though.

"This is going to be easier than I thought. Good. Makes getting on with our lives that much faster," Declan said with a chuckle. "I'm going to give him a little dose of his own medicine first, though."

Grabbing his arm, she tried to stop him. "Wait! He's out of it. He probably won't even understand what we're doing."

A look of confusion settled into Declan's features. "So? This was never about him, Solenne. This was about revenge. I've played this out in my mind so many times that there's no way I can just stake him and be done with it now. He's done too much to deserve to get off that easy."

She wanted to ask if that would make them as bad as Marc, but she knew Declan too well. He had waited all this time to finally make the one who raped and tortured her pay, and no moral arguments were going to stop him now.

"So, Archon Verrater," Declan began as he stepped around the desk to stand next to him. "Ready to play a little game?"

Marc sat up in his chair and looked up at him. "What makes you think I'll play anything with you?"

Typical Marc. Even when he's about to be staked all the way to the Underworld, he couldn't stop himself from being cocky. He made it impossible to feel even a hint of regret for what Declan was about to do to him.

Solenne watched as Declan pushed his forearm against Marc's neck to hold him in his seat. A few more responses like that and she suspected her husband wouldn't have the patience to follow through with his grand plan of revenge.

"Your time is over, fuck. The Archons have lost. By now, another Son of Navarus has staked your buddy Consera off to the next life. We walked the halls of this place for twenty minutes looking for you and only found two hunters, which we kindly staked the fuck out of. And soon you'll follow them and all your friends to your judgment. But first, I thought we'd spend a little time letting me give you exactly what you deserve."

Marc didn't seem to understand anything Declan said. Looking over at Solenne, he asked, "What does he mean, Lena? There will be guards here any minute, so you better hide, or they'll stake you."

Taking a step closer to the desk, she planted her palms on the top of it and leaned forward toward him. His eyes focused on her, but the drug's effects still made him dopey.

"It's over, Marc. The Archons have lost the war. Any who haven't been staked yet will be soon enough when the Sons and their troops find them. We're going to stop the Bliss from getting to any more vampires. Hades isn't sending any more daemons to fight us. You've lost."

Suddenly, his eyes opened wide, and he jumped up out of his chair, catching Declan off guard. She didn't know what she'd said to shake him from his Bliss stupor, but whatever it was, Marc was now fully aware of what was happening.

"So you brought your husband to stake me?" he asked, his voice verging on panic. "What have I ever done to deserve that? I made you immortal, Lena. Every Archon knows your name and sees you as a goddess."

"Made me immortal? You stole my blood after torturing me and created a drug that has enslaved vampires around the world. What the fuck is wrong with you, Marc? You raped me over and over. What did you do to deserve this? Are you crazy?"

Out of the corner of her eye, she saw Declan move toward him, his arm raised to stake him. "Fuck your immortality, Verrater. You hurt the woman I love. Whatever else you've done in your miserable life, that's enough for me to kill you."

As if suddenly all they'd said finally sunk into his brain, Marc shook his head wildly and flailed his hands toward Solenne. "I never meant to hurt you, Lena. I loved you. I adored you. You were a goddess to me. Tell him I didn't do anything bad. Tell him so he doesn't stake me!"

She didn't know how to respond to the madness coming out of Marc's mouth. That he could even say the words he didn't do anything bad to her was nothing less than stunning, but she had the feeling he truly believed that. To him, he'd adored her by forcing himself on her and then stealing her blood to hurt other vampires.

All of it was nothing less than pure evil. Maybe that's why she couldn't understand it.

"I can't tell him anything. You did what you did to me. That you thought you'd never have to answer for that is a prime example of why the Archon system needed to be eliminated. You've hurt millions, and you made me an accomplice to your crime, Marc. You're pure evil. That's all there is to you."

Declan had heard enough and grabbed the Archon by the collar. "Sit the fuck down, you son of a bitch! I'm tired of hearing your crazy shit coming out of your mouth."

He ripped the cord off the phone on the desk and forced Marc's hand down onto the arm of the chair. Quickly, he wrapped it around his wrist and then pulled the cord taut to tie the other arm down. It all happened so fast that Marc didn't realize he'd been immobilized until it was too late.

"And just for shits and giggles, this building has been secured by a witch who's made it impossible for any of us to disappear. You're not going anywhere until I stake you, Verrater."

Marc thrashed around for a few seconds before

looking over toward Solenne for help. "Don't do this. You're not this kind of vampire. I know you, Lena. You aren't a killer."

His insistence on using his pet name for her instead of her name made something snap inside her, and Solenne screamed, "My name is Solenne! It's not Lena. It's never been Lena. Solenne Collins! And you don't know me. You never knew me. You never bothered to think of me as anything but a female you could take from. Sex, blood, anything you wanted you thought you should be able to take from me! No more, Marc! Whatever Declan does from this point on is too good for you."

By the time she finished yelling at him, her hands were shaking like leaves in the wind and her mouth had not an ounce of liquid left in it. She'd waited for so long to finally tell him how he made her feel, and now that she had, it felt like she never wanted to stop.

But her husband had other ideas. He pushed up the sleeves of Marc's dress shirt to bare the skin on his arms and then stepped back to take out his knife. "Now onto the fun. Ready, Archon?"

Marc's eyes opened wide in terror as he watched Declan slice through the skin on his forearm. Just a tiny cut, but only the first of what Solenne knew would be many.

"Stop him!"

She knew the intention wasn't to let him bleed out, as painful as that would be. No, Declan had never been that patient. He'd do this for a little while, but she knew he'd grow weary of Marc's constant pleas and would just stake him after a short time.

For as much as he wanted to torture him for all he'd

done to them, her husband couldn't help but want to get on with their life together after this war.

"He'll stop when he's done, Marc," she answered as Declan sliced yet another cut into the Archon's skin.

After a few minutes, each arm had about twenty cuts that trickled blood, but he wasn't done quite yet. From his bag, Declan pulled out a salt shaker that looked suspiciously like the one from their kitchen table and lifted it up for Solenne to see.

"Did you bring that from the house?" she asked in disbelief how practical he could be in all of this madness.

"I've thought about this for a long time. I wanted to be prepared," he said with a smile. Turning his attention back to Marc, he leaned in close to him and laughed. "This is going to sting a bit, but it won't kill you. We're not there yet."

Declan held the shaker a foot above Marc's arms and began to pour salt onto his wounds. The Archon let out a blood-curdling scream, but Solenne sensed his cries were more for show than a reaction to real pain. Either way, it didn't stop her husband, who seemed to be enjoying the whole thing a bit too much.

"Just what I've always wanted—seasoned Archon. If we had a spit, we could roast him slow until the skin turned just brown enough to seal in the juices."

Terrified, Marc looked up at him and then over at Solenne. "He's going to cook me before killing me?"

Declan rolled his eyes, but she had a feeling this was all becoming too crazy. "Maybe we just get done with this and leave? You're freaking me out a little, honey."

Her husband screwed his face into an expression that made it seem like his feelings had been hurt by her suggestion. "Come on, Solenne. This bastard is the reason so many in the vampire world are drug addicts. He never gave a damn about anyone. Remember Emily? How about we get him to admit what he did to her since I severely doubt he let her go before all hell broke loose here?"

Guilt showed all over Marc's face at the mention of Emily. For all her flaws, she had helped Solenne escape, and for that, she'd be eternally grateful.

"Did you stake Emily?" she asked him, suddenly needing to know what had happened to her.

He winced at the question but refused to answer. In his silence, she found the truth, though. Had he ever been good to anyone?

"I think she cared about you, Marc. I mean truly cared about you. How could you stake someone who loved you?"

Declan pushed his knife against his throat and pressed until a spot of blood appeared. "You killed her because she helped Solenne, didn't you? Tell the truth or I swear I'm going to slit your throat and watch you bleed out, you motherfucker."

Still, Marc refused to answer, pressing his lips together like he had to work to keep the truth in. So Declan slowly began drawing the knife across his neck, leaving a thin trail of blood in its wake.

By the time he reached the Archon's Adam's apple, Marc couldn't take anymore and finally cried out, "Fine! I fucking killed her. Right over there near the wall. Why is that such a big deal? She was willing to help me spread lies about you, Saint, so what do you care if she died or how?"

Stopping his knife's slicing, Declan stepped back and grimaced. "You killed her because she helped Solenne. Admit it."

"Of course I did."

The way he so casually admitted the truth made Solenne sick to her stomach. She was sick of playing with this bastard. They needed to finish this and move on.

"Enough! I can't listen to this anymore. Just do it, Declan."

Both males turned to look at her with surprised looks on their faces. Marc had a flicker of hope in his eyes, a mistake because she wouldn't stop anyone from killing him, and her husband frowned like someone had taken his favorite toy away. She'd fantasized for so long about making Marc's death long and drawn out. He deserved it, after all, and the idea of seeing him suffer had always made her feel so good.

Now that the time had come, though, it didn't do that anymore. All it did was keep them from moving on to the next part of their life together, a much happier part not filled with vicious Archons and a war that could take one of them away before they ever got to enjoy the peaceful life they'd been promised.

A knock on the door made Declan take his focus off Marc, and a second later, a guard charged through the doorway. Wild-eyed, he looked like he didn't know where he was or what he had stumbled into, but it was too late for him. One swift stab of his stake to the male's heart and Declan sent him on his way as dust slowly filtered down onto the carpet.

Rattled from their unexpected visitor, Solenne closed her eyes for a split second, but that's all it took for Marc to pull free from the cords holding him to the chair. Her husband yelled something unintelligible, and she opened her eyes to see the Archon lunging at her, his blood-covered hands searching out her throat to strangle her.

Like when she killed that guard, her mind went blank, but her body did just what she'd been trained to do. Lifting her arm, she clutched the stake tightly in her hand and swung at the first chance she got. Then, everything turned black, and she heard nothing but the blood pounding in her ears.

She didn't know how long that went on, but when it stopped, the last thing she saw was Marc's eyes wide with surprise. Then he disappeared into a cloud of dust that seemed to hang in the air forever.

Stumbling back, she fell into a chair and began to sob, unable to stop herself. Solenne hated that she cried when she got angry. It made her look weak. She couldn't hold back the tears, though. For so long, she'd lived with the fear that at any moment, Marc or one of his men would pluck her from her life with Declan and enslave her for their evil purposes. Maybe they'd want more of her blood or maybe they'd want to do more tests on her.

Or maybe Marc would just want her for his to rape whenever the mood hit him.

She never knew, so she lived in constant terror. Even her husband didn't know how frightened she always felt. And now, the vampire who had nearly ruined her life was gone and from her hand.

Declan hurried across the room and crouched down beside her. She looked down and saw a strange look in his eyes she couldn't place. Was it concern? It didn't seem like that. It looked like pride.

"Are you okay? He didn't touch you, did he?"

Solenne had no idea if Marc had been able to touch her before she staked him. Even now, just a few seconds after it all happened, the entire event had become a blur. She knew how it began and how it ended, but she couldn't say anything about what happened between.

"I don't know," she answered, feeling like she was floating above herself.

"I thought maybe because you were crying that he hurt you before you got to him," Declan said sweetly as ran the pad of his thumb across her cheeks to dry her tears.

"No, I'm fine. I don't even know why I'm crying. It makes me seem so weak. God, I hate that."

Declan cradled her face in his strong hands and kissed her long and deep. Pressing his forehead to hers, he smiled. "You just staked the hell out of your enemy. Weak my ass. You are one tough vampire, Solenne Collins, and I couldn't be prouder of you."

Closing her eyes, she let the tears flow, needing to let out all the emotions Marc Verrater had created in her. He was finally gone. The one who had made her life a living hell was no more.

Finally, she wiped her tears away and kissed her husband. "Let's go home. I don't want to be in this place around everything that was his anymore. We've done our job, Declan. Now I want to find that house in France and never look back."

He chuckled as he pulled her up to her feet. "It only took us a hundred years, plus a few. We never were the kind to rush into anything."

As they walked out of Marc Verrater's office and out of

the Archon headquarters, neither one of them looked back. There was nothing there for them. They needed to focus on what lay ahead of them.

The life they'd wished for all those years ago when she was Teagan's vampire and he was the man she secretly loved could finally be theirs. The wait had been long, but in the end, they'd get that life.

Together.

## 20

Nyx held Theron's hand as the two of them walked down the dark pathway into the Underworld and she quietly warned him over and over not to let what he would see frighten him. He smiled and assured her nothing the Underworld could throw at him would scare him.

In truth, he had no idea what to expect. She'd been vague when he asked what he'd find, simply telling him to not let what he'd see rattle him.

The dim light that had shown them the way at the beginning slowly faded to nothing, leaving them in the pitch black. Nyx didn't slow her pace, practically pulling Theron along as they rounded a corner in the pathway.

"Maybe we should slow down since I can't see a damn thing," he mumbled as she tugged on his arm.

"I walk this every night at sunset and every morning at sunrise. Trust me. I know the way."

He hadn't thought of that. Knowing she likely wouldn't walk off a cliff made him trust her more, so he stopped hesitating and caught up to her pace.

"You should trust me, Theron. I haven't led you astray yet," she said in a teasing voice.

"You should stop reading my thoughts," he answered, hating how little he knew of her compared to everyone else in the world.

Nyx stopped suddenly and placed his hand over her heart. "You don't need to read my mind to know what I feel for you, Theron. Trust your emotions. They will show you the way."

He stood there next to her in the thick darkness and felt her heartbeat under his hand. "Is that advice only about you or what I'm about to do with Hades?"

"It's good advice for everything you're going through. Trust your emotions."

Theron didn't respond because he didn't know what to say. His emotions had done little but lead him into trouble since he never could control them. Now Nyx wanted him to trust them?

He trusted nothing and no one since his parents were taken from his life. Not even the only woman who ever made him want more than a single night got that from him.

They began walking again, slower as Nyx seemed to want to take her time now. In the blackness, he focused on her, trying to sense even a single, passing thought she may have. Just one would make him feel better.

But he couldn't penetrate the veil she kept around her mind.

"Again, you try to get into my head? Is it so important to you that you know what I'm thinking?" she asked in a sweet tone he hadn't expected when she caught him trying to invade her thoughts.

He wouldn't have reacted that way if someone tried to do the same to him.

For all the excuses he could give for his behavior, he simply answered with one word. "Yes."

Nyx walked a few more feet and then stopped. He sensed her turning toward him and then he felt her hands on his shoulders moving him so he faced her. Taking his hands in hers, she placed them on her face.

"Then here you go."

Suddenly, Theron's brain flooded with a rush of images and thoughts, pieces of ideas and full memories from the length of her life since the moment she came into existence. Thousands upon thousands of years raced past as he tried to grasp onto even a single thought of hers. Finally, just before he believed he couldn't handle not another second of her mind in his, he found a single thought so clear it took him by surprise.

It was what she thought of him. He hadn't known what to expect, but it wasn't all good or all bad. Just real with worries and emotions about him and what they were to one another. She craved him when he wasn't nearby. He scared her with how powerful he was without being a god. She wanted him to defeat Hades even more than he suspected. She was jealous, vengeful, and angry with most others in the world, but when she touched Theron, those traits in her faded away, replaced with a happiness she'd never experienced before in all her existence.

He stepped back, tearing his hands away from her face as he tried to take in everything she'd let him see in her. "I had no idea," he said as he tried to get his bearings once more.

"I am a goddess, Theron. I've been around since the beginning of time. You didn't expect me to be some empty-headed girl, did you?"

Still reeling from all he'd learned, he shook his head. "No. I didn't know what to expect. I guess I just expected something different."

"Something like you?" she asked with kindness in her voice as she took his hand in hers. "I've seen your thoughts. You think about much more than you let on. I'm sort of like that, except mine are a reflection of all time, not just a couple years."

When he didn't answer, she said, "Did you find what you were looking for?"

"I don't know what I was hoping to find," he said quietly. "I just didn't like you being able to know my thoughts without me knowing yours."

"Theron, you're on the precipice of the next step in your life. From now on, you'll have more to concern yourself with than what I think of you or anything else. That's why your emotions are so important. Focus on them and they'll show you what's right and what you need to do. Your ascension to ruling the Underworld has been prophesied for thousands of years. Now it's time for you to fulfill your destiny."

She released his hand and kissed him. "But now it's also time for me to go. What lies ahead is only for you, so I must leave you now."

"When will I see you again?" he asked as fear settled into him.

"When you meet the ruler of this kingdom, I will be there for you. Until then, you must take these next steps on your own. Remember your emotions. They will guide you."

A second later, he reached out for her, but she was already gone.

The darkness surrounded him, making him feel small and alone, and no matter what direction he looked, he saw no light. With Nyx gone, he had no guide, so he put his hands out in front of him and slowly began walking in the same direction as before, hoping he didn't walk off a fucking cliff.

Why had she left at this moment? Was it because she'd let him into her mind to see her thoughts? He couldn't help regretting his need to do that if the result had been losing the one soul who knew her way around this place. Regret quickly morphed into anger, mostly at himself for being so damn insistent about knowing what she thought.

"That's what a fucking child worries about," he said under his breath as he slowly made his way forward step-by-step.

Theron hated to think how young he seemed to a goddess who'd been alive since the dawn of time. He looked like an adult and had the thoughts and needs and desires of a grown man, but he'd only been alive for less than three years. No matter how hard he'd tried, he hadn't been able to experience all the world had to offer in that short time.

He knew as much as he could, yet still he felt like no matter what some damn prophecy said, he wasn't ready for what would come all too soon.

The moment that popped into his head, suddenly the

pathway he walked lit up, as if someone had lifted the cover off the world and let the light in. Theron stopped dead on the rocky path and looked around at faces poking out of the walls on each side of him. They looked tortured, like they'd been frozen in time as they screamed through some unbearable agony, their eyes wide and filled with terror.

Each one made him cringe at the pain they seemed to be suffering. He wondered if they were forced to remain in those spots for eternity. What had they done to be set in stone at the very moment they felt such misery?

The answer to that question came immediately when a voice said quietly in his head, "The god of the Underworld has the power to make one's afterlife ecstasy or agony. They chose the latter. What will you choose, vampire?"

Theron didn't have to ask who said that. He knew. He didn't know how he knew. He just did. So Hades could get into his head. Great. Another god who knew all his thoughts but didn't reciprocate the favor.

He waited for him to say something else, but after a few more steps, Theron heard nothing. All the better. He didn't need the god of the damned Underworld giving color commentary as he walked to meet him. They'd get to chat soon enough.

Before long, the anguished faces of agony in the walls disappeared, and he found himself in a smaller passageway like a hallway. A door at the end of it stood open a crack, and Theron made his way there, trusting his feelings like Nyx had advised him to. He had no idea what he'd find on the other side of that door, but he had to admit if it was Hades, he'd be disappointed. The god of the Underworld seemed like he'd be important enough to have something bigger than a room with a regular door on it.

Theron smiled as he realized Hades knew his opinion on that already. He knew from experience that reading others' thoughts did cut down on the time they had to spend talking. At least he and the god wouldn't have to make small talk when the moment came for them to battle for control of the Underworld.

Pushing the door open, he tentatively stepped into the room, not sure what to expect. There didn't seem to be anyone inside, which was disappointing. Theron had a feeling Hades liked to play games. The fate of every dead soul hung in the balance, and this asshole had him walking to empty rooms.

But the room had things in it. Just not another living being. Only furniture that reminded him of where he lived as a child. He took a closer look and noticed the couch exactly matched the one his parents had in Greece. What was this?

"I heard on my way here that nothing is real in this place. Did you get that little lecture too?"

Theron spun around to see his father standing there in front of him. Joy rushed through him at seeing Ramiel again and in one piece, unlike the last time he'd seen him in that Berlin Archon's office.

"Dad! I'd hoped I'd get to see you and Mom while I'm here. Where is she?" he asked, craning his neck to look behind his father for her.

His mother appeared in the doorway, hesitating for some reason behind his father. Didn't she want to see her own son?

"Mom, I'm here. I want to see you."

She slowly walked out from behind Ramiel and stopped. Tears welled in her eyes, and she covered her face as she began to sob. "Oh, honey. I had hoped it would be much longer before I saw you here with us."

"I didn't die, Mom. I'm not dead. I'm here to overthrow Hades and fulfill the prophecy."

She inched closer to him and reached up to touch his face. "Oh, Theron. You're all grown up. My little boy is a man now."

The sadness in her voice hit him square in the chest. She'd missed so much in the time since those Archons took her life and she ended up in the Underworld.

"It's okay, Mom," Theron said as she wrapped her arms around him and began to cry. "It's okay now."

"Nothing's okay," she said between sobs against his chest. "I realize that now. You had to grow up so fast, and now you have to fight Hades. It all happened so fast."

"I'm going to be fine. I promise. I won't let you down."

His mother lifted her head to stare up at him, and he saw in her eyes something he'd never seen in them before. He couldn't place the emotion, but she'd never shown him it before.

Then she spoke, and he recognized it immediately. Not worry or fear. Disappointment.

"Let me down? Theron, don't ever say that."

"I'm sorry. I didn't mean to upset you."

She stepped back away from him and shook her head, that painful expression still in her eyes as she looked up at him. "I don't want you to say that because you couldn't let me down, honey. Whatever else you are to the rest of the world and to the Sons, you're my child. I've loved you since the moment you first moved inside me. I will forever love you no matter what happens with Hades. Theron, I couldn't be prouder of you. Everyone demanded so much of you, and you've given them everything they required. The Archons are no more, and the vampire world is safe from everything they did to all of us. Whatever happens with Hades, you've done your part. You don't owe anyone anything."

He'd never let himself think any of that, but hearing his mother say those words nearly overwhelmed him. Nyx may have thought his emotions were helpful, but at that moment, all they did was threaten to ruin him.

"Your mother is right, Theron. Listen to her. She and I were so busy worrying that you weren't ready to be a Son, but you did everything you had to for our world. Whichever way this battle goes for control of the Underworld, just remember we're proud of you."

"And we love you, honey," his mother added. "We love you so much and we're so proud of you."

Until then, he'd simply assumed he'd defeat Hades because of the prophecy. He'd never thought about the possibility of failing. Strangely, now that he did, it didn't bother him as much as it probably should have.

The two most important souls in his world had shown him this battle truly didn't matter to them.

"We don't have much time, honey. I want you to listen to me carefully, okay?"

All the sweetness left his mother's voice now, replaced by that familiar tone of worry he'd so often heard from her in his life. She took his hand and held it like if she let go, something bad might happen.

"No matter what you see during your fight with him,

promise me you won't believe it. He uses tricks to fool you. Don't let him. I know you'll want to lash out, but stay calm."

"So don't let my emotions guide me?" Theron asked, confused at how different his mother's advice on how to handle the battle was from Nyx's.

She thought about what he asked for a moment and then frowned. "Don't ignore your emotions, but don't let them take you over. Trust your instincts and never forget we love you, Theron. We always have."

He began to ask why she thought he'd forget they loved him, but before he could, they disappeared from in front of him. Alone, his emotions began to swirl inside him as he wished so much to see his parents again.

Filing away his mother's advice with Nyx's, Theron took a deep breath and walked out of that room. But instead of entering the hallway he'd walked to get there, instead now he found himself in a cavernous room of black obsidian walls. He craned his neck to look to the ceiling and wondered what this place was.

"It's my throne room, and I intend to have it stay mine, little boy," a deep voice said, sliding over him like silk.

Theron looked around for any sign of Hades since that voice hadn't been in his head this time, but he saw no one. He was alone in that empty room.

"Not much of a place for your throne, it seems," he said, knowing his insult would land just as he intended.

"Didn't your daddy tell you that nothing is what it seems in this place?" Hades taunted him.

Looking over toward the right corner of the room

where the voice sounded like it came from, Theron tried to locate the god but couldn't. Best to keep him talking.

"He said something about this entire place being bullshit, if that's what you mean. I think he must have been referring to your need to play your little games. Personally, I'd say they're a bit beneath a god, but whatever floats your boat. I imagine having to be stuck down here all the time makes you go a little crazy, so maybe that's how you get off."

Hades didn't respond immediately to his insults, but when he did, Theron knew the time for joking had ended. The god appeared before him sitting on his black throne in the middle of the room, and along with him stood hundreds of his daemons around him.

The god sat back on his throne and draped his right leg over the arm. He looked perfectly casual, even though Theron sensed he'd roused his anger with his last comment.

"You lack the requisite respect you should have for a god, little boy," he said slowly, pronouncing every word perfectly.

Theron studied Hades for a few moments and couldn't help think he looked like a cross between a vampire and porn star. Knowing he would read his thoughts, he simply smiled and never broke his gaze as he waited for a reaction.

Surprisingly, the god of the Underworld didn't react angrily. He didn't snap or lash out. In fact, he seemed pleased by the thought, if the smile on his face was any indication.

"I'll take half of that as a compliment. The other half is trash, but I don't expect much better from the likes of you. What do you say we get down to business and stop all this foreplay?" Hades said, chuckling as he finished speaking and waved at one of his minions.

The young male wearing only a loincloth brought a male and female into the chamber and positioned them near Hades' throne. "I think you know one of my guests, but I feel like introductions are in order for the other one. My lovely whore is Noele, your mother, and this strapping young vampire with the oh-so-honorable look is none other than your father. Theron, meet Thane. Now you're all one big family."

Theron's blood began to boil at Hades' name for his mother, but he remembered his mother's advice telling him not to let his emotions control him, so he took a deep breath and pushed down the rage he felt for Hades. It took a few seconds for him to comprehend the other half of his statement. Why the hell did he think this male was his father?

"You've got your facts mixed up, dude. My father is named Ramiel, not whoever this guy is."

But one glance at his mother's face told him something was wrong. She didn't look sad or worried. She looked...guilty. Why?

He'd never invaded his mother's mind because he had trusted her implicitly, but now as he stood there confused as to why she didn't speak up and correct Hades, he focused on her thoughts and in them he found the truth that had been hidden all his life from him by every vampire he'd ever met.

He wasn't Ramiel's son. The one vampire he'd always looked up to as a model for how he wanted to be wasn't his father but just someone his mother loved.

Theron tore himself from his mother's mind as she stood crying and looked over at Thane. It didn't take more than a few moments for him to see how similar he looked to himself.

All this time, everything about his life had been a lie.

## 21

The sound of Hades' laughter filled the throne room, echoing off the obsidian walls as Theron tried to control his emotions about what he'd just learned courtesy of the god of the Underworld. Inside him, rage began bubble up, making him want to lash out. All his fucking life everyone around him had known the truth, and not a single one of them had thought to tell him who his real father was?

The list of names of those who had lied to him over and over by hiding this marched through his head. Did Dante know? Of course he did. Theron had no doubt every one of the Sons and their loved ones all knew.

But it wasn't their responsibility to tell him. He had parents, and even though his mother was taken early in his life, she'd had more than one chance to tell him Ramiel wasn't his father. Or even more, why hadn't he told him himself?

He watched as his mother sobbed, but even seeing her cry didn't change the betrayal that filled him. The male standing next to her who he now had to accept as his true father leveled his gaze on him as if he was studying him. Theron intruded into his mind to find out what he thought and disliked what he learned immediately.

They'd never been in love. She'd loved Ramiel but the Prophecy of Idolas required her to sleep with Thane. He hated having to do it, especially since he had finally fallen in love right before with Sasa.

For a second, Theron tried to figure out if he'd misunderstood what he'd seen in Thane's mind. Wasn't Sasa Vasilije's vampire?

Thane's memory of that time told him what he and his mother had done had been based on responsibility and nothing more. They had to have sex to make sure he came to be. Once they performed their duty, their time together was over.

"Let's bring the man who lied to you all your life in too," Hades announced and waved at his minion in the skimpy clothes.

Ramiel was brought in and stood next to Noele and Thane. Unlike the two of them, he didn't look guilty or upset. He held his chin up and met Theron's gaze evenly, as he always had.

Reading his father's mind, he found out what his mother and Thane remembered was exactly what he thought of that time. Like the two of them, he hated having her sleep with a man other than himself, but also like them, he did it out of duty.

"Don't let him confuse you, son. I'm your father and always have been. Your mother and I raised you as our son, and that's who you'll always be," Ramiel said with that same strength in his voice that had always made Theron feel safe.

Hades laughed, as if anything he'd heard sounded even remotely funny. "Says the man who lied to you all your life. Sounds like you can't trust anyone. No wonder you're so screwed up, little boy."

"Do you plan to insult me to death? Is that how this is going to go? I can't imagine how the Prophecy of Idolas explained that in all its lofty words." Opening his arms out wide, he mocked him. "The god of the Underworld shall bore to death the one who will fight him. All those around shall be put to sleep by his awful insults."

While Theron couldn't help but be amused by his jab, Hades didn't enjoy it at all. A low growl began to come from him, and before long, he showed just how angry he could get. Lifting Noele, Thane, and Ramiel into the air, he flung them against the walls of his throne room. They hit the stones with a thud and stuck there, all three crying out in pain as they slowly melded with the walls until all that was left were their faces protruding out from the stone. They looked like the ones Theron had seen on his walk into the Underworld, but now the agonized expressions he saw tore him up inside.

"Let them down!" he ordered as Hades chuckled with glee.

Looking on his handiwork, he shook his head. "No. I like them there. Should I let you hear the sounds of their cries? I might like that."

With a wave of his hand, the sound of Noele, Thane, and Ramiel's tormented sobs filled the room. They cried out for him to help them, to defeat Hades and save them. Each second that passed, their pleas ripped at Theron's heart, creating a rage in him he hadn't felt since that night his father was taken from right in front of him.

And then something inside him that had lay dormant for every moment of his existence came alive. His rage morphed into something wilder, something more terrifying even to him, but he had no control over it. It was as if the seed of whatever he was destined to be had been planted long ago, and the sound of their agony brought it to fruition.

Pain radiated out from the center of his body, down his arms and legs, until he let out a scream that stopped every daemon near him. They looked at Theron in horror as the creature inside him found its way out, changing his very appearance. His skin turned deep red, and he felt like he possessed one hundred times his strength.

Hades watched in horror, his eyes wide and full of fear. Theron screamed again, bellowing so loud the walls of the throne room shook, and then he couldn't hold back any longer.

The daemon closest to him experienced his wrath first. Like what he'd done to the two that night Ramiel died, he tore this one limb from limb and ripped his throat open with his teeth. He didn't know if what shot out of him was blood or something else, but it didn't matter.

This wasn't about feeding. This was about slaughtering all those who served the god of this realm.

One by one, he eliminated each daemon, leaving a trail of carnage behind him. When they tried to run, he scooped them up in one hand and ripped off their heads with the other. Their high-pitched screeches when he tore one apart warned the others their time was coming soon. He stalked each and every one of them around that throne room until the only thing left other than him and those he loved trapped in the rock above him was the god of the Underworld himself.

He liked those odds.

"Time for your reign to end, Hades."

Theron looked around at the room and reveled in the sight of nothing but daemon blood and body parts. Only one more to go before this place would be his to rule.

"Not so fast, little boy. Tearing into daemons isn't the same as defeating me," Hades warned.

And then just as Theron's beast inside had finally come, so did the god of the Underworld's. In seconds, he grew to ten times his normal size, and Theron realized why this throne room of his had such high ceilings.

Looking down, Hades shook his head and smiled. "You see, my monster is bigger than yours, so I just don't know how you can possibly win. But it's been fun playing your game, little boy. Time for you to die and spend the rest of eternity in the pit."

Out of the corner of his eye, Theron saw Nyx hiding in the corner of the room. For the first time since they'd met, he hoped she'd read his mind and knew if she ever wanted to help him, now was the time.

Hades' hand swooped down, but he jumped out of the way, barely missing being leveled. While the god had the benefit of being larger and stronger, Theron could run around and avoid him much easier at his size. That couldn't go on forever, though, so he hoped whatever Nyx had in mind to help happened sooner than later.

"Run away, little boy. I'll find you, though. There's

nowhere for you to hide here. This is my kingdom, and I know every inch of it."

As he spoke, Hades stomped around his throne room, squashing daemons and anything else that found itself in his path. Theron hurried over to where Nyx stood in an alcove, barely hiding himself before the god saw him.

"Why aren't you doing anything?" he asked as he kept a watchful eye on his enemy.

"I was waiting for the right time." Nyx stopped and then said, "I figured when you turned into this, you might not need my help."

Theron turned to face her in disbelief. "I don't know what the hell all this is, to be honest. It just happened. But I'll have to deal with being red at another time. Now I've got bigger problems, and if you have anything that will take down a giant god of the Underworld, I wish you'd bring it out. If not, I have no idea how I'm going to defeat a hundred-foot Hades."

From the other side of the room, the god himself called out, "Maybe I'll amuse myself by playing with the decorations on my walls. That should be fun."

Terror raced through Theron. He knew just what decorations he meant, and he couldn't let him do that.

He moved to leave, but Nyx caught him by the arm. "He's doing that to draw you out. Don't worry about them. They're fine."

"They're stuck in a fucking wall and screaming for help. Can't you hear them?"

She shook her head and smiled. "It's all an illusion. Most of what happens in the Underworld is. They can't feel anything. They're here. They're already dead,

Theron. What's he going to do? Kill them again. What you're hearing and seeing isn't real. Remember that."

"Like I was supposed to remember to use my emotions? You've got a lot of useful suggestions, don't you, Nyx? If you can't give me some help, don't bother me again, okay? I've got a god to defeat here. I don't have time for bullshit."

She touched his arm, instantly calming him. "I'll help. Give me a couple minutes and I'll be back with reinforcements."

"Great. In the meantime, I'll play hide and go seek with Hades. Any chance there are secret passageways anywhere around this room?"

"Not that I know of, but don't worry. You don't need them. I'll be back."

She hurried out of their hiding spot and left the throne room without Hades noticing. He was too busy abusing Thane's head by flicking it with his giant god fingers. Theron watched for a few seconds, trying to convince himself of what Nyx said about nothing being real, but his screams of pain and pleas for Theron to stop him made that next to impossible.

He had to get out there and distract Hades before he ripped Thane's head off.

"Is this really what gods do when they're upset? Don't you have a bolt of lightning or some major power to move the earth to use? It feels like flicking someone's face as they're stuck in the wall isn't much of a power," he yelled up at him, hoping it would make him focus on something other than Thane's nose.

Hades spun around and grimaced. "Lightning bolts

and controlling the seas are my brothers' powers!" he barked, clearly angry.

Theron had hit a nerve. Good. He'd need to do more of that to keep him away from Noele, Ramiel, and Thane and to pass the time until Nyx brought reinforcements, whatever they might be. He just hoped they were big.

"Oh, so what's your power? Getting tall and stomping around like some asshole? Doesn't seem very special at all. I feel like out of all the gods, you got the shaft."

For that, he got a hand swinging so close to his head he felt the breeze as Hades just missed lopping off the top half of his body. Theron took off behind him and ran around the back of the room. The god tried to follow him, but his size meant he had to maneuver too slowly to catch him.

Looking up, Theron saw his mother crying out in pain, but she no longer made any sound. She looked like some still from a horror film, and he had to look away as he silently promised her he'd rescue all of them as soon as he could.

As soon as Nyx brought back some help. One-hundred-foot help would be needed to defeat a hundred-foot-tall god. Where she'd get that, he had no idea, but she seemed confident whoever she was getting would be worth it.

"Come out, little boy. Come out, or I'll go back to torturing your family again. This time, I think I'll choose your mother. I'm coming for you Noele."

Theron cringed. Hades sounded like every horror film monster he'd ever seen. Before he could stop him, he had removed his mother from the stone wall and had her in his hand. She screamed for him to ignore what he was doing to her, but he couldn't.

How could he be expected to just let her be tortured?

"Run, Theron! It doesn't matter what he does to me. You're still alive. Run from this place and go back to your life!"

The terror in every word that came out of her mouth struck him to the bone. He couldn't just leave her there with Hades for him to punish her. It didn't matter if none of this was real, or she couldn't die again. He couldn't do that to his mother.

He had no choice.

Taking a deep breath, he calmed himself and stepped out where Hades could easily see him. Waving his arm, he yelled up, "I'm right here. There's no point in bothering with her anymore. Let her go. Take out your anger on me."

Hades threw his head back and laughed. "I knew you'd never be able to let her suffer. It's part of your weakness, boy."

"Then put her down and deal with me. If I'm such a little boy, you shouldn't have any problem defeating me."

Theron watched as Hades thought about his suggestion, and he silently hoped for Nyx to return at any moment before the god squashed him under his heel. Then, as he looked up and waited for him to focus all his attention on him and leave Noele alone, Theron saw Hades drop her from nearly a hundred feet up. He watched helplessly as she fell to the stone floor of the throne room, her body limp and broken.

"Okay, I put her down. Now get ready to meet your end, and when I kill you, I've got the perfect place for you to spend the rest of eternity. You'll be with the rest of your fucking kind, and you vampires will finally know your proper place in this world."

For a few seconds, Theron struggled to think of a way out of his predicament. He had no idea why Kali had ever thought he would defeat Hades and take over control of the Underworld. Maybe at his normal height, but as a giant, he was too much for anyone to overcome.

Just as he admitted to himself these were probably his last moments alive, a loud noise startled him. He looked over at where he'd last seen Nyx and there she stood surrounded by pieces of the cavern wall scattered around her and a creature standing behind her with dozens of heads and even more hands. It stood as tall as Hades but looked far more terrifying.

Theron had no idea what the fuck this thing was, but if it helped him defeat the god of the Underworld, he didn't care.

"Hades, your time here is over," the gigantic creature bellowed, shaking the remaining three walls.

The god shook his head, as if the thing standing there didn't frighten him in the least. "Briareus, who let you out? Go back with your brothers and return to work."

"Not this time, Hades."

And with that, the monster launched at the god with its dozens of hands and heads flailing in all directions. Hades stared at him in shock and didn't move, giving the creature an easier way to attack him. By the time he reacted, it was too late. The god teetered on his feet for a long moment and then crashed to the ground with a deafening boom.

"Theron, you must take the jewel from his throne!"

Nyx screamed from across the room. "Take it and you take his kingdom!"

He quickly turned and rushed toward the throne to find a giant red ruby embedded in Hades' throne. Looking around for anything to help him dislodge it, he saw a scepter nearby. He grabbed it and swung as hard as he could at the jewel, but it didn't budge.

"Hurry! The hundred-hander can't hold onto him forever. He's a god, and if he gets to that ruby, you'll lose!" she screamed as Hades tried to push the monster off him.

Finally, Theron noticed a tiny chip on one side of the throne next to the jewel. If he could remove it that way, he would defeat him. With all his strength, he pushed the scepter toward that weak spot in the throne. The end of it slammed into that spot, splintering the entire throne, and the ruby popped out and fell to the floor.

Hades heard it fall and pushed the monster off him. Theron rushed around the now-shattered throne and lifted the jewel into his arms. It weighed nearly as much as he did, but he had it.

"No! You can't take over this place! This is my realm," Hades screamed, and then in front of all of them, he shrunk down to his normal size.

"Not anymore," Theron said as he held the ruby with every ounce of strength he possessed.

"Hades will be going down to Tartarus, Briareus. Can you do the honors? He'll need a special cell all to his own," Nyx said with a smile as she made her way over to where Theron stood barely hanging onto the stone.

The monster nodded and with one of his many hands, picked up the god of the Underworld, who continued to protest with every step his captor took from the throne room. As they descended into the depths of the Underworld, Theron heard him promise to one day regain his kingdom and make all vampires pay.

With Hades gone, he finally dropped the ruby onto the floor next to him and rushed over to his mother. She lay in the spot where she fell, deathly still. Crouching next to her, he touched her face and hoped against hope that she would open her eyes and look up at him.

"Mom, are you okay? Look at me," he pleaded.

Slowly, her eyes opened, and a tiny smile appeared on her lips. "Theron, why didn't you leave?" she whispered in a soft voice.

"I couldn't," he said with a smile, happier at that moment to hear her speak than he'd ever been in his life. "I had no choice. This was my destiny. I was either going to defeat Hades or he was going to defeat me. Thanks to Nyx and that creature with the hundred hands and fifty heads, he lost. He doesn't rule the Underworld anymore. I do."

"My son, the ruler of the Underworld. Wait until your father hears that." Suddenly, her smile faded. "I'm so sorry we didn't tell you the truth about Thane and Ramiel, Theron. We never meant to lie to you. We just thought we'd have more time with you and then we'd talk to you about that. Don't let it change how you feel about Ramiel. He's been there since the moment you came into the world, and he would have given his life to protect us."

Theron took her hand in his and smiled. "I know. It's fine." Looking up toward where the two males had been trapped in the wall, he continued, "For now, I need to find out what happened to him and Thane once Hades was defeated."

From behind him, he heard his father call out, "Noele!"

Ramiel ran to her and fell to his knees. "You're alive. I thought I'd lost you when he let go. Are you okay?"

"I'll be okay. It's not like I could die a second time, honey," Noele said sweetly, bringing a smile to Ramiel's worried face.

Nyx joined them, so Theron stood to thank her, but before he could, he saw Thane standing a few feet away. He looked like he was unsure if he should be there or not.

Theron walked up to him and extended his hand. "I guess we should formally meet since the cat's out of the bag now. I'm Theron."

Thane's dark eyes grew wide and then he nodded. "I'm Thane. I know you never knew about me, but from the moment your mother told me we'd succeeded in getting her pregnant, I knew you'd be as wonderful as the prophecy predicted. It's nice to meet you."

They stood in silence sizing one another up, and Theron knew from his thoughts that Thane saw the resemblance between them now that whatever that red color was had faded away. That was okay. Ramiel would always be his father, but he didn't mind Thane having a part in his existence too.

He had to thank someone else, though, so he turned to face Nyx and opened his arms to hug her. "I don't know why nobody ever mentioned you in the prophecy. This wouldn't have happened without your help. Thank you."

She held him to her and rested her head on his chest as she sighed. "Promise me you'll do right by this place and all the creatures who've been mistreated by the former ruler."

"Like vampires?"

Lifting her head, she looked up at him and smiled. "Like vampires. We creatures of the night deserve better than we've gotten here."

That he could promise.

"The Underworld will no longer be a punishment for my kind. And now that I've decided that, I remember you saying something about standing by me as I ruled this place. Is that offer still good?"

Nyx nodded and sighed. "Are you sure you want the goddess of the night by your side, my lord? I suspect this new title comes with a lot of perks. At least it used to for Hades. Will one woman be enough for the god of the Underworld?"

Theron chuckled at her misuse of his title. "I'm not a god, so I think one woman will be just fine."

She tilted her head and with a shrug said, "Give it time. This place does things to all who stay here long enough. You may not be a god now, but I suspect a change is underway already."

The idea of being a god settled into Theron's mind, and he considered the possibility of what that might mean. He'd been many things and possessed many powers in his short lifetime. How would being a god suit him?

It didn't take long for him to decide it would suit him just fine. Damn fucking fine, in fact.

## 22

_____

The sound of footsteps rhythmically hitting off the sidewalk for the last three blocks told Vasilije he'd have a guest tonight. For the past few nights, he'd sensed he wasn't alone as he walked the streets of New Orleans, lost in his memories of a time long past but still so fresh in his mind. The interruption irritated him, but it wasn't wholly unexpected. He'd let his guard down lately, and now he'd pay the price.

He took a deep breath into his lungs and exhaled slowly. Heavy and muggy, the air tonight practically blanketed the skin, but to him, it felt like the kind of night she'd say was quintessential New Orleans.

The steps grew faster even as he slowed his pace to take in the beauty of City Park. He methodically walked up the steps of the stone arch bridge over the lagoon. A few ducks swam in the water, making ripples that spread out from them to the opposite shore. Vasilije watched them for a few moments and then let his gaze drift up to admire the Spanish moss that hung from ancient live oak trees. He'd fallen in love with this area when he returned to the city a few months before, a trip meant to heal his heart even now years after he lost her.

For the first months after she was gone, he would have been happy to let a hunter stake him. It would have put him out of his misery that threatened to devour him whole. But no one came to do it, so he continued to exist. Night after night, he silently wished to be relieved of all the pain that subsided.

One night turned into one week which turned into one month. Then before he knew it, he'd lived a year without her. He couldn't remember anything about all those nights. They simply passed one after another as he struggled to find a reason to go on.

Nearly twelve years had passed now since that night at the dragons' castle, but not a moment went by when he didn't replay the last precious moments of his time with Sasa. He clung to that memory of her dark eyes filled with love as she promised to wait for him. It tore him up while at the same time gave him a feeling of happiness he hadn't found anywhere else since.

His life had become a series of events to continue his existence without him making much effort. He found blood where he could, whether it was from humans he hypnotized or animals like chickens or rats. He consumed food and alcohol with little zest or enjoyment. They served their purpose and nothing else.

Although he had opportunities to spend time with his own kind, he avoided other vampires. He wanted nothing resembling community after he lost her. He lived alone as penance for his life before. Every so often, a tidbit of information about his old friends and fellow warriors floated into his life. He listened and filed it away, not interested in seeing any of them again.

That part of his world had ceased to be the moment he drove that stake into Sasa's heart. He'd fought enough. He'd killed enough. He didn't want to do either anymore.

So he didn't. He walked away and never looked back.

They'd tried to find him a few times. One time a few years ago Theron even succeeded, but he had nothing to say to the new leader of the vampire world. The others had joined with him, becoming his deputies and lieutenants, but that wasn't for him. He had nothing left for that kind of life anymore.

Vasilije closed his eyes and listened for the footsteps. Was the one following him alone, or did he have someone with him? His shoes tapped off the sidewalk, one shoe and then the other, telling the vampire it would be a one-on-one meeting tonight.

It would occur where he chose, so he walked over the bridge toward a group of live oaks. The swampy smell of the area filled his nose, making him feel as close to nature as possible. He reveled in the sensations this place brought out in him and waited for his guest.

The footsteps stopped on the bridge, and he turned to see the man who'd trailed him for the past few nights. A typical vampire hunter, he was human with round eyes that seemed too close to his nose and hair that needed a decent cut. He'd noticed both features when he first saw him at a café earlier in the week. Other than those distinctive traits, he looked like every other hunter Vasilije had ever encountered.

Years earlier, he would have slashed through his throat by now and feasted on his blood, but those times were long gone. He suspected his disinterest in the man confused him, but he'd soon understand.

"There's no point in running. I'll just keep tracking you," the man said with a bit too much bravado for the Romanian's taste.

"I'm vampire. I don't have to run. I can just disappear in front of your eyes and you'll never see me again."

This answer left him speechless, which Vasilije liked. Cockiness had no place in their meeting tonight.

"Why do I get the feeling you don't want to do that?" the hunter asked. "You've seen me following you all night. Why haven't you disappeared already?"

"I've seen you all week," Vasilije answered with a chuckle.

"And still you're standing here talking to me."

"Do you know who I am?"

The hunter shook his head. "Other than vampire?"

"I am Vasilije."

Even in the dim light of the moon shining through the Spanish moss, he saw the shock register on the man's face. That he enjoyed.

"The final Son of Navarus?" the hunter said, his voice hitching on the word Navarus.

Final Son?

Vasilije's chest tightened at those words. So of all the Sons, he'd outlasted them all.

"I didn't realize I held that distinction."

The hunter took a few steps toward him and stopped. "You're the last. Saint was staked by an Archon supporter two years after the end of the war. Terek lasted for a while, but once the born vampire he raised grew up and left him, he was easy for us to finish off. One of us got

Sion a few years ago in Germany, which seemed appropriate, I guess. And the clyten Dante I got a few months ago. He was a big catch considering how important he'd become in the vampire world. He was a two-for-one deal since I got his girl too that night. Now you're the only one left, the last of the Sons of Navarus."

His rundown of the demise of the rest of the Sons made Vasilije nostalgic for a moment. Saint gone so soon after the war? All that waiting to have his life with Solenne, and those Archons won in the end anyway.

He'd thought about Terek so many times after walking out of that room that night. He'd lost as much as Vasilije had, but he couldn't bring himself to find him throughout the years. Seeing him would open too many emotional wounds.

Sion had made a name for himself with those mechanical contraptions of his that had helped them defeat the daemons. It made Vasilije smile when he thought of all those human nerds working with a vampire. Did they even know what Sion was?

And Dante gone just a few months before. Vasilije knew he'd risen in the vampire world after the war when he joined Theron to reorganize the magistrate system.

"Your name and reputation are legendary among hunters. You're practically a myth."

"A myth?"

The hunter nodded and took a few more steps toward him. "Oh, yeah. The story goes that you disappeared after the war. Most of us thought you were long gone. Others put your name with Theron as just symbols of the old vampire world."

He stood just a few feet away from Vasilije now, his

stake pushed into the waistband of his pants. Back when he was a vampire to be reckoned with, the Romanian would have drained him and snapped his neck for being so poor at his job.

But not tonight.

For a moment, he considered telling him about how Theron wasn't just part of some long-told story. That he was real and had become as much a god as he was vampire over time.

But he decided not to. Humans believed what they wanted to believe, and he doubted he'd be able to convince this guy that a vampire born to fulfill a prophecy had become a god like the one he likely worshipped.

"I expected a fight. Even before I knew you were a Son, I thought you'd make me chase you at least."

Vasilije shook his head. He had no more interest in putting off the inevitable. Closing his eyes, he took one more deep breath of New Orleans air and slowly let it out of his lungs as he thought about Sasa and how much he missed her.

No more words. No more staving off the inevitable. His time had come.

A second later, the hunter's stake tore through his chest and pierced his heart. It stung for a moment, and then he felt nothing as the life he'd lived for over five hundred years came to an end there under the live oak trees and Spanish moss and he disappeared from what had become his favorite place in the world because of her.

.  .  .

VASILIJE OPENED his eyes and slowly focused his gaze on all the vampires standing in front of him. Saint and Solenne held hands and smiled, and he had to admit he'd never seen that Son happier. Terek and Ilona were reunited again, along with Ramiel and Noele. They all appeared content. As his eyes scanned the room, he saw Sion and Kali standing with Dante and Scarlett, and he began to wonder if that hunter had missed his mark and he was simply dreaming.

"You had to make sure you outlasted all of us, didn't you? Let me guess. You dared a hunter to get you, and he finally did," Saint teased.

Still the same vampire as always.

"Something like that."

Terek stepped toward him and opened his arms to embrace him. "It's good to see you again, my friend. We were starting to think you might be immortal."

With a laugh, Vasilije hugged him close, pleased to see his old friend finally happy with the one he loved. "That's what happens when you lay low. Nobody cares to come find you."

One by one, the former Sons of Navarus shook his hand and hugged him as they welcomed the last of their kind to the Underworld. Vasilije made light of the whole thing, joking around about how they'd all had to wait for him, but as he scanned the souls in that room, he didn't see a few and wondered what had happened to them.

When Ramiel came forward to shake his hand, Vasilije asked, "I don't see Nico. Where is he?"

Having little knowledge of the layout of the Underworld, he couldn't help but wonder. Had Theron found a special place to punish the one who betrayed them all?

Ramiel looked at Noele standing by his side and frowned before turning his focus back to Vasilije. "When Theron took over, he sent Hades to the prison here in Tartarus. That seemed like the right place to put Nico too, along with all his Archon and magistrate friends, once he admitted that it was him that tipped off the hunters to where Noele was that night they got her."

Still, all these years later, the Romanian had a hard time reconciling the vampire he'd known for centuries with the one he'd become in those last, crucial years before the Archon War. Stunned by what Ramiel said, he shook his head in disbelief at how Nico could have turned his back so brutally on her.

"I'm so sorry, you two. I didn't believe Nico could ever do that to any of us."

Noele smiled and brushed it off. "It was a long time ago, and we're together again, thankfully. As for Nico, he's where he belongs for what he did to the Sons."

When he looked around at the group, he didn't see two other faces. He feared even asking where they may be, but he had to know.

"Where's Thane?"

The room fell silent for a long moment that felt like it dragged out forever, and Vasilije silently told himself whatever the answer was, he'd have to accept it. The truth was he'd left Sasa alone for far too long again, and this time it had been all his choice. He couldn't claim he needed to protect his vampires like the last time he neglected her.

If she didn't wait for him, he only had himself to blame.

Nobody seemed to want to answer his question,

which made him sure he knew the answer, but then he saw Theron walk in and wave him over to him. As he made his way there, he couldn't believe how much Noele and Ramiel's son looked like his real father.

Enough that even talking to him made Vasilije more than a little pissed off.

"Finally decided to give up the ghost up top and join your friends, Vasilije. It's good to see you again," Theron said in a deep voice that sounded so different from the last time he'd spoken to him.

"I guess being the king of the Underworld made you grow up. Good for you."

Theron flashed him a smile that told him he may not have picked up on his sarcasm. "We never really did like each other, did we? Well, that's all in the past. This place is no longer a prison for vampires like it was under Hades' rule."

"Except Nico and the Archons who fought against us."

"True, but they got what they had coming to them. Not all Archons, though. Just ask Dante. His buddy Nero was an Archon of New York and when a hunter finally got to him, he came here and has an even better life now than he did before. I remember all those who fought on our side and make sure they know I appreciate their efforts back then."

"Life, or I guess it's death, is good for you then. That's nice."

Theron slid his arm around Vasilije's shoulders and began to guide him toward the door. "Let's take a walk. I have something to show you."

As they moved around the Underworld and its ruler

gave him a tour of the place while extoling all the wonderful benefits vampires possessed there now, Vasilije had a sense Theron was simply distracting him to avoid telling him the truth about Thane and Sasa. When they reached his throne room, he stopped him.

"I get it. You've won and won fucking big. You got everything you wanted. Good for you. But since nobody wanted to tell me what happened to Thane, I'm assuming it's because he and Sasa are together now. You can tell me. I'm a big boy. I can handle it."

In truth, the thought of spending eternity in the Underworld, no matter how great it was for vampires, knowing that Sasa had gone back to the one male who'd betrayed him more than even Nico made his stomach roil until he felt like he'd be sick right there in Theron's throne room.

"I'm assuming you knew Thane was my father too, like the others?" the ruler of the Underworld asked with an edge to his voice.

But Vasilije wasn't okay with calling Thane that or any other name of honor.

"He contributed some fluids. Ramiel has always been your father. I don't know what you all decided down here, but to me, Thane did nothing much. Ramiel raised you. He gets the title of father."

Halfway through his attack on Thane, it occurred to Vasilije that Theron may actually like the son of a bitch, but he didn't care. So he could send him to prison like he had with Nico and the Archon fuckers who deserved it. Whatever. Without Sasa, this whole fucking place had quickly turned into a prison for the rest of eternity.

"I heard you didn't like Thane. I see that hasn't

changed in all these years," Theron said with a grin that looked fucking smug.

"No, it hasn't, so why don't you just tell me where the hell he and Sasa are and stop this little cat and mouse bullshit thing you're doing. You must have better things to do with your time practically being a god and all now."

"It's more than practically, but we don't have to quibble about details now. As for Thane, he's gone from the Underworld. I gave everyone in the Sons family the same choice, and now I'll give it to you. You can stay here, or you can go back up top and live again. However, that life you choose on earth will be human, not vampire. Your choice."

Vasilije felt his mouth drop open as Theron's answer filtered through his brain. "Are you saying Thane chose to be human again and is alive up there?"

"Yes. He had nothing to stay here for after I imprisoned all of Hades' daemons, which included his girlfriend. So he chose to live another life as a human."

"Wow. If I had known he was walking around up there, I would have found him and ripped out his jugular."

Theron threw his head back and laughed at Vasilije's comment about Thane. "You do know how to hold a grudge. Well, I know you never liked me, but you did fight on my side. I've never forgotten that."

"Yeah? Does that mean if I choose to stay here that I get a deluxe suite in the Underworld, courtesy of your beneficence?"

Shaking his head, he answered, "No, but I have something that might help you make your choice for you. Follow me."

He led him to a room and opened the door, stepping back so Vasilije could see in. There on a bed Sasa lay fast asleep. Vasilije quickly worried she wasn't asleep but somehow dead unlike the rest of them, but Theron stopped him.

"I know what you're thinking, but no, she's fine. When she arrived here, she was despondent. She wouldn't leave this room. My mother told me she was worried you might think she betrayed you while she waited here for you. So I gave her the peace she needed for herself and wanted for you. She's been asleep since then and has never left this room."

Vasilije didn't know what to say. Shocked and thrilled at the same time, he stood there speechless as Theron walked over to the side of Sasa's bed and gently pressed his fingertips to her forehead.

He waited for her to respond, and a second later, her eyelids fluttered open, and he saw those beautiful deep brown eyes he'd missed all those years he lived without her. His heart swelled with love at the sight of her again.

"There's someone here for you, Sasa."

As he walked out of the room, Theron looked over toward Vasilije and smiled. "You're welcome."

"You're finally here. Did Theron tell you I've been here alone the whole time?" she asked as she sat up in the bed.

Vasilije walked over to sit next to her, pulling her close to him. He'd waited years to finally feel her next to him again, and to now experience it nearly overwhelmed him with emotion. Like she had so many times before, she rested her head on his shoulder as he answered her.

"He did, but this wasn't necessary. I left you alone for far too long again, so if you had gone with..."

Even now, after all this time, he didn't want to say his name to Sasa, so he let his sentence trail off as he held her to him. Just speaking that name would ruin everything, and he didn't want to do that again now that he had another chance with her.

She pulled away and looked up at him, shaking her head as worry filled her eyes. "I wouldn't have done that, Vasilije. No matter how long I had to wait this time, I wasn't going to make the mistake I made the last time."

He leaned down and softly kissed her lips to stop her from talking. He loved hearing her voice again, but she didn't have to explain herself anymore. She'd sacrificed years to be with him this time. That didn't require an explanation.

Sasa ended the kiss and hung her head as tears began to roll down her cheeks. "I was so afraid you'd think I betrayed you again. I just didn't want to mess things up this time. I would have stayed alone in this place forever waiting for you, but Theron offered to do that thing he can with his fingers on my head, so I said yes. Anything to make sure I could be here for you."

Vasilije gently touched her chin to lift her head and looked into her brown eyes still filled with tears. Wiping her cheeks, he wished he was worthy of such a wonderful creature. After all the mistakes he'd made, she worried she might not be there for him. No wonder he was madly in love with her.

"You had every right to be happy while I was gone, Sasa. I am glad you waited for me, though. I waited for you too."

She looked up at him in shock. "You waited all these years to be with me again?"

"I did. After I lost you, I couldn't imagine ever being with anyone again. I spent all those years existing, but nothing more. Life wasn't worth it without you. That's why when that hunter caught up to me, I didn't fight back. Missing you became too much to bear, so I let him send me off to you."

"Oh, Vasilije. I love you. I've always loved you."

"And I love you, Sasa. I'd forgotten what being happy felt like for so long, but just seeing you here has brought it all back."

She flung her arms around his neck and hugged him tightly. After a minute, she said quietly, "Did Theron tell you about what he can do? He can send us back to live again."

Vasilije heard hopefulness in her voice and leaned back to see her face. That hope he heard was in her eyes too. "He told me it means going back as humans, not vampires, though."

"I wouldn't care. As long as we were together, what would it matter? We'd get a second chance to do things right."

Even though he'd lived amongst humans for centuries, he hadn't been one since Queen Elizabeth I and Shakespeare were alive. A lot had changed in all those years.

"It's been five hundred years since I was human, Sasa. I'm not sure I could handle all their frailties. I've gotten used to be a vampire. Don't you think we could be happy here?"

She nodded and forced herself to smile. "Yes. I just

wonder what it would be like to be human again with you human too. We could start over and do things differently this time."

He didn't know if he wanted to do this, but he wanted to make her happy. "Maybe live in New Orleans?"

Her face lit up, and she smiled like she used to all those years ago when they were first together. "Oh, could we?"

"I'm not sure how we'd live. I was a prince in the sixteenth century. What would we do?"

Sasa thought about his question for a moment and shrugged her shoulders. "I don't know. We'll be together and that's the most important thing. No Sons of Navarus. No Archons. No war. Just Vasilije and Sasa living life together. And when our time ends, we'll return here to our friends."

Pulling her into his arms, he held her close and tried to think of a reason to tell her no. He had none. He'd promised her the world when he made her vampire. Now she asked for that promise to be fulfilled, except with the two of them as humans.

How could he say no?

Quietly, he whispered in her ear, "Okay. Just promise me no matter what happens, it's just you and me, Sasa."

She looked up at him and nodded. "Just you and me and a second chance to have that life I always dreamed of for us. Do you want to tell Theron now?"

Vasilije smiled and shook his head. For at least a few hours, he had other things in mind for their first night together.

Easing her back onto the bed, he looked down into her beautiful brown eyes as she gazed up at him. In them, he'd seen the world and more, and he'd see it again as a human man.

"Tomorrow. For now, let's enjoy our last night with you as my vampire and me as your sire."

He kissed her long and deep as his fangs slowly descended into his mouth. No other woman had ever excited him like Sasa, and he wanted to get lost in her just once more like this.

As she slid her hands down to palm his cock and she wrapped her legs around his waist, he wondered if once would be enough. They did want to have a memory of the Underworld that could get them through life as humans.

Maybe a few more times getting lost in one another would be better.

KEEP READING FOR MORE INFORMATION ABOUT
K.M. SCOTT BOOKS!

# BOOKS BY K.M. SCOTT

**HEART OF STONE SERIES**

Crash Into Me (Heart of Stone #1)

Fall Into Me (Heart of Stone #2)

Give In To Me (Heart of Stone #3)

Heart of Stone Volume One

Ever After (Heart of Stone #4)

A Heart of Stone Christmas (Heart of Stone #5)

Return To Me (Heart of Stone #6)

Forever With Me (Heart of Stone #7)

Heart of Stone Volume Two

Hard As Stone (Heart of Stone #8)

Set In Stone (Heart of Stone #9)

Silent As A Stone (Heart of Stone #10)

Heart of Stone Volume Three

All of Me (Heart of Stone #11)

**CLUB X SERIES**

Temptation (Club X #1)

Surrender (Club X #2)

Possession (Club X #3)

Satisfaction (Club X #4)

Acceptance (Club X #5)

Complete Club X Series Box Set

NeXt SERIES

Notorious (NeXt #1)

Infamous (NeXt #2)

Ravenous (NeXt #3)

Ambitious (NeXt #4)

Flirtatious (NeXt #5)

Mysterious (NeXt #6)

Sensuous (NeXt #7)

Desirous (NeXt #8)

CORRUPTED LOVE TRILOGY

If I Dream (Corrupted Love #1)

If You Fight (Corrupted Love #2)

If We Fall (Corrupted Love #3)

Corrupted Love Trilogy Box Set

ADDICTED TO YOU SERIES

Crave (Addicted To You #1)

Adore (Addicted To You #2)

Shatter (Addicted To You #3)

Claim (Addicted To You #4)

Addicted To You Series Box Set

PROJECT ARTEMIS SERIES

In The Darkness (Project Artemis #1)

After The Storm (Project Artemis #2)

Behind The Scenes (Project Artemis #3)

Project Artemis Box Set

FINDING THE ONE SERIES

Hard Work (Finding The One #1)

Big Love (Finding The One #2)

DIRTY BOSS SERIES

Sweet Things (Dirty Boss #1)

Private Secretary (Dirty Boss #2)

Play Date (Dirty Boss #3)

Dirty Boss Volume One

K.M.'S BOOKS ARE IN AUDIOBOOK TOO!

# BOOKS BY K.M. SCOTT WRITING AS GABRIELLE BISSET

### SONS OF NAVARUS SERIES

Vampire Dreams Revamped (A Sons of Navarus Prequel)

Blood Avenged (Sons of Navarus #1)

Blood Betrayed (Sons of Navarus #2)

Longing (A Sons of Navarus Short Story)

Blood Spirit (Sons of Navarus #3)

The Deepest Cut (A Sons of Navarus Short Story)

Blood Prophecy (Sons of Navarus #4)

Blood Craving (Sons of Navarus #5)

Blood Eclipse (Sons of Navarus #6)

Blood Ascendant (Sons of Navarus #7)

The Sons of Navarus Box Set #1

The Sons of Navarus Box Set #2

### DESTINED ONES DUET

Stolen Destiny (Destined Ones Duet #1)

Destiny Redeemed (Destined Ones Duet #2)

### VICTORIAN EROTIC ROMANCES

Love's Master

Masquerade

The Victorian Erotic Romance Trilogy